M000158419

THE TWO-WEEK PROMISE

REGINA BROWNELL

CHAPTER 1

$\mathcal{A}$s my best friend twirls on the dance floor with the man of her dreams, I stand off to the side as her maid of honor, trying to hold myself together. It isn't the sudden text from the man I'd been dating for a year telling me that I was getting too serious. It's because this moment signifies the end of an era, and from here on out she will be married and I'll forever be their third wheel.

Charlotte Fields was one of those little girls who dreamt about the day when Prince Charming would sweep her off her feet, and ask for her hand in marriage. The best part was she found him, just as her mother had found her own Prince Charming all those years ago. Charlotte's parents were a fairy-tale couple straight out of the story books.

Henry and Josephine Fields' love story began with a puddle of spilt milk in the cafeteria of their high school that almost took Josephine to the ground. Henry briskly dove across the cafeteria and caught her before she could tumble. I might be exaggerating, but that's how the story is told. At least her parents showed Charlotte how to love.

I'd heard their story a million times growing up. Today I

1

heard it again as Charlotte used it in her vows to describe how Bryan was her own savior. She spoke with admiration of that cold morning when she slipped on ice and he was the officer who came to her call.

I hope that Charlotte and Bryan's love story will carry them through until they are old.

Unfortunately for Henry and Josephine it didn't quite end that way. They would have still been in love, but an accident at work claimed his life four years ago. His memory is still strong, and his presence lingers in the room, in the shape of an empty seat beside Josephine decorated with a beautiful floral arrangement. Old family photos sharing all of their favorite memories, and a beautiful white tribute candle sits beside the DJ booth.

"I've never seen Charlotte shine so bright," Mom says, sniffling.

She takes her hand in mine, squeezing gently. Her green eyes twinkle. Charlotte is like a second daughter to her and Mom's emotions have been as erratic as mine through the entire ceremony.

"She's the most beautiful woman I know," I say.

It's my turn to tear up as I turn my attention back to the dance floor.

Dan and Shay's big hit bleeds into an old familiar tune. Charlotte breaks away from Bryan and her eyes meet mine. We deemed "Love Bug" by the Jonas Brothers as our song as a joke many years ago. Charlotte shimmies her hips, lifting the lace bottom of her ball gown wedding dress as she glides across the freshly polished dance floor. Her face lights up, small crinkles forming at the corner of her eyes as she curls her finger at me to step forward. The bass of the music vibrates my chest as the lights strobe in several colors, illuminating the dance floor and Charlotte's white gown. The guests turn their attention to me as

Bryan steps to the side. I shake my head at her. My auburn hair skims my face, covering my flaming red cheeks.

"Come on, Ellie Garner, you know you want to dance!"

I scowl at her as my feet defy me and start moving forward. The hairs on my neck stand on end. Lifting my eyes I scan the intimate hotel reception hall, only to have my attention land on Logan Fields, Charlotte's older brother. His warm, bright eyes glimmer with the flashing lights, but I'm mostly caught up by the Cheshire grin on his annoyingly perfect face.

Hands grasp me, but I'm still entranced by him. After four years of playing a disappearing act following their father's passing, he's finally here. I was a little worried that he wouldn't show up, and although he ran when things got bad, I knew he would never let his sister down on her wedding day.

I'm pulled forward and distracted by Charlotte's voice shouting the lyrics to the chorus. I can't help it. It's like the song is a part of me, and I belt it out along with her. We wait for that pivotal moment where the Jo Bros rock out. When they finally do we are shaking our heads and rocking out along with them, as if we were at a concert. Charlotte's dark curls bounce with each step. She pulls me into her arms and we sway back and forth, and nearly crash to the ground together as she attempts to dip me. The tight purple mermaid-style dress I've somehow managed to squeeze into makes it difficult to perform this maneuver. Yet somehow, I'm more flexible than I thought.

While I'm being dipped, my eyes catch sight of Logan watching us and shaking his head. *You're ridiculous*, he mouths to me. I raise my hand above my head, and casually throw him the bird with a smirk as Charlotte lifts me.

"You had them play our song," I yell over the music as it fades into an upbeat Ed Sheeran song I've heard on the radio.

"Of course I did, we all know I really married *you*," she says. She pulls me into a hug and I rest my head on her shoulder. Her sweet strawberry shampoo fills the air as we rock slowly to what should be a fast-moving song.

"I can't believe you're married."

We pull apart and walk off the dance floor. It's not much quieter on the other side of the reception hall, but it's a little more bearable. We take a seat at the beautiful table set up for the bride and groom. Their initials sit on the floor, lit up with twinkling white lights against the violet tablecloth, giving the area an angelic glow. There's a fancy wicker arch over it intertwined with faux flowers and vines.

I take Bryan's spot. He's still working the dance floor in his crisp black suit. His tall, lean body sways to the rhythm. That man can dance. His friends are all drunk and shouting the wrong song lyrics. It's an amusing scene.

"So, are you excited about the honeymoon?"

She stabs the leafy green on her plate. The waiters and waitresses in their black and white tuxes are starting to bring out some dishes as the crowd dances around.

"Yes! But how can I ever get over the fact that we broke friendship rule number seven?"

The rule list was written on an old looseleaf piece of paper and had been changed and updated many times over the years. They were never meant to be serious—well, most of them weren't. Rule seven was that we would get married together, maybe not the same day, but we wanted to plan our weddings at the same time, and hopefully have children simultaneously, although I'm nowhere near as ready for that as Charlotte is.

I chuckle and bump into her with my shoulder. "It happens. Matt wasn't the one, and plus, why would you want to share a wedding day with me? Remember *Bride Wars*?"

"That would never be us," she says with a mouth full of lettuce, some sticking out.

I hand a napkin to her. She smirks and mumbles thanks while chewing. "Plus," she pauses to swallow, "they fought over having to find a new venue for one of the weddings. You and I wanted a dual ceremony. Too bad Bryan wasn't a twin."

I chuckle. "As a twin, I think it would be really weird if Arthur and I married two people who were best friends."

She sighs. "We'll find you a man. Someone really amazing, and your love story will be straight out of a Taylor Swift song."

"Aren't all of her songs about breakups?"

"No, not all of them." She points a fork at me. "What about the one she did with Ed?"

I shrug. "As much as I would love to meet the man of my dreams, I think I'm destined to be alone for the rest of my life. Maybe I'll move out from my mom's and adopt several cats. They can't break your heart like men do."

She sets her fork down and scowls at me. As her mouth opens I get that skin prickling feeling again. Tiny goosebumps crawl up my arm. I look briefly around the room, hugging myself and rubbing along my skin. Charlotte's rambling on about how when she returns from honeymoon, we are going to find me a husband, and as the word crosses her lips Logan comes into view. His cocky smile doesn't fade as he catches my gaze from across the room.

Leaning against the bar he lifts a glass with dark colored liquor inside, like he's toasting to me, then tips it back and rests it on the counter. His intense honey brown eyes never leave mine. It's like he's challenging me, and to be honest I could use a drink or two.

"Hello, earth to Ellie!" Charlotte waves her hand in front of my face.

"What?"

"Who are you looking—" She adjusts so that her body is straight and she's facing the bar across the way. Logan being Logan purses his lips and wiggles his brows. Her shoulders sag and she shakes her head.

"Is he bothering you? Because I can kick his ass if he is."

Logan is rule number five. I've already made a vow from deep within my heart to never ever break that rule.

I huff. "Nah, but I think he wants to do shots."

"My brother has a stomach like a tank. You'll be on your ass in one drink." She narrows her eyes as if she's speaking to him through their sibling bond. They are probably yelling at each other. I can hear them in my head, her telling him to go easy on me because my heart is fragile, and him telling her I can handle it.

Charlotte and Logan, although he left for a few years, are very close. Logan has never treated either one of us badly. He's always been there in a brotherly sort of way for me too. He's attractive, I'll give him that, with his perfect jawline and sexy dark eyes, but he's also a player, and off limits. Although I highly doubt he would ever look at me in that way.

I make the mistake of glancing over his way again, and somewhere inside of me there's a growing desire to find out what it would be like to have Logan. It's an awful thought—no—it's a *dangerous* thought.

To get Logan out of my head I scan the dance floor. Josephine is a stunning vision in navy blue. Her hair is set atop her head in an updo with two strands curling against the sides of her face. She's dancing with her new boyfriend, Tommy. His tall sturdy frame envelopes her as they sway. It's nice to see her smiling and happy once more. Through the crowd on the dance floor, my gaze catches Logan again. His eyes are on his mom and Tommy. The grin he held for me has changed to a frown, while his hands rest at his side in closed tight fists.

"May I have my wife?" Bryan towers over me, eyeing Charlotte with a love in his eyes that you don't find every day. A soft smile dances on his lips as he regards her.

"Of course. I'm gonna get a drink."

Charlotte's brow raises, and I shrug, but give a smile to let her know I promise not to get myself into trouble.

But I'm not entirely sure I can keep that promise.

CHAPTER 2

"Are you sure this is okay?" eight-year-old me questioned a young doe-eyed Charlotte.

I glanced around the bedroom, biting my nails. The walls of Logan's room were a dark forest green back then. It was neat and organized by Josephine. You could tell it was her touch, because everything was labeled, even his underwear drawer.

"Logan's at soccer practice, we have plenty of—"

"What are you two doing in my room?"

Even at eight years old my heart thudded hard in my chest every time Logan was in the room. I'd been well aware of how cute he was since I was five.

"Logan, where is your suit that you wore for your Communion?"

Logan shifted his black duffel off his thin shoulders. It landed with a thud on the wood floor. He walked past me and his arm brushed against mine. I could feel my face light up like a Christmas tree. As he reached the closet he turned back to give me the Logan smirk.

Charlotte stood on a stool as she rummaged through. He pushed her out of the way and she screeched at him.

7

"Why do you need it?" he asked.

Charlotte walked down the "aisle" with me several times when we were kids. She wanted to act out every moment of her future wedding for it to be perfect. We spent hours looking through bridal magazines for floral arrangements and dresses. She even had a scrapbook with cut-out images.

"Oh, it's not for me," she said and pointed in my direction. "I'm making Ellie my husband."

Logan snorted.

I can still feel the flush creeping up my face, even now.

"Why didn't you say it was for her?" He reached into the closet, grabbed a random tux, and inspected it for damages. It was still perfectly pressed and not a speck of dust was on it.

"So you're marrying my sister, huh?"

"Do I have your blessing?" I had no idea what that meant at the time, I heard it on some movie my mom was watching.

He smirked at me. "I mean whatever floats your boat, but I have one request."

I looked up at him, into his beautiful dark eyes.

"You let me be the priest."

I smacked my hand over my mouth and giggled.

"What, you don't think I can be a priest?"

He crossed the room back to where I stood and gently pushed my shoulder. I was swept away by his smile. He handed me the tux and I held it against my body.

At eleven he had already had two girlfriends, so the thought of Logan being a priest was hilarious. I shook my head. "You'll have to break up with your girlfriend. It's against the rules."

"Already done." He smirked.

"Dude, you're eleven, and does Mom even know you've kissed a girl?" Charlotte asked.

"Nope, and you're not going to tell her. Kissing is fun. You'll see."

"Ew," I said. I don't think I fully meant *ew*, because as I said it, my eyes went to his lips. Being eight didn't stop me from being boy crazy or maybe just crazy for one boy.

As Logan reached the door he turned back around. "I'm going to shower. Don't rip my suit, 'kay?"

I nodded. I would take good care of that suit, because he said so. I could feel Charlotte's eyes on me, but ignored her.

That afternoon when Logan finished his shower he came to Charlotte's room and married us. She had notes on how the wedding should go, what dresses everyone would wear, and the exact time of her ceremony. She would always make us redo parts, because Logan and I were never serious. We laughed the whole time, and even though it was the dumbest thing in the world, I can still recall how much fun we had.

❧

An unfamiliar phone alarm jars me awake as the memory fades. The ground—or maybe it's my body—shifts and I plummet to the floor with a loud thump, taking the soft white linen sheets with me. I groan and pain shoots up my left arm. From where I am I scan the room to get my bearings. A suit jacket is draped over the back of a floral hotel chair in the corner. My purple bridesmaid dress is strewn across the seat.

A black suitcase sits beside the chair. Tipped over beside it is a bottle of golden liquid, the pi symbol in black on the side. There's only one guy I know that uses Givenchy cologne.

I attempt to get to my feet, but only wind up on my knees. I peer over a foreign queen-sized bed at a smirking figure lying there baring it all. I'm half thankful I know the man on the bed.

He props his head up with his hand. "You look a little lost there, Ellie."

I narrow my eyes at the naked man before me. It's Logan Fields, the only guy who has ever been off limits. What a way to start a Monday.

"Oh, hush you, I..." I try to stand, but lose my footing as I get more tangled in the bedding and wipe out for a second time.

His dark eyes find mine over the edge of the bed. I cringe. I can't believe what I did. There's no way I'm getting back into that bed, even if it was the best sex of my life (though I'll never admit it out loud).

Scanning the room around me, I come to the conclusion that we are in a hotel room at The Hilton, the SAME Hilton at which his sister—and my best friend—had her wedding last night.

Rubbing my temples I moan. "Why me!" I collapse on the floor in a heap along with the sheets.

A pillow lands on top of me and I hiss like a cat, because I'm weird like that. Logan chuckles, then rolls onto his back looking up at the ceiling. I do the same.

"What are we gonna tell Charlotte?" I ask. Really, I'm talking to no one, but of course Logan butts in anyway.

"That you slept with her big brother and then she'll never speak to you again."

I reach for the pillow he threw and chuck it back over at him. His laughter is muffled, so I know I got him.

"Not funny!" Ugh! Maybe if I pinch myself I'll wake up from this awful dream. I reach over, grabbing the skin of my arm, and squeeze tight. Instead of waking up in my room I'm still here. I whimper. Logan's laughing should make me want to punch him, but some recollection of last night passes through my mind and I find myself having to squeeze my legs a little to stop the buzzing sensation.

"Look, she and Bryan left early this morning for their two-week honeymoon. You can at least keep it quiet till they get back, and who knows, maybe you'll have forgotten all about it. Or maybe..."

"Don't finish that sentence!" I say.

I get to my feet and start to untangle from the sheets when I realize I'm naked too. Half my boob is hanging out. *God, when will this nightmare end?* I quickly wrap the sheet back around me and start shuffling for the bathroom.

A deep chuckle fills the room. "No need to cover up, I saw a lot more of you last night." He grins.

"Ugh! Bite me!" I growl at him like an angry dog ready to maul off his head.

"Did plenty of that last night."

I stop walking, and peer over my shoulder, he winks, and I shoot him the bird. With whatever pride I have left, I gather the bottom of the sheet, square my shoulders, and walk straight into the bathroom to wash away Logan Fields.

I scrub my skin so hard it turns a fiery shade of red. I am still fuzzy about how I ended up in Logan's bed. There was definitely a shot or two of tequila at the open bar. My stomach lurches from the memory, triggering the start of a migraine pressing at my temples. I vaguely remember Logan mentioning something about how his plus-one bailed on him because he wasn't serious enough. We connected on that fact, because my plus-one decided I was far too serious for his liking.

Prior to Friday night's rehearsal dinner, I hadn't seen Logan since my twentieth birthday four years ago. He never said it out loud, but I've known Logan my whole life, enough to understand that the memories were too much.

A pounding at the bathroom door tugs me from my thoughts.

"What are you doing in there? Thinking about last night?" His voice is muffled through the closed door. It's playful, and too sexy for my liking.

I groan, scrubbing hard at my face, but no matter what I do the memories keep coming.

"Go away!" I yell, closing my eyes.

I allow the hot steaming water to rinse the soap and whatever is left of him on me.

"Oh, so you are then."

The door whines as he opens it.

Way to go, Ellie, you forgot to lock it! Immediately I go to wrap my arms around my body, only to realize I'm hidden behind the glass. The shadow of the door dances off the reflection of the soft yellow lighting above. For him to get a visual, he'll have to stick his whole head around. The glass is grainy, and I hope my body is nothing more than a silhouette, but that doesn't actually make me feel any better.

He's too quiet. I pull the screen open to peek my head out.

"Why are you still not dressed?" I ask, attempting not to look down.

His eyebrows perk up, like he's waiting for me to invite him in. My eyes remain focused on his every movement, as my hand reaches down into the soap dish attached to the wall. I feel around until I find what I'm looking for. I chuck an unopened box of hotel soap. It hits him square in the chest, and lands with a thud at his feet. I'd intended for it to shoo him away but instead he comes into the bathroom.

He steps over the soap box. I don't know what made me think sleeping with my best friend's brother was a good idea. As the moments become clearer the tension in my body releases. How could something so good feel so wrong? I have the urge to scream, cry, punch something—maybe Logan. The emotions running through me need to calm themselves, because it's all a bit overwhelming.

As he gets nearer I begin to recollect the sloppy kisses in the elevator on the way up. The way his tongue hungrily devoured mine, and how his dry, coarse hands slipped up my purple dress. My eyes dart to his mouth and my cheeks burn with the memory. He grins as if he knows exactly the scene playing out in my head.

Between my legs aches like it wants to remember the way it

felt last night. His crooked grin beams as he leans against part of the wall that juts out near the tub. Our faces align. Both his eyes and my own land right in the spot we're both craving.

"You want to remember too, don't you?" he questions in a low, velvety voice. His eyes meet mine, and I try to pull away, but I'm stuck.

I say nothing, but he already knows I'm contemplating his question. More of the night falls together, piece by piece like a large puzzle. I squeeze my legs closed wanting the pressure to subside on its own, but there's only one way it can release —well, two.

"Just say what you want, Ellie." His voice makes it hard to breathe.

My eyes flicker down towards his length and the way it hardens for me the moment I give it some attention. Glancing up, his smile never falters.

"One more time." My voice comes out raspier than usual. It's deeper than most females normally, but never have I heard it in this way.

I slide the door open and he gets inside the tub, shutting it behind him. Backing up for him, my foot catches a puddle of shampoo. He reaches for me, grabbing my waist, and pulls me into him. Skin against skin, he hardens even more.

"Wait, what about a condom?" I ask, nearly out of breath even though we haven't begun yet.

"You said you're on birth control, right?"

I nod; I vaguely remember telling him, but we chose to use a condom to be safe. At least we had some sense of what was happening last night.

He tightens his grip on my waist. His eyes are locked on mine. "I get tested regularly, did it recently, if that makes you feel any better."

Logan has always been a responsible person, making sure he contemplated every outcome before actually doing something, minus when his dad passed. Although I think from the moment they got the call about the accident, his mind had already started the process of deciding to leave and all the pros and cons that went along with it.

"I trust you," I whisper.

Lifting my right leg allows him to slip inside. I toss my head back and moan out his name. His smile widens—proud of his accomplishment. Now that all the memories surface, there's no way I could forget anything, even if I tried. We went three rounds last night before we collapsed in each other's arms.

I would be lying if I said I never fantasized about him while we were growing up. He had girlfriends, a lot of them, and I was just his kid sister's best friend. I don't know when his view of me changed—or maybe it hadn't and he'd hidden it all those years. Three years isn't a lot, but when you're a senior dating a sophomore it is a bit skeezy.

"Am I jogging your memory now?" He bites down on the lower part of my ear. My insides twitch, tightening around his length.

"This will be the last memory we have of this. We can't do this again." Even as I say it, part of me knows it's not true.

He shakes his head, grinning. I'm trying to be convincing but with each thrust it grows harder and harder to tell myself this could never happen again. *Off-limits, Ellie, he's always been off-limits.*

A moan threatens to escape as he lifts me, allowing him in deeper. I bury my face in his neck and release a high-pitched half-scream half-moan that has been sitting at the edge of my throat. He joins me, and the sound of his moans along with him saying my name causes my entire body to shake with an intensity so strong that I have to grip him tighter. The pleasure doesn't stop, not for one heartbeat as I let whatever this is play out.

This is it, I tell myself. *I'm going to treat this like what happens in Vegas; except this is whatever happens at The Hilton stays at The*

Hilton. One can only hope I keep that mantra. My heart squeezes at the thought of losing Charlotte's friendship over this. As good as this feels, after today Logan and I will go back to whatever it is we were. I'm still reeling over breaking this rule. It was an important one.

My twin brother, Arthur, broke her heart. She didn't want the same for me. And now here I am receiving the best orgasm of my life with the one person I'm not supposed to have one with. I'm so screwed.

CHAPTER 3

"Honey, why don't you go outside and play. Or call one of your—"

"I don't have anyone to call." Nine-year-old me huffed a sigh and pointed the remote at the TV. *Zenon* was playing on the Disney Channel. It reminded me of Charlotte, but I left it on anyway.

Charlotte had gone off to band camp for a few weeks. Her mom signed her up and she wasn't too thrilled, but had to go since her mom spent a lot of money on it.

Mom sat down on the edge of the couch and ran a hand through my hair. She sighed. "There's got to be someone."

"She has no one." My brother, Arthur, appeared, dressed and ready for his friend to pick him up for soccer.

"Why don't you go with Arthur—"

"No way. I'll go outside in a little while. Can I please finish the movie?" I asked, adjusting so that I could see the TV instead of Mom.

"She can't come with me, she's a loser."

Mom scowled at Arthur. "Arthur, please, if you can't be nice to your sister you won't be going anywhere."

16

Arthur flopped down on the love seat on the other side of the room. "Fine. Sorry."

After a few minutes Mom shooed him out and the two of them left the room. I had promised Mom I'd go outside and once the show was over, I did. I sat on the front steps with a Cam Jansen book in my hand. I was deep into the book when I heard something fall. I glanced up to find Logan's bike on its side and him walking towards me, a cup of ice cream in his hand. His face was red with beads of sweat rolling down his face. He had very light blonde hair then and it was wet with sweat.

I put the book down behind me and moved to give him room. He sat beside me and stared into the cup. Inside the ice cream had turned to green soup.

"I owe you an ice cream," he said. His shoulders slumped and he looked defeated.

I moved closer, our bodies touched. I'd never seen Logan so sad.

"You rode your bike all the way here for me?"

His eyes never left mine as he shook his head. "When Charlotte left you were sad. I wanted to cheer you up."

It didn't matter that the ice cream was soup. All that mattered was that Logan had done the sweetest thing anyone had ever done for me. I smiled. It was the first time that week that I had. "Well it worked," I said.

His mouth opened and then closed. "It did?"

I wrapped my arms around him. Back then Logan was like a bean pole. He was skinny with not a single ounce of muscle. It was easy to hold on.

"Yeah. Thank you."

"Hey, do you want to ride bikes?" he asked.

"I'd love to. Let me go ask my mom."

For the rest of the afternoon Logan and I rode bikes around my neighborhood. He asked Mom if he could take me to the ice-cream shop that was a few blocks over, and she allowed it. Logan was twelve and I was nine; we were so young to be riding off on our own, but we did. From that day forward he showed up on the days he wasn't hanging out with his own friends, and he made it a point to make my summer something special. I will forever be grateful for what he did for me.

Out of Logan's arms is the perfect place to be. I'm glad I have work and a reason to check out of The Hilton. I have no idea how long he'll be in town, but from the looks of it this morning he wasn't planning on leaving any time soon. Josephine still lives on Long Island. I can imagine him staying for her, even though he refused to stick around to help following his father's funeral. Maybe he's changed. I can't think about that right now, because I'm almost late for work.

Sheer Threads is a small clothing boutique in one of the most high-traffic malls on Long Island. The lot is somewhat full for a Monday morning. I pull into a spot near the free-standing Barnes and Noble on the south side of the mall.

I have three minutes before I have to clock in. It was a good thing I chose to stay at the hotel, even though my room was wasted and only occupied for an hour prior to the wedding. At least I had everything I needed for work today, including the Tylenol to rid me of the migraine that peaked after our fourth round this morning in the shower.

I grab my mini brown backpack and swing it over my shoulder as I step out of my old gray Toyota. My grass-green pleated skirt blows in the soft summer breeze as I stroll through the lot towards the main mall.

Behind the Barnes and Noble is a small outdoor area with a beautiful array of small trees and shrubs along the center and some seating for the Cheesecake Factory.

As I reach the glass doors my phone buzzes in my bag. I pull it to the front to get it out. I gasp. Charlotte's beautiful brown eyes stare at me. I took the picture of us a few weeks ago while we were at our last dress fitting. I should answer it; I can't ignore my best friend. She would know immediately that something was up.

"Hey!" I say, pushing through the door.

Voices of customers carry through the large hallway. On Charlotte's end the call is a bit muffled by announcements overhead. She must have gotten in a little while ago. She said her flight should take about ten hours.

"Hey. I didn't get to say goodbye. You disappeared on me."

The words stick to the end of my tongue. There's no way I can play it cool. If I can't speak over the phone, what will happen when she comes home? How will I face her knowing what I've done? She can be mad at Logan all she wants, but it would kill me inside if she hated me for it.

"You okay over there?"

"Yeah, sorry." The words finally make their way to the surface. "I'm walking through the mall on my way to work. Sorry, I had a headache." It's only half a lie. "You were busy having the time of your life."

"I almost knocked on your hotel room door before I left, but since you disappeared I imagined you were having one of your migraines."

I laugh, but immediately recover with a cough. "Yeah I definitely was. I'm sorry to cut this short," I say as I reach the center of the mall.

The space in the center is bare right now, aside from a few chairs scattered around near a large white column. "I'm going to clock in late as it is, but I want to hear all about your first day."

"Okay. I'll call you tomorrow. Can you believe I'm married?" she squeals. Bryan says something beside her, I can't hear what it is over the commotion on the other end. "I should go anyway. Have a good day at work."

"Have fun in Hawaii!"

I'm not jealous. No, never. Okay, maybe a little. I've never been anywhere other than Jersey and Florida, once. I'm not too big on travel and airplanes.

She hangs up and for the first time in our twenty-year friendship, I'm relieved when she does.

I hurry through the mall to the small boutique nestled into the far hallway past the FYE. There are two floors of clothing, men's and women's. I work in the women's clothing area, and have had to swap my sweats and ripped jeans for pleated skirts and crop tops. The clothing here is very chic and fashionable. Thank God for the paycheck or else I would have stood out like a sore thumb. Prior to this job I dressed more like Anne Hathaway in *Devil Wears Prada* pre makeover, with my sweaters, vests, and penny loafers.

Even though we are inside the mall, the space the store occupies is bright with faux windows that display around the top of the wall with white lights behind them. Large spotlight fixtures hang from the lowered ceiling. Beautiful mahogany wooden shelves against the walls hold various folded clothing and black metal racks take up the center of the sales floor. There's also always a wafting scent of lavender, but we have never figured out where it's coming from.

Lily waves from behind the register in the far back. In this area alone we have three registers perched on top of a counter. Her long flowing floral print skirt crinkles as she struts around the cash-wrap. She's not Charlotte, but she's been a constant in my life since I started working here after I graduated high school. My plans to take my mass communications degree and turn it into something slipped far away, as all of my internships never led anywhere. After countless resumes and demos, I felt like it was time to move on.

Lily is happy here at Sheer Threads. Her plans are to take over as manager one day. She's already a key holder—we both are, but the only difference is she wants to retire here. This is what she loves. I would be lying if I said I wasn't jealous that she had her life planned out, while I'm still over here figuring things out.

She wraps her pale, brawny arms around me as if she hadn't seen me in ages, but it's only been a week. I took most of the week off to help Charlotte do last-minute wedding errands. But the hugs are Lily's way of greeting everyone she likes. She pulls back and tugs at her sun-kissed blonde hair. "How was the wedding?"

My face turns a ferocious shade of crimson. I check it in the mirror plastered to the wall to the left of the register.

Her brow rises. "Did you and Matt..."

"Matt thought it would be fun to dump me over text." I step around her so that I can clock in. Sliding behind the register I note the time on the computer. It's ten past three and that means I'm ten minutes late. I type in my passcode and employee number as quickly as possible. Lily struts over and her fingers slide along the counter as she slips by me.

"Oh no, hon, I'm so sorry. Is there anything I can do?" She glances up. There's pity in those big blue eyes.

I shake my head. "Thank you. I thought I'd still be in bed today eating a tub of ice cream, but there I was staring down at the text and I almost felt nothing. Which is strange, because he was my everything, like I thought he was the one. I'll probably feel the repercussions in a few days once this hangover wears off."

Her high-pitched giggles causes two women browsing the jewelry at the cash-wrap to turn their gaze to us.

"Maybe you didn't really love him. Did you ever think it's possible that you were in love with the idea of love and not him?"

I shrug and bend down to place my belongings in the small safe under the counter.

"You know I never thought of it like that. I felt like I'd been punched in the gut, but not hard enough that I couldn't catch my breath, ya know?"

21

She nods. "I do. In fact, when I was dating Carly last year and she cheated on me, I expected to curl up in a ball and not want to move for days, but I never did."

I get to my feet and give her a sympathetic look. At least I know there's nothing wrong with me for not getting overly emotional about it. I'm more angry than anything.

"Then Jett came into my life, and he flipped my world upside down. He's even up to opening our relationship." She winks at me.

Lily is bisexual and since I've known her she's dated both men and women. She's had some of the sweetest romances and some that were pretty raunchy. This one is teetering on the edge of the latter, but who am I to judge? She's never smiled more than she has since Jett strolled into the store searching for a tux. He asked her to direct him to the men's department, and instead of directing she led him there. By the time he had his tux she had his number.

"So, the wedding," she prods. "Any cute guys there? You were a red ripe tomato when I asked you about it before. I have to know what happened."

It's not that I don't want to tell Lily. She's a neutral party; She knows Charlotte, but they aren't friends. Lily is my work friend and I've never really combined my outside life with my work life.

"Nothing happened, just a lot of drinking."

As she's about to open her mouth to ask for more a customer walks up. I know she won't let me off the hook. Her devilish smirk says she's going to poke around later until I spill my guts. I'm grateful for the sudden rush, as one of our regulars asks me about a pair of shoes, which are across the store.

❦

It turns out the world must have known that I wasn't ready to tell anyone about my night with Logan, because once the first rush hit, we were faced with multiple waves throughout the night. It was so busy at one point I almost didn't have a chance to take my break, and when I did I cut it short by ten minutes to make sure the sales floor was covered.

By closing time we're both too exhausted to hold a normal conversation. We only have enough energy to chat about sales figures or the horror stories our co-worker Jess told us about her day in the fitting rooms. Jess offered to run to the bank with Lily, so we don't walk out together either, and I can leave before they do.

Lily shuts the gate behind me and wishes me a goodnight. The mall is eerily quiet at this hour. I pass by some other employees and a few members of the custodial staff cleaning up after the long day. Other than that it's quiet, except the soft music that still plays overhead.

I push my way out of the mall and into the damp summer night. A shadow of a man leans up against the brick siding of Barnes and Noble. I pick up the pace. I'm not in the mood to get mugged. He steps out of the darkness and into the spotlight of the overhead lamp.

My pulse kicks up a notch until my gaze lands on his face. Eyes wide, I glare at him. "What are you doing here? And how did you know where I worked?"

"You told me your schedule for today."

I did? I wish I had never gotten wasted last night. No matter how attractive Logan is, this was not, and still isn't a good idea.

He doesn't seem to understand the concept of space. When I left this morning I told him we should keep our distance—as in no communication. Only here he is standing in front of me with his sexy tousled short brown hair.

He closes the gap between us so that the tips of our shoes are touching. His eyes roam my body and under his intense stare my insides tickle with a pleasure I wasn't expecting. I hate the tremor that races through me. It makes my whole body shake.

23

"But that doesn't answer the *what are you doing here* question."

If it's possible, his grin grows wider. He leans forward grazing his lips against my cheek and letting them tickle my ear. "I can't stop thinking about what it felt like to be with you."

Be with you. His words catch me by surprise. I expected his mouth to spout dirty words, but instead he's reeling me in with that charm of his. I sway backwards trying to escape, but he's got some kind of strange power over me. I'd blame my childhood crush, but I'm well past that stage now. As a grown adult I should know better, but for some reason I can't help myself. It's like telling a dog to not chase a squirrel.

"I see you've been thinking about it too." He lifts his arm and gently caresses my cheek with the back of his hand. Under my skirt I close my legs trying to stop the friction steadily growing down there.

"No." The word comes out in a whisper.

He chuckles, then gently presses his lips to my jawline. I gasp at the wetness growing between my legs.

"We can't. I can't. She…" My words are broken. My head falls back as he grazes along my neck, slowly nipping in all the right places.

"One more night. Just give me one more night," he says between kisses. His voice has a desperation in it. He's pleading with me and I like that he wants more. I try to erase the image that anything can come of this. It could be fun. I've never had one of these—flings? Is that what they are called? I don't know. I don't care, but oh God, what is he doing now? His finger slowly swirls down into my cleavage.

I shouldn't do this. I need to stop. It's only going to make things more complicated.

"But, I…Charlotte."

He tucks his pointer under my chin, and when I open my eyes, he's watching me with an intense gaze.

"Charlotte isn't here. We're grown adults and we can do what we please."

"She's my best—"

"I know. What she doesn't know won't hurt her. I like whatever this is."

I shake my head and try to pull away. I'm reluctant as his hands cup my breasts. I gaze around the area. It's quiet, there's no one here, but what about the other employees? What if Lily finds me here? I'll never hear the end of it.

"Fine," I say through gritted teeth. "I'll meet you back at the hotel."

He smirks like he's won. "Looking forward to it," he whispers as he lets go and struts away like he didn't just try to have his way with me right here in public.

I fall back onto the soft white sheets of the hotel room bed, and collapse into them. I should be exhausted. We've been back and forth all night between kissing, sex, and watching reruns of *Friends* on Nick at Night.

"I got you all worked up that time."

I roll my eyes. "Don't be so smug about it." I flail my arm over, smacking him across the chest. It bounces with laughter while I leave it there. He bites down a little on the soft flesh near my wrist. I hiss and roll on my side so that I can face him.

"Come with me!" He sits up suddenly.

My brows rise as he stands, baring it all to me again. He slips into his green plaid boxers and throws a black T-shirt over himself. There's a roughness to him that I've never noticed before. He was always the clean-shaven boy that got straight As and was homecoming king his senior year. Now he's this man with a grungy look about him.

After tugging on his pair of blue jeans he walks around to my side of the bed and reaches his hand down. "What are you afraid of? It's not like we've never hung out before."

It's true, we spent almost a whole summer together, but that was before it turned sexual. Things are different now. We've crossed a line and there's no turning back.

I take his hand anyway. "First, I need to use the bathroom."

"You women and your desire to 'freshen up' after sex."

I shove at his chest playfully, getting a laugh out of him. In the bathroom I shut the door and lean against it. I need a few minutes not only to clean up, but to screw my head on in the right direction. After I do what I need and clear my mind I grab my clothes from the floor. I pad over to where he's leaning against the door waiting for me. His foot is propped up on the wall, head buried in his phone. In his free hand is an empty coffee cup. I'd question it, but it's Logan and he's probably devised a devious plan. It's written clear as day in the smirk on his face.

"Ready?" he questions, looking up.

I nod.

He opens the door, allowing me to go first, then takes my hand and pulls me down the hallway. His eyes dart around like he's about to pull off one of his signature stunts. He was an all-around nice guy, but he was still the first to pull a prank or TP the neighbors' house.

"We aren't doing anything illegal, are we?"

He peeks over his shoulder at me and winks. This can't be good. He may have been the good boy, but he had his moments of late-night trouble-making as a teen.

"You know me better than that, Ellie."

"Do I?" I ask a little too loud.

"Shh."

We reach a dead-end with a door that says NO ACCESS ROOF. He checks over his shoulder and tugs on the door, grinning when it opens for him as if he had magic powers. In his free hand he's holding a coffee cup from the room, and he wedges it between the door and the frame before we slip through and head up the stairs. Thankfully, there's no alarm and we make it to the roof without anyone noticing.

It's still dark, but on the horizon there's a bit of a purple glow in the sky.

"You and your devious ways haven't changed one bit."

Smiling, he says, "Just watch."

He points towards the eastern part of the sky where the purple color is fading into a lighter shade of blue. A yellowish tint glows beyond the buildings and trees in the distance. The cars below us whiz by. Rush hour should be starting soon. If this wasn't some random fling I'd say he was trying to be romantic.

"There." He points back in the same area, but this time the glow is so radiant that it's almost peaceful. Even with the overpowering sound pollution on Long Island, the sunrise is beautiful.

"Why did you want to show me this?" I ask.

He shrugs. "I remember driving two young girls around who were eager to watch sunrises. They would beg me to take them to the beach every Saturday in the summer."

Charlotte was the one with the camera and I was the one with the idea. We spent many summer Saturdays at the beach awaiting the sunrise with Logan. Sometimes he'd bring one of his girlfriends and they'd make out in the car the whole time. Charlotte and I would take pictures and enjoy some bagels by the beach. Other times he joined us as we waited.

"And I remember someone sucking face with every girl at Babylon High School while Charlotte and I enjoyed the beautiful sunrise."

He chuckles and wraps his arm around me. I'm confused by the gesture. It makes the moment feel romantic and I don't like it. I step out from his touch and immediately my body regrets it, but I don't let on that I feel anything.

"Where have you been, Logan Fields? You kind of disappeared

off the face of the earth. Then you show up at your sister's wedding and try to woo me with your..." I try to find the right word.

"Quivering member?" He wiggles his brows.

I push his shoulder, smiling at his jab at one of my favorite movies of all time, *Ten Things I Hate About You*. Growing up I thought our playful banter was part of our sibling-like bond, but maybe as I grew older it was something more and I was oblivious because he was off limits.

"Seriously though, what happened to you?"

He shrugs and stares off at the rising sun. I shouldn't press him for information, especially since, after today, whatever there is between us will be pushed aside as if it never happened. I'm totally fine with that, but not hearing from him for four years makes me want to know more.

"I moved to the mountains of Pennsylvania got a job as a high school gym teacher right out of college, and lived my life. I guess. What about you? Why aren't you a famous DJ yet?"

I'm surprised he remembers. "Wasn't cut out for it."

He glances over at me briefly, before returning his eyes to the sky. The sun is already fully up, and the traffic below comes to a halt. Horns honk and tires screech. It is the State of New York after all. It may not be the city, but us New Yorkers are brutal when it comes to driving.

"I don't believe that, not for one minute. You and that girl, Bonnie, had that kick-ass radio show in high school."

High school feels like so long ago. I look over at him and I really take in his appearance. He's aged more than I imagined the heartthrob of Babylon High School would. At the wedding I noticed his tired heavy lids, and how his shoulders sagged more than they ever did. He used to walk tall and act like nothing in the world bothered him. Until he lost his father

"Bonnie moved out to California and is now a morning show host, so maybe it was her that was the kick-ass one."

"Nah." He bumps his hip into mine. "It was you."

I smile, but stare down at the pebbles at my feet. I kick a few with the toe of my sandal. A heavy silence falls between us, like we're unsure what to say next. It's unlike him or maybe that was the drunk version that talked my ear off. He had babbled the entire way through, from the moment we arrived to the point where we kissed. Now, as we stand here unsure of what the future holds, he's quiet. For him that means he's contemplating something. A quiet Logan is a dangerous one.

"What if we did this?"

I narrow my eyes on him. "Did what?"

"This. Whatever this is. For two weeks. I was supposed to go back tomorrow, but Mom could use a hand around the house, and I don't know, it's kind of nice to have a distraction."

His words hit me hard. I'm a distraction, but maybe that's what he is for me too. There are plenty of other things I'd like to forget right now. I've had so many thoughts on how my life isn't nearly what I expected it to be when I graduated high school. I thought I'd work for Z100 or some top radio show, but here I was twenty-four nearing twenty-five and working at the same clothing store I've been at since I was eighteen.

"What do you propose?" I can't believe what I'm saying, that I might actually agree to whatever terms he wants to set. My mind drifts to Charlotte. Would she ever forgive me if she found out? Am I willing to take that chance? I've never done anything like this. I'm the good girl, the one who believes in love and relationships before sex.

"Two weeks. No strings."

"And what happens after the two weeks? We pretend, just as we were going to?"

He tilts his chin up towards the now perfectly clear blue summer sky. "It's probably for the best. Pretending. You can say no. It's only a suggestion."

I set my eyes back up on the rising sun. Not even a cloud rolls by. The traffic is still busy on the street level, but there's a strange kind of silence between us that fills the roof. If only I could get a sign that this—

"Hey what are you two doing up here?"

"Shit!" Logan grabs a hold of me as the man in a blue button-down security uniform steps out from the stairs. And here's our sign.

"Sorry, sir, the door was open and I wanted the perfect sunrise for our engagement." He gives the man every ounce of emotion, as if it really did happen. Logan grabs hold of my hand, lifts it up, and stares at the empty space on the left ring finger. "I couldn't afford a ring, and a sunrise was the next best thing."

His acting skills are on point. He could pull it off much better than me. I lean into him, trying to play the part.

Glancing up I give him a doe-eyed look. "It was absolutely perfect."

He stares at me wide-eyed, shocked that I'm playing along. "No," he whispers, "you're perfect." He leans down and plants the softest most realistic kiss to my lips.

I suck in a breath hoping he doesn't notice. I hate that his fake words have this effect on me. Maybe I can't pretend as well as I'd hoped.

"I'll let you both off with a warning," the security guard says, crossing his arms. "Please return to your room, and don't let me catch you up here again." The man adjusts his belt, his pot belly spilling over his waistline. "Go. Skat!" He steps aside.

"Come on, beautiful, let's go celebrate." Logan swoops his arms underneath me and scoops me off the ground.

As I tuck my hands around his neck, he winks.

"What did you have in mind?" I ask, half playing the part and half turned on by his ability to carry me out of here.

"You, me, every piece of furniture in that hotel room." He smirks like he means it. Without another word, he whisks me off past the guard and down the stairs. His quick steps make for a bumpy ride down. We flee to the room. He easily takes the key card from his back pocket.

"You act like you've done this before."

"Done what?" he questions, with a grin.

"Swept a girl off her feet."

He chuckles, shaking me and almost dropping the key card. He slides it through, the door opens, and we stumble inside. The door shuts behind us.

"I'm just really good."

It's that comment that makes me realize: this can only be exactly what he says. No strings, no emotions, just good old-fashioned sex. It will take some getting used to, but maybe it's what I need in my life right now.

"Yes."

"Yes what?"

We stop in the middle of the entryway, the mirrored closet doors reflecting our image. I try to ignore the way seeing him holding me makes my heart jump.

"Two weeks. After that we forget it happened. We'll both move on. You go back to Pennsylvania; I'm here. We live separate lives, and never speak of it again."

He licks his lips and regards me in a way I've never seen him do before. His eyes rake over my face, gauging how serious I am. "So, does that mean I have permission to have my way with you right now?"

I stare up into his warm brown eyes. All of his attention is on me. It doesn't even slip as I squirm out of his arms and begin undressing in front of him. "Actually I think it's the other way around."

I step out of my pants and toss them aside, then pull my shirt up over my head. I'd been so rushed to see what he had planned I'd forgotten a bra. Without hesitation, he leans down and takes my breast in his mouth. His tongue dances in circles over my hardened nipple. I throw my head back and glance over at the mirror.

His eyes follow mine. "You like watching?"

I nod, and moan as he takes my other nipple between his thumb and pointer. Without another word he removes his clothing and lifts me back into his arms. I wrap my legs around him and we both watch in the mirror as we lose ourselves in each other again.

CHAPTER 4

"C'mon, Logan, please." Thirteen-year-old Charlotte whined from outside Logan's bedroom door. "You promised."

At that point, Charlotte and I were running on zero hours of sleep. Our hair was in messy buns on top of our heads, but at least our faces were refreshed with some cucumber mask we stole from Josephine. We had been up all night doing what girls our age did at sleepovers. We chatted about boys, bands we loved, and more boys. We ate junk until our bellies hurt and had a marathon of old teen rom-coms.

Logan's door flew open. He stood sleepy-eyed in boxers with no T-shirt. Thirteen was a rough age for me. My body bloomed later than most. My boobs had finally come in, but looked lopsided and awkward, and my period had struck with full force. By this point I had liked boys for a while, but all of the urges that came along with puberty had hit. Logan worked out back then and I would be lying if I said I didn't have fantasies about him. Him and his ridiculously sexy tousled brown hair, and his almost six-pack.

He stared both of us down, but his expression somewhat

33

softened when his eyes landed on me. "Be ready to go in ten minutes, and I'm bringing Jennifer."

"Ugh!" Charlotte said, groaning. She turned to me and whispered, "At least it's not Sophie Michaels or Carrie Johnson."

I was in agreement with that. Those girls always had a bone to pick with everyone, but they liked to torture me because they knew I liked Logan.

"Fine, but if you're gonna screw in the car at least put a towel down so we don't have to sit in your sex juice." She turned to me and curled her lip, exposing her bright pink braces. I swallowed hard, unable to look at Logan. The thought of what he did with those girls disgusted me. It was like there was a new one every month.

Logan drove us to the beach before the first light peeked through. Thinking back, I'm sure if we got caught he probably would have gotten in trouble. He had his license, but at his age should have had an adult in the car with him. We always made it back before their mom woke up.

We picked up Jennifer along the way. She made the car smell like a funeral home with her floral body spray. Charlotte and I coughed for the first ten minutes straight. She was not amused.

The moment we arrived Charlotte and I ran out of the car, while Logan and Jennifer hung back doing God knows what inside the car. It wasn't only Jennifer; there'd been others on different occasions, but on this particular day it was her.

We stayed over an hour, and I still couldn't help feeling creeped out while I sat in the back where something probably happened. As we drove back over the bridge towards home Charlotte and I sang along to the Taylor Swift song on the radio.

"I can't listen to this shit," Jennifer moaned from the front seat.

She turned the music down, but Charlotte and I knew every lyric to "You Belong With Me", and it didn't stop us from singing louder and out of tune. I remember for a few moments I caught

Logan's eye in the rearview mirror. While Jennifer scowled with her arms crossed, Logan smirked at me and made silly faces. When he didn't know I was looking I saw him narrow his eyes at Jennifer, which confirmed that by the end of the day Jennifer would be old news, and someone else would take her place. It was never me, and no matter how hard I tried to forget it I always wished it had been.

Yesterday was a whirlwind. Who is the person that agreed to such a ridiculous arrangement with her best friend's brother? Oh right, that was me. After the sunrise and another round of amazing sex, I went off to work. I spent my entire shift contemplating all of the things that could go wrong between now and next Sunday when Charlotte arrives back home. She never called me back and for once I'm okay with it, because I'm not even sure what I'll say.

It's Wednesday, and while I'm usually grateful for a morning shift, I'm uneasy about what my evening holds. I haven't heard from Logan and I want to believe that's a good thing. The morning has been slow, which is great in the long run because I find myself buried in shipment. I also think Lily is rubbing off on me, because I'm starting to love the new items we've gotten.

Lily takes the register and has offered to check in all the boxes that arrive through the day. Wednesday is our normal shipment day, while the rest of the week we receive drabs here and there.

I tug out some new jean shorts, frayed at the bottom, with some tears in the leg. There's a mixture of short and long versions of the same pants. I fold them carefully onto the shelf against the wall near the main entrance to the store. As I shift back to the box, two familiar warm eyes find mine. He's crouched behind the box hiding the rest of his face.

"Stalking me again, Fields?"

He stretches his neck to uncover the sly grin on his lips. "I have another proposition for you."

I narrow my eyes as I pull out another sheer tank.

"No, I will not go on a date with you." I smile. I mean it, but at the same time I'm enjoying teasing him. Our banter is the one thing that has never changed throughout the years and it's familiar.

"I'm wounded." He stands and clutches a hand to his chest over his heart. He towers over the large shipment box and myself.

"Should I be worried? I won't do a video either."

He chuckles. "For the next two weeks that body is for my eyes only."

"Oh, so it's an exclusive no strings proposition."

"I'm a little selfish when it comes to the women in my life." He pauses, licks his lips and purses them like he's contemplating his next words. "Especially you."

I'm taken aback by his comment. *Especially me.* What does that mean? Is it because I'm like a sister to him? I grimace.

"Well, I'm not sure if exclusive is going to work." I tease, tugging my phone free from my back pocket. "What if I had a date next week?"

I check for my boss, Maryann. She's nice, but if she caught me with my phone on the sales floor I'd be done for.

"Look at this guy." I flip through one of the dating apps on my phone. I haven't actually looked at it since I met Matt through it, but I kind of like messing with Logan.

I pull up a guy with big round glasses and Cory Matthews type curls on his head. In the corner of my eye I watch Logan's brow raise. He snorts. "Nice try."

I shrug, and place the phone back into the rear pocket of my dark blue jeans. "So, what do you have in mind?" I check around me again to make sure I'm not being watched. Aside from the phone, fraternizing is a big no-no. Lily catches my eye, her brow arching. I spin back to Logan waiting for a response.

"Bryan called me and he asked for a favor. He saw what I'd done at the house I rented in Pennsylvania and wanted me to do a small renovation on their bedroom, plus add some of my interior decorating skills. I'm here to recruit you as my apprentice."

"So, role-playing?"

"You won't let me get a word in today, will you?" He smirks.

"What will this apprenticeship consist of?"

He folds his arms at his chest. "I'm so glad you asked. Painting the walls and each other, mostly the walls though. Adding a new window—" He drones on.

I shake my head, and cover my face, trying to hide the sly smile forming. I blink up at him through my lashes.

"Bryan wants to surprise Charlotte, so it's a secret. Can you keep one of those?"

"So far I haven't told her about us, so I think I'm good."

"Good, so are you in?" he questions.

"For my best friend, sure."

His eyes flicker over my face like he's trying to read me. He tilts his head, keeping his attention all on me. He shifts his weight and I catch a flicker of something more than hunger in his deep brown eyes. I can't quite figure out what's hiding behind them, but whatever it was vanishes as quickly as it came.

"Will you be off work before four?"

"I get off at five, but I have to go home and change."

"I'll pick you up and we'll head to Home Depot. He also sent me a vision board of how she always dreamed her bedroom would resemble."

"I don't need one of those, I'm pretty sure I know exactly what she wants."

"Great. So tonight we go to Home Depot, tomorrow the furniture store, then over the weekend we start painting. Should be done before they come back next Sunday."

He spins to leave, but then turns back, glancing over his

shoulder he whispers, "I think your friend back there is going to ask you a lot of questions."

I turn my neck and sure enough, Lily has her elbows perched on the counter, her head in her hands, and a dreamy look in her eyes. I definitely have a lot of explaining to do. I turn to tell him off, but he's already gone, leaving me with a very curious Lily on my hands.

⁂

Almost my entire shift is taken up by the shipment we've received today. It's almost as bad as the ones we get during Christmas. Finally done, I trudge over to the cash-wrap to throw away some of the paper and plastic the clothing was wrapped in.

"So, who's the hottie?" Lily questions.

She's caught me and there's not a customer in sight who can distract her. After stuffing the garbage into the pail, I straighten and stare at her. "Logan."

"You moved on pretty fast."

"I wouldn't say that exactly. It's more of a casual thing. Two weeks."

Lily wiggles her brows. "Are you sure that's casual? I only saw him for less than five minutes, but did you see the way he watched you? It was as if you were the only one in this entire store. Nothing else mattered."

I snort, loud enough for the customers walking in to eye me. The customer's lip curls upwards.

"It's not like that with Logan. It's a mere high-school fantasy."

"Oh, so he's not some random guy then? The plot thickens, dun dun." She brings her voice down into a low baritone.

Laughter fills my lungs. "No, he's not random at all."

Her lips twitch. "Casual." She shakes her head. "You keep telling yourself that."

Her words slice through me. Of course this is casual, what

else would it be? Logan and I can't be more wrong for each other. Not only because of the promise I made to Charlotte, but because he's Logan Fields, the guy every girl wants to date. I was the awkward girl with a mouth full of braces who wore Jonas Brothers tees every day for an entire school year.

Maryann struts up to the front of the store, her hands behind her back, as she observes the two of us chatting. I don't give her a chance to reprimand me as I pretend to busy myself with organizing the cash-wrap. She scowls, but gets distracted by a customer yelling in the lingerie department.

"You'll see," Lily smirks.

I don't get a rebuttal, as the empty space before us becomes filled with customers ready to be rung up.

CHAPTER 5

$\mathcal{I}$'m grateful Mom is working late tonight. She knows Logan all too well. I'd be bombarded with questions if she knew I was hanging out with him. I sent her a text to let her know not to wait up that I'm going out again. She suspects I'm seeing someone, but hasn't pried.

Mom works part time as a waitress to keep herself busy. Although she retired from her many years of teaching, she wanted something to do, especially after she and Dad divorced. They didn't separate until I was eighteen. I was going into my first year of college, and the thought of being alone all day made her anxious. She hated the silence in the house, especially since my brother, Arthur, got up and left for his dream career in California. Mom expected him to come back home after college. There were plenty of opportunities in Manhattan for him, but he chose to stay in California.

I remember the phone call like it was yesterday. Mom pretended that it didn't hurt, but I knew when she retreated to her room and shut the door, that it bothered her more than she let on. By that point both Arthur and Dad had been out of the house for four years, so we were used to it being only us. Deep down I knew Mom wanted him to come back and make the house feel more like home again.

I feel bad, because even now I'm rarely home. My time is consumed by work. Even if she is lonely, Mom doesn't mind the extra work. She enjoys being a waitress.

The Skype app on my phone comes to life. Excited to see Charlotte's name and face pop up, I answer. Her dark chestnut curls fall at her shoulder, grazing a red line of sunburn along both shoulders where her bathing suit must have been.

"Why do you look like you're going on a hot date?" she questions.

I catch a glimpse of my outfit in the large mirror that leans against the bare white walls of my childhood room. I recently revamped the space by tearing down lingering posters of Nick Jonas and Harry Styles. I went on a purge last spring when life felt as if it was going nowhere. Knowing I couldn't, and still can't, afford my own place on Long Island with my salary put me in a funk I'm still not completely out of yet.

"No. No date. I'm—" I pause. Lying to my best friend is going to hurt my heart in more ways than my breakup with Matt did.

I take another look in the mirror at the flowy olive tank and tight black dress pants. I realize that an effort was made to pick out my clothing tonight. My subconscious must have taken over. I'm a bit overdressed for a trip to Home Depot.

This almost reminds me of the time Logan offered to take us to the movies and stay with us, since their mom couldn't. When I got into the car Charlotte commented on my makeup and low-cut shirt. I honestly don't remember what I was thinking, but I'm pretty sure my little crush on Logan had something to do with it. What girl didn't have a crush on him?

"Lily invited me out tonight. Co-workers, drinks, the usual." I bite the inside of my cheek, and try to keep the knot in my throat at bay. Lying to Charlotte again feels like having a wisdom tooth pulled sans happy gas and Novocain.

"Oh, well that sounds like fun. Oh check out this view!"

It's a little past noon in Hawaii, so the sun shines bright through the sheer white curtains of her hotel room. I'm in awe as the camera pans out into the ocean and clean sand on the beach below. Waves crash to shore, surfers ride them in. There's nothing but clear blue skies and the ocean as far as the eye can see. I'd be lying if I said I wasn't jealous. Long Island beaches are nice, but don't compare to the true paradise displayed before my eyes.

"I wish you were here with me, I mean, look at this place. We should do a girls' trip, just you and me one day."

I'm not into traveling as much as Charlotte, but a girls' trip does sound tempting.

"That could be fun. That view is unbelievable. How's married life treating you?"

If I ask a bunch of questions maybe she won't put her attention on me.

The camera pans back to her face as she flops down on the white fluffy bed to her left. A pink blush forms on her cheeks. "Amazing. Bryan is like the perfect man. Seriously. We need to find you one."

I choke on my spit and it takes me a few moments of painful coughs to get past it. "I'm okay. You enjoy your amazing man. I'll have my chance one day."

The most obnoxious horn wails outside my window. I close my eyes and sigh at Logan's childish behavior.

"What was that?"

"Neighbors?" I shrug.

She narrows her eyes at me. "Are you sure you're not meeting a guy at this work event tonight?"

An awkward laugh passes through my tight lips. "Positive. I should get going though. Can you send me some more pictures of that view, please. I want to live vicariously through you."

She smiles, but I've known her for so long that it's obvious by the scowl on her face that I haven't convinced her that this "work thing" is not a date.

"Of course. I'll send you a ton. I miss you though. Bryan's sexy and the best husband ever, but I want my best friend." She pouts.

I chuckle. "Live it up, you're in Hawaii and I'm back in New York spending eight hours a day in the stuffy old mall."

She smiles. "True. Well, have fun at your work thingy. I'll call you soon. Love you."

"Love you too."

As I hang up the sound of the front door opening startles me. I slap a hand to my chest. I swipe the small black purse off my bed, and slip my phone inside, then race out of my room and down the stairs. The beige carpet cushions my steps. Taking a left out of the living room I stop at the entryway of the mudroom. Standing there glancing around at the floral portraits hanging on the soft cream walls is Logan.

"Ever hear of knocking?"

"Ever hear of locking the door?" he mocks me.

I scowl and stick my tongue out. He runs his eyes over me, and it takes everything in me not to self-consciously want to cover up, but my lower half has other plans and tingles under his dark stare.

"Ready?"

I slip on my sandals at the door, and wave my hands out in front of me.

"Are you home alone?" he questions, brows wiggling.

I smack his arm hard. "Just get in the car! You promised food and I'm starving."

A mischievous chuckle escapes his lips. He closes the small gap between us, grabs hold of my waist and leans forward. "You know you've imagined me in your bedroom."

I'm trying hard to not let him see how much his breath dancing along the edges of my ear turns me on. I squeeze my legs together. My stomach decides to help out and growl like there's a monster attempting to break free.

"I've got the perfect plan for dinner." He leans back with a grin.

"Oh really, and what's that?"

⁊

"This is your perfect plan?" I ask.

We park in the dirty lot on the side of New Highway, across from the airport. He turns off his engine and faces me. The loud roar of jet engines rumble overhead. I look over his shoulder at the old white hotdog truck a few cars over. It's a staple in this area.

"We agreed on no dates, right? So this is the least date-like dinner."

I scratch my head and glare at him. "You could have taken us to White Castle."

He hums. "True, but nothing like a good chili dog. That and White Castle might lead to a fartgasm, we don't need any of that."

I glance over at him, brows arched. "Fartgasm?"

"Yeah. Fart and orgasm."

"I think I got that. Is that really something people say?"

He chuckles and shrugs. "Don't know, I may have made it up."

"Have you had one?" It's hard to hold back the smile hiding behind my lips. The conversations he and I have are one for the record books.

"You'll find out if you make me eat White Castle."

"Should I worry about what that chili dog you're drooling over is going to do to your stomach?"

He chuckles, shaking his head. "Can you really only think about sex at a time like this? Gosh!" He sends me a flirtatious smile then hops out of the car, towards the food truck.

"And can you only think about food at a time like this?" I shout back.

He throws a grin over his shoulder. Reluctantly, I follow him to the truck and wait in line. Once we've got our hotdogs we head back to the car. He hops up onto the trunk and pats the empty space beside him.

The summer sun is fading into a swirl of purple and pink. I settle down beside him, leaving plenty of space so that our bodies won't touch, yet he still finds a way to rub his leg against mine. It's like he's trying to get a rise out of me, like he's had all these years of pent-up sexual desires regarding me, and now that he can, he's trying to live it all up at once.

"First, the sunrise, now the sunset. We might be eating hotdogs, but this is a little too date-like for me."

He smirks. "We could go eat in the cemetery." He throws his thumb over his shoulder at the large plot behind us.

With my free hand I rub the right side of my head, shaking it. "So, what do we need from Home Depot?"

"Paint, spackle, and brushes. Charlotte created a Pinterest board to give Bryan hints that she wanted this done, she requested—"

"Wicker furniture?"

One side of his lip pulls up. "You really do know my sister well."

I put my hotdog back into its container and take a deep breath. He has no idea what I know. Charlotte has been planning her life since we were practically babies. "For the rest of the room she wants, a balance of olive and macaroon cream walls, throw rugs to match, and a new custom window to replace the old one with a half circle on top—"

"Are you sure Bryan didn't call you?" he chuckles.

Half the meat of his chili dog spills out into the small cardboard box, and topples over hitting the trunk of the car.

I laugh. "I told you, she's my best friend. I know these things."

45

I grow quiet. She's my best friend and I'm lying to her. Lying about a fling with her older brother. It feels so wrong, yet right at the same time. Not that I want to go beyond the two weeks. Maybe I am trying to fulfill this high-school fantasy.

I stare off at the beautiful sight before me. A plane soars overhead as it takes off from the runway to our left into the setting sun.

"Are you going to finish that?" he questions, eyeing my hotdog.

I stare at him, and shovel it into my mouth as if I were competing in a hotdog eating contest. He chuckles and shakes his head, shoving the rest of his own meal into his mouth.

As we enter Home Depot a mixture of wood and soil fills my nostrils. A large forklift beeps a few aisles over and echoes through the large building. Tall orange shelves that almost reach the ceiling line each aisle. We veer to the left, Logan leading the way—like any man he knows the store layout as if he lived here.

We head for the paint first, and Logan pulls out one of the swatch cards from the display. The first card he chooses has different shades of green on it.

"That one." I point directly to a smooth olive color on the card.

He glances up at me, then back down at the one I've chosen. He shakes his head, and grabs for a puke green color.

"No way, that's like vomit. She wants an olive color."

Logan sighs, and puts two of the cards back. He hands me the one with the olive then searches the peach swatches for the perfect macaroon one. When he finds one close to what I imagine she wants I grab the cards and head for the small counter in the center of the paint aisle.

46

The older gentleman behind the counter immediately begins to get to work mixing up the paint.

"I'm going to go grab a cart, I'll be right back," Logan says and jogs off back towards the entrance.

"Ellie, is that you?"

I turn to find Ethan Thomas, one of my co-workers from the men's department, walking towards me. We went through training together at Sheer Threads. He's a sweetheart and always remembers my birthday. He once decorated the break room with balloons and streamers for me. Lily at one point swore he was going to ask me out, but he never did.

"Hey. Fancy running into you here," I say.

He wraps me in a tight hug, but doesn't linger. It's good that he doesn't because as I pull away Logan walks up. His eyes narrow at Ethan. It's weird to see Logan's eyes so feral towards a guy who's paying attention to me. Back in the day I was the one to throw the stink-eye at the girls he dated.

"I'm putting in new flooring in my apartment. Can't decide what I want. Are you doing some renovations to your house?"

"Oh, no." I shake my head.

Logan struts around Ethan, sizing him up as he passes, then slips his hand into mine. I fight the urge to enjoy him being a little territorial. It awakens something within me. I have to shake the thoughts, because this is for two weeks only and those feelings will get me into trouble. I have to think about Charlotte and how this could impact our relationship. The thought alone brings my body back into check. Well that is until Logan rubs his fingertips over my hand.

"I'm helping renovate my friend's house." I finally speak, and clear my throat out of a nervous habit.

"That's really cool." He pauses and turns to Logan. "Hey, man, I'm Ethan."

Logan's eyes wander down the size of Ethan's body. Ethan's a bit shorter than Logan, but still an inch or two above me. I watch

Ethan give him the same look. All I can think is there's going to be a showdown right here in Home Depot. I nudge Logan.

"I'm Logan, the friend's brother."

"Oh. Well that's really cool. Um—" Ethan stalls. "I should probably go."

The weight of Logan's stare causes Ethan's pale face to turn red. Ethan holds his hand out for Logan to take. "It was great to meet you." He holds his hand out, waiting for Logan to shake it.

It takes him a minute, but he finally releases my hand and grabs Ethan's. I notice the firm grip Logan gives Ethan. *Save me!* The testosterone is running high here.

"I guess I'll see you at work. It was nice to meet you, Logan."

Without another word Ethan waves goodbye, and heads off. I smack Logan's chest.

He smirks. "What?" he chuckles.

"What was that all about?"

"I have no idea what you're talking about. Oh look," he says, pointing towards the gentleman mixing our paint. "Our paint is ready."

He can't store the items that we picked up tonight at the hotel, so we find ourselves parked in front of Charlotte and Bryan's brand-new two-story colonial. It's just the right size for a starter home with three bedrooms and two baths. The best part is, it's down by the bay and the view from the end of the cross street is gorgeous, especially on a clear summer day.

Charlotte and Bryan haven't yet paid much attention to the exterior. They moved some of their belongings prior to the wedding, but still have most of their things in the small apartment they rented together across town.

Along the side of the house is a short stone wall. Inside is empty with fresh dirt laid out along the entire path. I imagine a

48

rainbow of flowers blooming from it one day. Charlotte has a green thumb, unlike me and my black thumb. Mom knows never to trust me to water her plants: I've killed more than I can count.

Logan parks the car right outside the two-car garage in the cemented driveway. We quietly empty out the trunk and set things down inside the house. The house isn't old or run-down, but Charlotte has always had a vision for her bedroom. I remember coming with her and Bryan when they were looking to buy the house. The first thing she said she was going to change was the bedroom. She was pretty upset that it didn't get done before they started moving their things in, but I guess Bryan had planned to finish it without her knowing.

Most of the space is bare. The cedar wood on the floor shines like it's been recently polished. We bring what we can upstairs to the master bedroom. A light gray carpet currently occupies the floor at our feet.

"You New Yorkers and your expensive waterfront homes. Seriously, you know how much cheaper it is to live in Pennsylvania?" Logan sets down a can of the olive paint, and glances around the bright, eggshell painted room. His voice echoes in the empty space. "You could have so many more acres for half the price."

"It's always been her dream to live near the water. It's like she got the fairy-tale life she always wanted. Remember when she used to make me play pretend weddings when we were like seven? I was always her groom. What she wanted was to live in one of those raised houses on Gilgo Beach."

He snickers. "I remember that she used to wear Mom's white doily tablecloth over her head. You borrowed one of my suits once."

Him remembering it brings a smile to my face. We had some of the best times growing up. That feeling returns, the one where the pain takes over and I'm ready to call this thing with Logan off.

I stare out the old two-pane curtainless window. From here I catch sight of the bay in the moonlight. I step forward and lean against the windowsill. A ping of jealousy hits me. When Charlotte returns from her honeymoon, she will be living her dream. She's got the husband, the perfect job—special education teacher —and the perfect house. She'll get pregnant soon and I'll be Aunt Ellie, and turn into a resident cat lady. It's inevitable.

I gasp at the feeling of my hair being brushed to the side. Logan's soft, aggressive lips ignite a fire deep inside. Tossing my head back I rest it on his right shoulder. His lips find mine and his hands grab at my waist, spinning me to face him as he devours me whole.

His calloused fingers gently rub at the skin on my hips. They wiggle along the waistline of my pants, and slip underneath. I hiss when he touches me at the peak of my sex. My underwear grows damp from his simple touch. With most guys it takes me a while to warm up, but with him, it's instantaneous.

With his hand flat against me, rubbing in a circular motion, I push into him moaning while he kisses and nips at my neck. There are some spots that are tender from previously being bitten by him, but it feels too good to care.

"You're always so wet for me," he murmurs.

I whimper. His finger slides in, pumping up and down. On the next thrust he pushes a second finger deep inside of me, rattling my bones with a deep chill. I am rendered speechless by the way his warm fingers feel in there. He pulls them free. His face lights up.

There's no furniture in this room, so we have to improvise. He shimmies down my pants crouching in front of me. This part of our arrangement is new: we haven't gotten to the oral. I go weak in the knees the second his tongue hits me. I grab onto the windowsill and throw my head back. He lifts his gaze, but he keeps his head in place, and his tongue pressed inside of me. I wish he wasn't so attractive, it would make this so much easier, but damn, I can't get over the way he looks at me.

The room is still dark; we never turned on the lights. The only light is streaming in from the neighbors' house and the streetlamps. A ray glides across his face. I catch sight of his lips curling up as he gets to his feet and kisses me with my taste on his tongue.

I finish getting out of my pants while he unzips and discards his. It's my turn, and it's not my strong suit, but I get down on my knees anyway. I take his length in my hands and stroke gently.

I fit him inside my mouth making delicate motions with my tongue.

He writhes from the touch, moaning and calling out my name. "Ellie."

My name on his lips causes me to tense. I reach for myself with my free hand to try to release the building pressure. I glance up through my lashes to find his eyes lit from his devious smile.

"Are you getting yourself off?" His voice is rough with a velvety tone that drives me to the point of leaving a small puddle on the floor. His dirty words make it easy for the pressure to build and release.

He chuckles, and reaches down, hooking his hands under my arms to pull me to his level.

"That was so hot," he growls, nipping at my ear.

For a second he reaches down to feel the wetness pooling between my legs and sucks in a deep breath. His touch sets my skin on fire and once again, I'm screaming out in another orgasmic twitch. He pulls his hand away and sucks on the fingers that touched me. I never imagined something like that turning me on, but my core tightens at the sight of him licking me off his fingers.

He scoops my leg up and slides inside, the moment he's in I yell. He sighs heavily and whispers, "Where do you want this?"

"Against the wall," I reply in a breathless growl.

He's the only man that's been able to hold me up to a wall and fuck me. The pleasure is far greater than anything I've ever experienced. It's pure ecstasy.

He purses his lip, a smile hiding behind them as he lifts me into the air and presses me against the wall. I let him thrust into me as he holds me in place. His lips crash into mine, feverishly and hungry, he devours them whole.

"Fuck, Ellie. You're so perfect." It's his turn to throw his head back.

Lowering his gaze, his eyes meet mine for the briefest moment, but in that time he lets me in, the want and need in his eyes is laid right out for me to see, like he's baring his soul. As quick as he allowed me in, he shut me out. I wince as if an actual door slammed closed.

His thrusts become more urgent. His chest heaves in and out from exerting all that energy. I push forward to urge him deeper and my name slips out of his mouth again with plenty of dirty words to follow. The sound against my lips unravels me. His body tenses and he shakes as he releases at the same time.

He keeps me wrapped tight in his arms against the wall for moments after he comes. His face sits nestled between my shoulder and neck, as he takes slow, deep breaths. The racing beats of his heart pulsate under me.

I hate when he finally lets me go. There's a coldness between us, but I refuse to let it bother me as I saunter off to the bathroom to clean up.

We pull up to my house half an hour later. Mom's car is in the driveway but all the lights are out. Mom and I live in a small, old restored Tudor on the north side of town, not far from where Charlotte and Bryan bought their home.

Logan idles in the driveway. Our banter has calmed since we

christened Charlotte's bedroom, but I'm too tired to read deeply into it.

"What's your schedule like for the week?" he asks.

"I'm working an early shift again tomorrow and Friday. Saturday I'm off, but I'm working all day Sunday."

"What time do you start tomorrow?"

"Uh, nine. Why?" I raise a curious brow.

The lamppost above the car illuminates his face.

"It might be easier if I take you to work, then pick you up and we can go to the store. If you want Friday night into Saturday you can come back to the hotel and then I'll bring you back home Saturday night so you can get to work Sunday."

I contemplate this. I don't know what I'd tell Mom. Although I am a grown woman, she still likes to keep tabs on me. I'm her only child still in the nest. With my brother, Arthur, living in Hollywood, it's kind of like I'm an only child. We hardly hear from him, like Dad he's kind of disappeared, so it's just her and me. She usually works overnights at the diner on Friday and Saturdays, so I should be able to formulate something to tell her. I don't want to worry her.

"Okay. I'll see you tomorrow."

"Yeah. See ya."

Logan reaches for his phone that's on the center console. It lights up with a picture of a dark-haired woman, the name Marisol written on the screen. Her breasts are pushed up and there's a sexy grin on her face. The only words I see are "when you're back". Ignoring the stupid tug on my heart, I grab the door handle, pushing to get out when his hand wraps around my wrist. I snap my head toward him. I don't mean to scowl at him, but I do.

He tilts his head. "Are you okay?" His tone is serious.

I check my phone, then look back up at him. "Yeah, why wouldn't I be?"

He shrugs, then lets go, setting his attention back on his

phone. Of course, Logan Fields hasn't changed one bit. It shouldn't affect me. This isn't a real thing that we have, it's just fun. This time I slip out without him stopping me. I don't watch him leave; instead, I run upstairs to shower and rid my body of his touch.

CHAPTER 6

Charlotte stood in my doorway, her face flushed and lips a little swollen. I sat up in bed and took in her appearance then searched for the ice pops she'd gone downstairs to get, but there were none in her hands.

It was the summer before sophomore year. Charlotte and I had spent most every day together. I had noticed that when she did come over she was always looking for Arthur. When he was home she always made it a point to get him to notice her. He was nice, and never rude like he was with me. I feared for her heart. Arthur wasn't popular like Logan, but he had his fair share of girlfriends. Mostly, he kept to himself though.

"We didn't have ice pops?" I asked.

She turned her hands over in a daze. Her mouth opened, then closed. She stood there in silence for a few seconds.

"I…Uh…Your…your brother. Arthur kissed me." She put her hands to her lips as if she were remembering the kiss.

"He what?"

She carefully examined her face and lips with her hand, like she was trying to figure out what happened. I wasn't mad at her, it was him. I knew he had been on a few dates with Missy Harper

55

the week prior. I thought maybe he'd called it off. But why would he kiss Charlotte? Out of all the girls he could have, why my best friend? My first thought was that he was doing it to rile me up. But who wouldn't want to kiss a girl like Charlotte? She was perfect. In my eyes she was supermodel beautiful. Guys started to notice her a lot more than me, but what happened made no sense. I didn't even think Arthur was interested.

"I'm sorry. That was really bad of me," she said. She flopped down onto the bed beside me and covered her eyes, looking at me through her fingers.

I was speechless. Of course I wanted her to be happy, but I was confused. Sure I liked Logan, maybe a little too much, but I always thought kissing him would be wrong. "No. No, it's just... I'm worried about you."

She got up from the bed and paced back and forth. She reached for my desk and grabbed the ridiculous Joe Jonas doll she had gotten me as a joke for my birthday. She hugged it to her chest. "It was dumb, wasn't it? He could never like me."

I stood up and walked over to my window. I looked out onto the front lawn. My eyes wandered, while listening to her footsteps.

"Who kissed who?"

"I don't know." She paused in the middle of the room to think about it. Her eyes rolled up. "Him? I think. It all happened so fast. We went to the basement, because he said there would be ice pops down there. We chatted and laughed, and I leaned over to help him pull out some pops and our lips crashed together." There was another long silence. "His tongue was in my mouth."

I made several gagging noises. Arthur jamming his tongue down her throat was not something I wanted to imagine. I looked back over my shoulder as she started pacing again. My eyes landed on movement below. Charlotte came to the window the very moment the two figures came into view. It was Arthur and Missy and they were making out in my front yard.

The world stopped at that moment. Even if it wasn't me hurt, the idea that my brother could take Charlotte's heart and stomp on it in a matter of ten minutes made my blood boil.

"Oh I'll—" I was about to rush outside to tell him off when I noticed Charlotte's wobbling lip and watery eyes. Instead of unleashing my anger I closed the space between Charlotte and me and hugged her.

I dealt with Arthur later that night after Logan picked her up. It wasn't a pretty conversation. There was a lot of cursing and swearing. He deserved it.

But at that moment in my bedroom with Charlotte, the only thing on my mind was to make her feel better. She was the only thing that mattered.

The doorbell rings and I spring out of bed. I check the time on the small alarm clock on my desk. I realize I've overslept. It's Thursday morning. The week is flying by. There's a small part of me that wishes it would slow down, but that's my heart playing tricks.

My lavender sheets have piled up on the floor at my feet. I lose balance, and wipe out, narrowly missing landing face first. The thud vibrates the house.

My knees ache as I shake myself off. The doorbell is silent now. Mom! Without thinking, I race downstairs and stop short when I round the corner into the mudroom. Logan is smiling down at my petite mom wrapped in her sky-blue morning robe. He's said something funny that has triggered her light airy laugh.

He lifts his gaze straight at me with a grin. He's well aware of the power he has with that smile, so he milks it some more. Mom spins, her green eyes meeting mine.

"Oh. Hi, sweetie. Logan says you are helping out with Charlotte's house."

I've lost my voice as my attention darts back and forth between them. "I—uh." This doesn't look suspicious or anything. "Yeah. Anything for Charlotte." I smile.

If Mom can read me she doesn't let on that she knows. My tense shoulders fall, but tighten again when I catch sight of Logan raking over my entire body and my pajama choice. He snickers when his eyes land on the white shirt. Not only am I NOT wearing a bra, but the shirt has two avocados with a cartoon faces, holding hands, and it says, "I want to avo-cuddle with you."

I scowl and let out a growl before covering my chest. "I should go get ready."

"Logan, come to the kitchen. I've got a freshly brewed pot of coffee with your name on it." Mom reaches for his arm, and nudges him down the hallway.

Mom always liked Logan. He'd sometimes pick Charlotte up when he got his license and Mom would bug him to stay for dinner. He was very respectful when it came to speaking with adults, and they all loved him. My father even enjoyed his company.

Before disappearing into the kitchen, Logan throws a watchful glance over his shoulder at me and winks. I narrow my eyes at him. I can only hope he doesn't give Mom any clues that we are doing more than renovating a room for Charlotte. I hesitate to head upstairs, but I can't go to work wearing this, and I don't want Logan to get any ideas with my boobs running free.

"So, are you and that guy serious?" Lily questions. She tries to keep her voice low. With our boss Maryann on the clock, there would be no fooling around.

"Me and Logan? No." I continue to ring the customer up in front of me. I smile at the woman, then back over at Lily. It's not that I don't want to share my feelings with her; it's that I'm trying

58

my hardest to forget that I have those feelings. Logan is Logan and he will always be Charlotte's older brother who's hot. There is nothing real between us.

"Well just so you know he watched you walk all the way into the store and didn't leave until he knew you were settled."

My cheeks burn, but I try to hide it as I untuck a few strands of hair from behind my ear. "He did not." I briefly smile at the customer again. "That will be sixteen twenty-eight."

She swipes her card through the PIN pad and waits for the prompts to come up. I turn back to Lily. "Did he really?"

"Either that or he was checking out your ass."

The customer I am helping turns several shades of red, and as I hand her her items, she doesn't even look me in the eye.

After the customer left Lily and I chatted some more, mostly about Logan, until Ethan showed up to return some items. He was awkward about it, scratching his neck and fidgeting. He didn't ask about Logan, thank God. We discussed the renovation and his project as well. It was a quick friendly conversation that was cut short by Maryann giving me the stink-eye.

The day dragged by, but when it was time to leave I was relieved. Lily walked me to the parking lot, and I hopped in Logan's car so we could go furniture shopping.

Despite the way we left things last night, Logan is acting like his usual self. I can't understand why I want to ask him who the girl was that sent him a text. My heart and my head seem to be at war with each other. Both know that this is not a relationship in any shape or form, but my heart has other plans. As much as my worries lie with the fear of losing Charlotte because of what I've done, part of me is afraid to lose him too. Friends without benefits is much less confusing.

59

"What about this bed?" His voice pulls me from my thoughts. He falls onto a bed with a dark wooden frame and headboard.

I curl my lip up, glaring at it as if it disgusted me.

After Logan picked me up from work, we ate at the PF Changs in the mall and now we're browsing through furniture. We've been here for all of ten minutes and he's already trying to get us kicked out. I don't think there is one bed he hasn't made himself comfortable on.

"Do you even know your sister at all? Seriously." I grin.

He pats the fluffy white down comforter beside him.

"I don't think we're allowed to have sex in a furniture store." It's hard to hold in my smile. I stand at the foot of the bed with my arms crossed at my chest. My eyes narrow at him.

He sits up and I try to step out of his grasp, but I don't move in time and go falling down on top of him. Laughter tumbles between us. Beneath me he's hard and ready to go. The thought alone leaves moisture pooling between my legs. I don't know what it is about him, but the littlest things have me all hot and bothered.

"Is that your wallet? Or are you just happy to see me?"

Chuckling, he says, "That was the cheesiest line, but coming from you it somehow turned me on."

Laughter fills my lungs as I roll off him. I sneak a peak of his skin-tight jeans and his growing bulge. I snort, failing to suppress a giggle. He lifts his head ever so slightly to check on his pants, then back over at me. Propping my head up with my hands, I stare back. He smirks and rests his head back against the soft sheets.

I roll onto my back and join him, leaving no space between our bodies. I release a shaky breath as his fingers dance over mine, and clasp together. For a minute his breathing slows as a long silence passes between us. We've fallen into this routine that will be hard to break come next week when it's all over.

Someone clears their throat above us, breaking the moment.

I'm grateful for the interruption; there were way too many feelings in that moment.

A man in a purple button-down, black pants, and the shiniest shoes this side of New York, stands over us. "I'm sorry, but we don't allow customers to test the beds. Is there something you need help with?"

Logan chuckles, and I shove his arm hard enough to rock him. Continuing to smile, I roll off the bed and land on my feet. He follows me, then wraps his arms around me. My eyes widen at his touch. There are way too many feelings passing between us right now as his heart pounds hard enough for me to feel. It's different than the other night on the rooftop.

I hold my breath for a moment, then plummet back down to reality, because this isn't real and he's just fucking with the sales associate. I'm angry with my body for misbehaving and sending me mixed signals. I don't know why I even have to remind myself that there's NO STRINGS ATTACHED! Not even a thread.

Setting his chin on my shoulder, he glances up at the man. "Yes, we're looking for a bed that won't squeak..."

I elbow him in the gut. He grunts and laughs, then steps away. I give an apologetic look to the man.

"We are looking for a bed with a wicker headboard, preferably gray, white is okay too. And some matching furniture to go along with it."

"We have a really great set—" the sales associate starts to ramble, but I've half lost him and have thrown myself on autopilot.

We end up with a whole wicker bedroom set that is all in stock and can be delivered by next Thursday, which is perfect since Charlotte and Bryan aren't coming home until next Sunday. It gives us plenty of time to set it all up and have everything prepared. Logan is planning to get ready for spackling tomorrow morning and by the time he picks me up from work, we can get things underway.

We slide inside the car. The bright light from the tall lamppost in the parking lot fills up the darkened car. My phone vibrates in my bag. I reach in for it to find Charlotte's name. I'm frozen in place, debating whether or not I should answer it. Logan notices my hesitation and hits the green button for me.

I'm about to reprimand him when Charlotte's voice vibrates through the speakers. "Ellie, you there?"

I bring the phone to my ear and almost drop it from my trembling hand. "Hi. Sorry. I just got in the car."

"Oh, that's okay. You leaving work or—"

"Yeah, work. I'm leaving work." My words come out cut up and choppy. If she notices, she ignores it.

"That's cool. I had a giant-ass piña colada." She giggles. "I swear, they taste better in Hawaii than they do in New York." Her laughter fills my ear. She's probably a bit tipsy, so it could be why she ignored my hesitation.

Logan's gaze falls on me. I close my eyes and pretend I actually did leave work, and that I'm in my car about to head home. He isn't here and the thought of having sex with him is only a fantasy I'll never live out.

"Are you okay? You're kind of quiet. Are you upset about Matt? I promise, when I get back we are going to—"

"No, no. It's not Matt. I've had a hard time sleeping the past few nights. I'll be okay. I have to go take the deposit to the bank." I squeeze my eyes even tighter, trying to persuade the tears forming behind them to go away. Lying feels awful. I take several deep breaths to rid my chest of the tightness that strangles me.

"Oh. Sure. I just wanted to tell you about the piña colada. It reminded me of you. Anyway, I'll let you go. I'm going to send you a pic of last night's sunset. You'll die when you see it! Oh and Bryan in a hula skirt."

A mixture of a laugh and a sob escaped my lips. "I can't wait to see that."

"Goodnight, love!" She hangs up before I have a chance to say anything.

I continue to hold the phone to my ear. I'm the worst friend ever. I gasp loudly as Logan's warm fingers dance over my skin. He tugs the hand holding the phone back down. With my free hand I wipe a warm tear that falls.

"We can stop."

I open my eyes, blinking. His lips pull into a straight line as he carefully regards me. Worry lines make creases in his forehead. I sneak a peek down at his hand still wrapped around mine and the phone.

Lying to my friend is the most painful thing in the world, but do I want to stop this arrangement? His thumb swipes under my eyelid, gently brushing away the plump silent tears cascading down my cheek. *No.* The answer is I don't want to stop. I have enjoyed every moment of this fling with Logan. I hate lying, but being with him feels good. I like no strings attached and that he lives in another state and hardly visits. It will be easier to cut ties.

"No," I whisper. "I don't want to stop, but for tonight—I want to go home."

"That's okay." He leans over the center console and wraps his arms around me tight. Slowly, he runs his fingers through my auburn locks, carefully twisting the ends around his pointer. I breathe in and out enjoying the feeling.

"Thank you," I say, softly, staring down at the warm phone in my lap.

He pulls away, confusion blanketing his expression. "For what?"

"Understanding."

"I'm not going to force you into anything. Of course, I'd love more than anything to drive us over to my hotel room and for you to have your way with me, but I'm not saying we have to."

I smile. "I'm sorry. I promised I wouldn't get emotional."

"I'm asking you to lie to your best friend. You don't have anything to be sorry about."

He slides his fingers down my arm and connects them with mine. He gives a soft squeeze before pulling away. I don't have it in me to look at him as he turns the key and drives me home.

CHAPTER 7

*A*fter a good night's rest, I'm ready to take on Friday. I pad down the stairs towards the kitchen. I'm up early enough to have a bite to eat before Logan picks me up to take me to work. Behind me, I drag my rolling duffel bag. I'll only be spending one night in the hotel with him, but as I learned that night on the hotel rooftop, I should be prepared for anything.

Mom sits at the small round kitchen table beside my favorite four-pane window. The bright yellow curtains are pulled back to allow the light in. The suncatcher hanging in the middle of the window casts a rainbow across the maple wood table.

Mom lifts her gaze at the sound of the wheels rolling onto the green and white tiled floor. "Morning, sweetie." She smiles, taking a sip of coffee from her favorite *Buffy The Vampire Slayer* mug. I practically grew up with the show as she watched it religiously every week when I was a toddler. Eventually, when I was old enough we binged it together during one cold, miserable winter break.

"Morning." I lean the bag against the counter that juts out in the center of the kitchen from the back wall where all of our appliances are. I stand in the enclosed rectangular space.

65

"Are you staying out tonight?"

"Oh. I'm helping Logan with the renovation and it's just in case it gets late."

Mom raises a brow as she brings the mug to her lips. "Is something going on between you and Logan?"

"Oh, God no, Mom, ew." I can already feel the nagging stabbing in my heart from the lies piling up.

She chuckles. "Relax. I believe you."

"He's like a second brother to me." And the lies keep coming. I hate it. "Mine isn't much of one anyway."

She sets her mug down and narrows her eyes at me. "That's not fair."

"Hey, he's the one who left for California and never looked back. I texted him, showed interest in his career. Hell I even promoted that god-awful sci-fi show about a man-made tornado that he was in."

She sighs. "I wish you two would get along."

"And I wish he would stay in touch for more than five minutes." I hate snapping at her. Mom has been through a lot and more recently she's been plagued by Dad trying to contact her. I don't like stressing her out more than she already is. It seems all the men in my life run away when they can't handle things. Makes me wonder if I'll ever find a man who sticks around.

"I'm sorry. I've got a lot on my mind." I apologize. I make my way around the kitchen, grabbing a bowl, some milk, and my favorite cereal, Frosted Flakes.

"Do you want to discuss it?"

I shake my head. "I'm not sure I know where to begin."

She gives me a pity smile.

I cringe. "Maybe another time. Logan is picking me up in a little while. He's going to drive me to work too."

Her eyes twinkle.

"Mom." I laugh, the tension rolling off of me like a morning fog on its way out.

The doorbell rings as I'm about to pour the milk. Mom slides out of her seat. "I'll get it. You eat."

I continue to pour myself some cereal and top it off with milk. I step away to put it back in the fridge. I turn to find Logan scooping up my flakes into his mouth.

"Aw, you shouldn't have," he says, a smirk tugging at his lips.

I stalk across the room, give him a light playful tap on the back of his head, then steal the spoon. Our arms collide as I lean in. He's watching me closely, his grin never fading. His laughter fills the room, a sound I'll never get tired of.

I'm vaguely aware of Mom observing us from the entryway of the kitchen.

"Do you want some? Because you know where everything is."

"Nah, that's okay. I had a huge helping of oatmeal before I left."

"And yet you had the audacity to steal my breakfast," I tease.

He shrugs, steals the spoon back, takes another large bite, then hands it back to me. I purse my lips and scowl. Pulling the bowl from him, I cover it like I'm hiding something, and scurry off to the table and settle in across from Mom. I was so wrapped up in Logan I didn't notice her sit back down.

Logan makes himself at home, grabbing a mug from the cabinets above the sink, then pouring himself some coffee, like this is his new routine. He slides in beside me and smiles.

"So, what are you two working on today?" Mom asks, her eyes darting between the two of us.

He's left almost no space, and I nearly knock into him as I lift my spoon to take a bite of cereal. You would think he'd move away, but instead he scoots closer so that our legs are touching under the table. My cheeks grow warm from the feeling of his skin pressed up against mine.

"Spackling. Shouldn't be too bad, the walls aren't awful but there are a few imperfections that are driving me nuts," he says.

"You're gonna spackle?" Mom watches me closely.

I shrug. "How hard can it be?" I've never in my life painted or spackled, let alone done any kind of renovation work to a house. I wouldn't count myself stealing a can of paint my dad had left hanging around when he was redoing Arthur's room. I was maybe eight, I dragged it into my room and drew a large smiling face on one of the walls. Dad was not pleased.

"Should I be worried?" Logan jokes.

Mom dives into the story about the smiling face, and the two of them go back and forth teasing me about it. It's a nice, light conversation and although it means I'm being picked on, the witty banter puts me in a good mood.

※

After a full day of work, I'm exhausted, but ready to jump into the work in Charlotte and Bryan's room. I'm excited to put it all together at the end of next week. Logan pulls up to the mall. I'm waiting outside the food court for him.

I slip inside the car and the aroma of greasy burgers and onions fill the car.

"You got White Castle?" Eyes wide, I stare at him.

"It's the perfect non-date food, right?"

"Is this fartgasm inducing?"

He chuckles. "Guess we'll find out, won't we?" I can't help but enjoy the devilish grin. This arrangement might have no strings attached, but Logan is an attractive guy, with his boy-next-door chiseled jaw and warm brown eyes. It's hard *not* to enjoy him.

"Oh, so you think you're getting some?"

The banter between us is so easy. When we were younger it didn't include any sexual remarks, but we had our little game of who is the most sarcastic. I think I won, but he would claim it was him if anyone asked.

He rests his hand over me, rubbing along the crotch of my

jeans. I try not to show him the effect he has on me, but it's hard not to.

"Admit it, you can't think about anything other than fucking me."

I roll my eyes up and move them left and right. He grips the seat of my pants tighter and I hiss. His chuckle wakes the tumbling gymnast low in my belly.

"You're so full of yourself, Logan Fields."

He laughs. "Yeah and you like it."

There's no denying that.

Over twenty minutes later we arrive at Charlotte and Bryan's house. The summer sun is beginning to set, but still high in the sky. Inside we set up the White Castle in the living room. We sit with our backs against the soft gray couch on the shiny hardwood floor in front of the small glass coffee table. They have already installed their TV and Bryan provided us with a Netflix password. We throw on some random movie with David Spade where he invites the wrong girl to a resort after having two girls with the same name in his phone.

"You know he's going to fall in love with her at the end. I mean, it's not a rom-com, but it kind of is," he says, chewing on the tiny burger in his hand.

"I think I like her better than the other Missy. I mean, quirky is better."

"You know, I see why you like her. She's just like you."

"Hardy-har-har." I bump into him.

We finish our dinner as the movie ends. Logan and I clean up our mess. While he prepares the spackle I go and get changed so I don't ruin my work clothes.

I enter the room wearing some old ripped up jeans and a black tank that shows maybe too much skin. I don't have a massive chest, but in this tank they look a little fuller than usual.

Logan does a double-take, his eyes landing right on the cleavage. "You're distracting me, Garner."

"That was the plan." My sarcasm shines through. "Okay, so how do we do this?" I ask.

He bends down and I check out his ass in his skin-tight jeans. He straightens and strolls over with a swagger. I roll my eyes as he hands me a tool. "This is a putty knife." His hand grazes mine as he slips the knife into my grip.

"Putty knife. Got it!"

Smirking, he continues. "That." He points to the white bucket with orange writing. "That's the spackle."

I cross my arms at my chest and purse my lips. "Why are you stalling? We only have a week to finish this."

"I'm not stalling." He whistles and looks around the room. "Now the trick is to angle it the proper way." He glops the spackle onto the knife and goes over to one of the imperfect spots that he claimed was driving him nuts. He slaps the goop on with a loud thud, then angles it using downward strokes. "We want to cover the imperfections. There are a few spots where the previous owner must have had something hanging and there are tiny holes in the wall. Cover those."

"Cover imperfections and holes. Got it."

I imitate him, grabbing a big glob. Searching the wall I find one of the spots he's talking about and slap it on. "Like this?" I ask, eyeing him.

He observes me as I attempt to cover the small indent in the wall. He places his knife on one of the closed buckets of spackle and heads over to me. Gripping my wrist he slowly presses the knife to the spot and angles my hand in the correct position. His erection is pressed into me.

"Can't you control that thing? It's like it has a mind of its own."

He chuckles, his warm breath tickling my ear. "He does what he wants."

"He?" I tilt my head back, glancing up at him. He smiles with his eyes. Add another crazy conversation to the record books.

"Got a problem with that?"

"Does he have a name?" It's the dumbest question I've ever asked someone, but I'm just rolling with the punches here. There's no one else in this world I can talk to about fartgasms, and penis names with. Charlotte would probably get a kick out of naming a penis.

His deep, hearty laugh powers through me. "I had one girl name him Spike."

I snort. "He's no angel, I guess."

He rolls his eyes. "You and your *Buffy* references."

He's quiet for a moment. In the corner of my eye I catch him staring down at my jawline like he's hungry for a snack. There's an electric vibe in the air around us. It takes everything in me to hold back and not start something right here in the room.

"We should get to work," I say in an unconvincing tone.

"We should."

He steps away with a dumb grin and crosses the room to work on the far wall while I work on the one closest to the door. Over the next hour or so we swap spots, checking over each wall carefully. Halfway through he put some music on his phone. I dance and sing along without a care in the world. He doesn't seem to mind, and I may have even caught him bobbing along to my favorite Andy Grammar song, "Don't Give Up On Me."

We finish cleaning up and pack our things for the night to head back over to the hotel. Both of us are still covered in the spackle dust, but we were waiting to get back before we cleaned up. Inside the car he's quietly humming along to Long Island's rock radio station.

"Why aren't you staying with your mom?" I ask, as we pull into the hotel lot.

His demeanor changes almost immediately. "Tommy's always there."

Tommy and Josephine met six months ago, and she's been happier than I've seen her in a while. After Logan's father passed from a heart attack while working construction, she was hit hard with depression. In my opinion, Logan should have stayed to make sure she was okay. Leaving it all on Charlotte's shoulders was wrong.

"He's not that bad of a guy."

Logan flicks his flaming angry eyes at me.

I sink back into my seat. I'm not trying to push his buttons, but I also feel as if he's being a little childish. I'd be a bit skeptical if Mom started dating, but if she was happy and the relationship was healthy, I think I'd be okay with it.

"You'd save a lot more if you stayed there."

"I know. I just don't want to." He runs a frustrated hand through his short hair as he releases a trembling breath. "Can we drop it? No strings means no diving deeper."

He'd helped me overcome my emotions last night, yet won't let me do the same for him. He's right. This isn't a relationship, it's two friends fucking. Or—are we even friends? I'm not sure. Friends talk to each other.

The minute we get upstairs I start to run the shower. Logan seems a little less agitated with me. I haven't said a word since the car. I'm not keen to piss him off then be stuck here all night.

I'm about to step inside the tub, but I'm pulled back and spun around into his arms. He throws his mouth over mine like he's hungry for my touch. I press my hands against his smooth, naked chest. Our breathing is heavy as we devour each other.

Steam from the shower rises and swirls around us. The heat in the room causes me to sweat. He nibbles aggressively at my neck, while I throw my head back enjoying every bite. He hisses and reaches his hand around my ass. Lifting me, he steps into the shower. He seems to be a big fan of sex in the shower. I'm not complaining, that's for sure.

Inside, he sets me down, and spins me so I'm facing the faucet. He gently pushes me so that I'm bent forward. The warm water cascades down my back and head and between our naked bodies.

"Are you ready for me to fuck you?" he asks.

"What are you waiting for?" I growl.

That electric charge is back, but there's an aggressive heat behind it. This position is so much better, looking at him sometimes makes it tough to distinguish that this is only temporary.

He thrusts himself inside, and places both hands on my shoulders, gripping hard as he rocks into me. I throw my head back enjoying it from this angle.

"Oh my—" I don't even finish the sentence before a powerful orgasm takes over me.

It doesn't take him a long time to release. We need a few seconds to catch our breath. Between the hot rising steam and the powerful thrusts we're both spent. I count each silent beat that passes. By the time he's done soaping me up and I do him, I've already counted well past three hundred.

I step out of the shower first, towel myself dry, then get dressed. He emerges from the bathroom a few minutes later. The small white hotel towel sits low on his waist. I try to encourage my eyes to look anywhere but at the "V" etched into his muscles, but they defy me, as usual. *Ellie, turn away, before you have to change your underwear again.*

The corners of his lips rise like he knows. Slipping on a pair of boxers he turns to me, shaking his head as he takes in another one of my famous avocado shirts.

"'Rock out with your guac out', really?"

"I thought it was cute." I turn back to my bag on the edge of the desk, searching for my phone to check for messages. As I dig into the bag the entire thing slips off the table and crashes with a thud, spilling the contents onto the floor.

Logan kneels down beside me, helping to clean up the mess.

"Thank you."

"Sure," he says, reaching for the book that fell. "*After?*" he questions, eyebrows raised.

I reach for the book and he pulls it away with a smirk.

"Are you reading smut?"

"It's not smut, now give me that!" I yell.

He gets to his feet and dangles it high up. I stand in front of him and try to jump for it, but he's too tall. Lifting it high, he opens to a page and begins to read in an over exaggerated, passionate voice. "I can't believe no one..." He barely gets the words out before doubling over in laughter.

I smack him in the stomach. He grunts, but continues on reading more of the scene until he loses it at the words on the page.

He shuts the book. "What is this anyway?"

"It's *After*, Anna Todd. She's a goddess in my eyes. Her books are like—"

He raises his brow. "A virgin and let me guess..." He hums for a moment tapping his lip. "...and a bad boy."

"First off, she's an amazing author, secondly, what novels have you written that they've based movies on? None. So shush."

He groans. "There's a movie too?"

"Yeah, on Netflix."

He grins and swipes the remote from the dresser beside the desk that holds the large TV unit. He jumps onto the bed and scrolls through until he finds what he's looking for. He starts up the movie as I pick up my bag.

He chuckles at Tessa's monologue and grins. "This is gonna be good."

I grab a small bag of chips from off the desk that we'd gotten at the vending machine when we arrived, and settle down beside him on the bed. I fluff the pillows setting them up and crawl under the heavy down comforter.

We spend the rest of the night engrossed in *After* and *After We Collided*. A quarter of the way through the second movie my eyelids grow heavy. I miss huge chunks, until my body relaxes. I fall asleep to the sound of Logan's laughter at the scene where they have sex in her office.

CHAPTER 8

The day Charlotte and I made rule number five I had another argument with Arthur. I was sitting on my front steps waiting for Mom to drive me over to Charlotte's when a friend of Arthur's dropped him off in front of the house.

He strolled up the walkway as if it were no big deal. "Move," he said.

I growled at him and stood still. We were the same height then, still are now, but as I stood on that first step I was slightly taller. He ran a hand through his shoulder-length auburn hair and let it fall. We have the same hair, and eyes. Our noses are a bit different. His is rounded, mine a little pointy.

"I'm going to Charlotte's to make her feel better. What you did yesterday was fucked up."

"So?" He shrugged. "She'll live."

I narrowed my eyes. "Why did you do it?"

"She was there, her lips were close by and I went for it. It meant nothing. Charlotte's hot, but there's no way I'd date my sister's best friend. Plus she's weird like you." His tone fell flat like it didn't matter. I hated him for that.

I crossed my arms. "So do you like her?"

"I said she was hot."

"God, you are so shallow. That was not what I meant."

He shook his head. "No. I don't. Now move so I can go inside."

I wasn't in the mood to fight anymore, so I stepped aside. Mom came out a minute after and drove me to Charlotte's.

It was a beautiful day so we decided to head to the backyard. Back then they had an above-ground pool with a deck in the center of the yard. Charlotte and I sat in lounge chairs with the notebook paper in our hands.

"So, number five." She scribbled down the words with a green marker, keeping her eyes on the paper. Her shoulders were slumped. I hated that my best friend was hurting because my brother was an asshole.

"No dating each other's siblings, no matter how much we like them," I said.

She picked up a second marker to write it down when the back door to the house opened. Logan appeared and a girl with long platinum blonde hair trailed behind him. My attention focused on them. She jumped on his shoulders as they exited the house. A few of his other friends came out behind them. They didn't see us at first. They were loud and obnoxious, their voices carrying through the yard. Charlotte ignored them. Her mind was somewhere far away.

The girl dropped from Logan's back, and he spun her around and grabbed her. He pulled her close and kissed her. I couldn't take my eyes away. This rule would change things, but it had to be put in place. At the time I thought Logan would never look at me as anything other than his little sister's best friend. Rule number five was good. It meant there would be no chance of either of us getting hurt again.

"Ellie?"

I glanced back at Charlotte. "Right, yeah. Sorry."

Her eyes followed mine to Logan and she sighed. She placed a hand on my shoulder. "It's for the best."

Logan's head shot up at that very moment. He squinted as the sun beamed down on him. Our eyes met, and we shared a moment. It caught me by surprise and I gasped out loud. It didn't last long because the beautiful blonde in his arms grabbed him and brought her lips to his.

"Yes. It's for the best," I repeated.

I made a silent promise to myself that day that I would never break that rule. I knew even then that I could never handle the hurt if Logan broke my heart.

Too bad I couldn't have kept that promise.

In a sleepy daze, I hit the accept button on a phone call—no wait —shit—it's a video call. I blink several times as a dark-haired beauty comes into view. Realization strikes me. I gasp. It's Charlotte. She's going to know I'm not home. I'm lying in a hotel bed beside her brother. What is she doing up so early?

"Where are you?" she questions, squinting.

I burrow down into the sheets attempting to conceal any evidence that this isn't my bed.

"Home. Duh." My cheeks burn at the lie that forms on my lips.

Beside me Logan groans and kicks me with his long naked legs. With quick fingers, I slap the mute button on, and try to muster the best smile I can.

"What was that?"

Pivoting the phone with my right hand, I use my left to shove him away. He groans again before falling into another deep slumber, lightly snoring. I wait a few seconds to be safe before I press the button to unmute. As my finger taps it, Logan, still dead asleep, rips one so loud that it vibrates the bed. I almost want to check to see if he tore his boxers. I slap a hand to my mouth, not only to protect my nose from the odor, but to suppress the giggle climbing its way up my throat. The first thought that passes through my head is, thank God this is only for two weeks, because imagine waking up to that every morning for the rest of my life.

Charlotte stares back at me wide-eyed. "Did you have Senor Taco without me again?" She snorts.

I hold on to my sides as the giggle finally surfaces, but keep one hand tight over my mouth in an attempt not to wake the sleeping giant beside me.

"You know I love my tacos." Lowering my hand, I pause, checking the time. In Hawaii it's around five in the morning. Charlotte is not an early riser. "What are you doing up? Isn't it super early over there?" Maybe if I veer away from the fart she'll be less suspicious, because that definitely didn't sound like one of mine.

She yawns and I realize she's still in bed too. She rests her head on the soft cream-colored headboard. Her bed looks like heaven with all the fluffy white surrounding her. "My darling husband wants to do a sunrise tour."

"You're gonna love it, baby, I swear." His voice is muffled in the background.

"Hi, Bryan."

He shoves his round face in front of her and waves with a toothy grin. "Morning, Ellie! How's New York?"

It may be five in the morning, but he looks as if he's been up for hours. His bright blue eyes shine and there's not a sign of any sleep deprivation, unlike Charlotte, who carries some light bags under her dark brown eyes. Bryan is the type of person who could go to bed at two in the morning and be ready and raring to go at five.

"Same old crap, different day." I smile.

He looks over his shoulder and then back at me. "How's work?" He winks, and I know he's not talking about my day job at Sheer Threads.

I peek over at the spot occupied beside me. After his

79

disgusting display a few moments ago, Logan's now peacefully passed out and content. I hate myself for gazing at him for a second too long. I snap my attention back to Bryan. "It's uh—a bit messy."

His right brow lifts, but he doesn't question it.

"You know how customers can be, always making a big mess and then I'm stuck cleaning up. It's a never-ending cycle, but the project I've been assigned this week—" I narrow my eyes at the screen. "It's going well." I realize seconds later how stupid that sounded, but he catches my drift and nods.

"Glad to hear. I hope the mess becomes bearable." He grins.

At that, I chuckle a little, glancing over at my side again.

"You two are acting weird." Charlotte's voice pulls me out of my trance.

"He's so bossy," she teases.

In the background, Bryan shouts out, "Heard that."

We both chuckle lightly.

"Anyways, chat again soon?"

I nod. "Of course. Go enjoy your sunrise in paradise." I pretend to cry.

She smirks. "Later!"

I release a steady breath as the screen goes blank, then my eyes return to the sleeping man beside me. I scratch the back of my neck, antsy to get out of bed and start the day. There's still so much of it left and the idea of spending it with Logan turns my mind into this weird state of both wanting it to last, and wishing this week would end.

We enter Charlotte and Bryan's quiet house after 1pm. Logan decided he was going to spend his Saturday morning snoring away. Typical Logan. While he slept, I did some stretching to my favorite exercise guru on YouTube. Once Logan finally woke up, we ordered room service for breakfast—or brunch.

Today's plans include sanding down the spots we spackled yesterday. He plans to prime the walls while I'm at work tomorrow. As long as it looks good and dries well, we should be able to paint on Monday. The colors are almost identical to the ones already there, so it shouldn't cause too much of an issue, at least that's what Logan says. Apparently, he's an expert at this stuff.

He hands me a sanding block and a white dust mask and we get to work.

"You know you almost busted me this morning," I say, over the light scratching sound of the sandpaper against the wall.

"And how's that?"

"Remember I said Charlotte called?"

"Uh-huh," he says, but doesn't look at me, he's busy concentrating on one specific spot on the wall. He scowls at it like it angers him.

"Well, you decided to let one rip. She gave me a look as if she knew, but then somehow blamed it on me eating tacos without her."

Logan chuckles. "Are you sure it wasn't you?"

I pick up the roll of paper towels on the floor beside my feet and chuck it at him. Instead of his head, it nails him in the leg and falls on the ground beside him, unrolling slightly. He scowls at me and smiles. "Nice shot!"

I glower at him. I would have stuck my tongue out, but the mask was in the way.

It didn't take us too long to finish. There weren't that many spots that needed touch-ups. He rolls in the shop vac and stops for a moment in the middle of the room. His eyes dart around. "Can you start vacuuming? I forgot something in the car."

"Sure." I shrug, ignoring his odd behavior and take it from him.

He jets out of the room like someone told him a delivery truck of Twinkies crashed outside the house. Those are his all-time favorites. He has been known to eat three in one sitting. I don't know how he never vomited.

I start up the vacuum and work it in along the edges of the molding and all across the sides of the walls. I watch out the window as I work. It's a beautiful mid-August day, not a cloud in sight.

I scan the upmarket neighborhood. Charlotte's created this amazing life for herself, while I continue to bask in the fact that I'm nearly thirty, living at home, working in retail, with no steady partner.

Charlotte always knew the direction her life was headed. She fought for her dreams and never gave up. I wish I was more like her, but sometimes the fear of screwing up gets in the way and brings me back to square one. Like with radio. I feared I'd never be good enough, held back, and got stuck in a dead-end job instead. Logan sort of has his life in check too, at least the career part. Being a gym teacher and coach is a good career, especially for someone as active as he is.

I try to forget my downfalls and concentrate on the task at hand. On the other side of the street sits a freshly painted white and blue ice-cream truck. My mouth waters. I can't remember the last time I splurged on Mr. Softee.

Neighborhood kids start flocking over like the music is some sort of demon summoning them to his lair. Mom, Arthur, and I lived on a small street and we were always deprived of the ice-cream man as a kid. All the other kids had the truck come down their blocks, except me. There were times she and I would wait two blocks over near the main highway so that I could get my favorite waffle cone with vanilla ice cream and chocolate sprinkles.

Ignoring the urge to run out there with the kids, I continue to clean up around the window frame, staring out every few minutes, watching them waiting in line. I lean down to get around the floor, then stray from the window. I wonder what Logan is up to; he's taking a long time getting something from his car.

I adjust the vac to the next corner, glancing over my shoulder to grab the cord so that I can unravel it. My eyes land on hands holding two very large vanilla ice-cream cones doused in chocolate sprinkles, looking like the Leaning Tower of Pisa ready to fall.

I flip the switch on the shop vac. That's what he ran out for? My eyes wander up to his face. There's no devious or sexy grin, only a kind one.

"Are you going to eat one or not? They're about to melt in my hand."

Smirking, I run to him and grab hold of one. "We should eat this outside before we make a mess."

Out in the backyard, we stand on a small rectangular deck, trying to devour our cones before they melt. Their yard is small, but the perfect size for a starter house. Beyond the old rickety wooden deck is a field of lush green grass enclosed by a weathered fence.

"I'm so sad I missed you running after the ice-cream man."

"I was first in line." He grins like a child. "I heard that sucker coming from down the block."

I chuckle. "You always did have an ear and eye for food on wheels."

He scowls.

"Well, it was nice of you to buy it for me, so thank you."

The devilish grin returns. "If I recall, a certain someone always complained that the truck never came down her street. Remember the time I rode my bike to your house with melted ice cream in a cup?" He watches the melting mess in his hands, a light blush creeping up on his cheeks.

I laugh. "Yeah, of course I do." My voice wavers a bit as I think back to that summer.

Underneath all of that uncaring exterior, Logan has a sweet side, from protecting me from bullies to bike riding the few miles through town to my house.

"We had some good times that year. Remember when we wrote a letter to Charlotte?" He's still focused on the ice cream, but from this angle I catch sight of his smile as he recalls the memory.

"Yes." I nearly shout. "We pretended to be Joe Jonas. She wrote us back with a drawing of a middle finger." I chuckle at the memory.

He nods, taking another bite, "Mom was so mad that when Charlotte got home she was grounded for a week, and I was too, because Mom blamed me for teaching her about the middle finger."

At this point the ice cream has cascaded down the cone, and is melted between my fingers. I'm a sticky mess. I attempt to get it all down before it melts, but it's proving to be difficult in the late afternoon heat.

Logan watches me attempt to lick it all up. A determined look crosses his face. With his narrowed eyes on me, he crosses the old wooden deck, the boards creaking under his weight. He grabs hold of my hand and sticks my sticky fingers in his mouth, licking off the ice cream. Lowering his head and lifting his eyes he watches me through his sexy dark lashes. There's no denying this man is sex on fire, but that's all he can ever be.

I suck in a breath enjoying the way his tongue feels scraping across my fingers. He takes the cone and carefully tosses it into a large, black outdoor garbage pail on the ground below the deck.

"I wasn't done with that yet," I whisper.

"You can have some of mine." He leans forward and presses his lips to mine, devouring me. When his mouth opens the coolness of the ice cream lingers, sending a shiver down my spine.

"I think you need to be cleaned up a little," he smirks, resting his lips against mine.

"What did you have in mind?"

He jogs down the three uneven steps at the base of the deck. I follow, wishing I hadn't. A dense stream of water hits me, soaking my clothes. By the time I reach him, I'm dripping wet. We wrestle with the hose. Laughter fills the space around us as we break our relationship boundaries and have some much-needed fun, and for the time being I don't mind, not one bit.

※

"You'd love the storms where I live, the way they sneak up over the mountains. The crazy lightning. It's fucking beautiful." He stares up at the cloudy sky, allowing the light misting rain to drizzle over his face. "Long Island always gets duped."

I lean over the rail of the deck. The sunny afternoon turned gray in a matter of thirty minutes. After our little "hose-off" we dried in the sun, cleaned up our mess, and ordered Dominos. We just finished eating, and it's perfect timing as there's a storm rolling in, fogging up the choppy water of the Great South Bay.

"I'm a little jealous, not gonna lie," I say.

He leans in beside me, leaving no space between us. His body warms me enough that when a cool breeze rolls through I don't even shiver. I rest my head on his shoulder, and the motion flows so naturally through me, my pulse speeds up. His breath hitches as my head touches him, but it doesn't stop him from leaning into me and snaking his arm around my lower back.

"You should come visit, you'd love it. I have the perfect screened in porch for storm watching. We could also go and visit the Amish areas. It's a bit of a drive from where I live, but worth it. There are some sweet places to stay, like farmhouses and B&Bs—"

As Logan rambles on, I can't help but imagine what it would be like to visit him. Sitting on his screened porch watching severe weather sounds like a dream. He and I have always had a fascination with storms. Charlotte used to hate that whenever I was over and one rolled in, he and I would curl up in their bay window and watch.

He continues to talk about a vacation in Amish country. He knows that's another one of my bucket list items. I'm surprised after all these years he still recalls those tidbits from our conversations. It's like he's locked all of it away in the back of his mind to pull out on a rainy day.

"We could also do some horseback riding too. Like the summer my folks took us to the dude ranch and we went on that trail ride together."

"Your dad warned you that if I got hurt you'd be grounded for the rest of your life."

He chuckles. "Yeah. I told him he couldn't ground me because I was eighteen and leaving for college the following week. Plus, we had a guide with us."

Charlotte was terrified of horses, so when I wanted to go, Logan offered to take me. It was memorable because he knew I was nervous. The entire ride we talked about everything going on in our lives. It was a good distraction from the fact that I was riding a horse and one false move could send me flying. That memory is one that, like Logan, I've stored it in a safe place in my brain.

I love how he always finds a way to bring us back into the past. As much as living in the now is a big motto for myself, it's nice sometimes to relive those moments, especially the fond memories with the people that we love who are no longer a part of our lives. If you do it in a positive light, there's no harm in it.

"What do you think? Would you come visit?"

Our eyes meet and I'm stuck in his gaze. I open my mouth to speak as a bolt comes crashing down over the bay. Both of us jump back at the sizzle and bang that comes seconds after the flash.

"We should probably get inside," he says as plump droplets of rain smack us in the face.

We make it in as the skies open up and several strikes happen all at once. I pull my wet shirt from my stomach. It clings to it a bit.

"Oh no, your shirt is all wet, again. Whatever shall we do," he says, closing the space between us.

"Charlotte and Bryan are going to be pissed to know that they weren't the first to christen their house."

I'm entranced by his wide-mouthed grin, and the way his fingertips tickle the skin beneath the hem of my wet shirt.

A short, sensual laugh tumbles from his moist lips. He leans down to suck feverishly on my neck, and whispers, "It'll be our little secret."

I didn't want to add any more secrets onto the list, but as Logan lifts me into his arms, I melt. He smirks. I can't help being swept up by his Logan charm.

CHAPTER 9

$\mathcal{I}$n order to fill my craving for some UV rays, I head outside during my break. Working in one of the larger malls on the island has its benefits. Like the small quad behind the Cheesecake Factory. It's filled with shoppers and restaurant patrons, but still gives the fresh air I need.

My phone vibrates beside me. It flashes a brief summary of a text from Logan. In the sun it's hard to see, I squint as I fix the brightness level to read his words.

Hey, I went to Charlotte's last night to do some priming after I dropped you off. I drove through the night and I'm in Pennsylvania. I have some things to take care of today. Not sure when I'll be back, but tomorrow we paint!

I stare at the text for a few extra minutes, then set the phone down, but can't keep my eyes off the words on the screen. My thoughts jump to the text he received a few nights ago. I don't know why it worries me, it shouldn't. We are nothing more than friends who have a sexual attraction towards each other and are doing something to relieve that tension. Two weeks should be plenty of time, shouldn't it?

The screen goes dark, and I close my eyes. It's been a week since the wedding, and my emotions are all over the place. My stomach feels like it's weighing me down. I can't shake the feeling. It's frustrating to want something you know you shouldn't have. Our conversation last night has me on edge. The way he acted like this relationship could go beyond our little arrangement hurt more than I expected it to. Unless, he believes what is happening between us is real too, but I doubt that.

The sun beats down over me, feeling hotter than usual, as I lean against a cement planter in the center of the quad. I open my eyes blinking towards the Modells on the other side of the small street, passing between the mall and the free-standing store. Lily rounds the corner, her pastel-colored skirt waving gently in the soft breeze as she walks up. She has the later shift today, but we get a few hours together at least.

"Hey!" she says, lowering the dark shades off her eyes.

I push away from the planter and smile.

"You forgot your sunblock again. Your face is so red." She laughs.

I reach up and touch my cheek. Warmth radiates from it. I've been out here since my break started about forty-five minutes ago, so I'm not surprised I've gotten a burn. I swear my skin calls the sun to it. I never tan—only burn. I'll be regretting my decision to catch some rays later.

"Good thing my break is over. I'll walk with you."

We turn and head for the glass doors at the entryway.

"So, I have a question," she says, her voice light and bubbly.

"Of course."

"Are you still seeing that hunk of a man that visits you sometimes?" She wiggles her brows.

I don't know if it's her calling him a hunk or her assuming we are actually dating, but whichever it is, I can't help laughing. I want to tell her everything, and maybe I should: it's not like she knows Charlotte. Then there's that voice inside my head that says what I'm doing is wrong and that I'm a terrible person for it. For lying to my best friend.

The cool mall air hits our faces, leaving a sting on my sunburnt face.

"Uh, yeah, I guess, it's..."

"Complicated, I know. So, I was thinking we don't get to hang out much outside of work and I know your bestie is on her honeymoon. Do you guys want to come to dinner with us Wednesday night? I checked the schedule and it seems we're both off. Come on, what do you say?"

I always say Lily and I don't spend enough time together outside of work. We've both known each other for a long time and have only done mostly work events together, with the exception of one or two things. I don't know what Logan would say though.

"Jett and I were thinking of going to the pub up the road. They have the best food and it will be a Wednesday, so the crowd will be minimal."

We stop at the front of the store.

"Hey, ladies!" Ethan rushes past us back into the store. He's pulling the cart we use to dump the garbage at the far end of the mall. The wheels swivel and grind along the floor. We both wave as he passes by. I give a kind smile, but don't let it linger.

Lily taps my shoulder. "Do I smell a love triangle?"

"No way!" I chuckle. I reach into my back pocket for my phone to see the time. I have five minutes before I have to check in. "Can I get back to you about Wednesday? Logan drove up to Pennsylvania today."

The heaviness from earlier returns. Admitting that I've always wished he could be mine is harder to say out loud than it is in my head. I try to push it back down, deep into the depths to be forgotten.

"Oh yeah, sure. I hope you both decide to come. It could be fun to double date."

"It definitely will."

With nothing to do after work, I head to my favorite sushi place around the block from my house. It's only just after seven. On Sundays the mall closes early, so there's plenty of time to sit, relax, and enjoy my food. I plan on bringing it home and binging through the entire *Shadow and Bone* season one on Netflix, because well—Ben Barnes, need I say more?

I pull up to the front of the strip mall and park a few stores down from The Sakura Tree. I walk under the overhang on the old beat-up sidewalk towards the place. There's a few people meandering outside. The scent of tuna and miso wafts out the door as a couple holding hands exit. The man holds it open for me. I thank them and slip through.

The tables to my right are filled to the max. Small, round, mostly for two, only a few with four. There's more tables out back for outdoor dining. The line thankfully is short. I stop behind a dark-haired man, trying to see the menu above the counter. I know what I want, but I always scan to see if there's anything new.

"Ellie?"

I'm frozen like a deer in headlights as the man in front faces me. His intriguing hazel eyes, the ones with a hint of gold, captivate me as they had when we first met.

"Matt?"

Of course, he'd be here. We had our first date in this very restaurant, and many others following. Seeing him again in person is making way for several emotions to surface.

His eyes wander the length of my body, from the hem of my ankle-length button-down beige skirt, to the slate-gray V-neck tee I've tucked into the waistline, then finally reach my lips. He licks his own and swallows hard. "How are you?" he asks, his eyes flicking away, but he can't seem to keep them astray for very long.

"Trucking along. Yourself?" The way it comes out sounds aggressive, I clear my throat. "I mean, I'm okay."

"You look amazing."

I want to snap and say, it's only been like a week since you dumped me, nothing much has changed aside from my sex life. Could that change the way a person looks? "What about you?" I ask.

"Pretty shitty, actually. Are you taking your order to go or do you think we can talk?"

Now he wants to talk? He could have talked a week ago, could have given me more than a single text. As if my brain isn't confused enough by whatever is happening between Logan and me, now I have to process *this* as well. I spent a year of my life with this man. He does owe me an explanation, but it couldn't have come at a worse time.

"I don't know. I really—"

"Please," he whispers like he's desperate.

"Next!" the petite dark-haired woman calls from behind the counter.

I nudge him, and he turns to her. Her smile widens as he closes in. I lose myself in deciding what I should do. I see her deep red lips moving as she takes his order, but hear nothing. The world around me has turned silent. I didn't cry when he broke it off with me, but seeing him today, there's a deep pang of hurt bubbling up inside of me.

"What are you having?"

I shake my head as his eyes fall on mine.

"What?"

"Are you having the usual?" he questions, his voice taut.

I step forward behind him, the woman smiles at us. All I can do is nod, afraid I'll look like a bitch for denying the request. He turns to her and rattles off my usual order of three spicy tuna rolls, two regular tuna rolls, and a miso soup.

He hands her his credit card and I want to protest, but hold back. We slide over together and wait in front of a large display of fish inside the refrigerated display unit.

"Thank you for staying."

I grunt, not sure what more I can say.

"How was the wedding?" he asks.

I clench my hands into fists at my side, needing to take deep, steady breaths before I lose it on him. If I were braver I would outright say something like, *You would have found out if you'd come with me*, but that's not how I—Ellie Garner—roll. Allowing my feelings to leave my lips is never easy. The thought causes my chest to constrict. "Fine. It was fine."

In the corner of my eye I catch sight of his hand reaching out for me, but he quickly pulls back. He shifts on his feet and clears his throat. "Where did they go on their honeymoon?"

"Hawaii."

He knew that. I'd told him many times. Even brought up that maybe one day he and I could go together. Maybe that was the last straw for him, the one that told him I was too serious about our one-year relationship. If only I'd seen the signs sooner that he wasn't in it for the long haul, I would have tried to grow the balls to end things myself.

We wait in silence for ten minutes before another woman hands us our food. I follow him down a long corridor out into the back. There's a parking lot, so it's not an amazing view. Large trees hover over a chipped red-painted fence on the opposite side of the lot. Cars pull in and gravel cracks under the pressure of the tires.

We find a spot against the white wall on the left side of the outdoor deck. The sun has nearly set, and the twinkling lights hanging from the wall are starting to illuminate the deck.

"What did you want to talk about?" I open up the container of sushi. The plastic snaps and cracks as I bend it upwards to release. He does the same.

"What I did to you was messed up." He scratches at the back of his neck. "The last time I broke up with someone they stalked me for a month. You—" He pauses. "You just disappeared." He lowers his gaze.

I've had myself a few minor breakups and even when they made me sad, I never reached back out. If they don't want you around, what's the point in trying? "The past week has been a little strange—complicated—strangely complicated." I can't quite figure out how to explain what the past week has been like.

He lifts a brow as he brings a piece of salmon to his mouth. "Are you with someone?"

"No. Yes. Maybe."

"Oh." He rubs at his neck again. "Already?"

I raise a brow. He told me in the text I should move on, so I did the next best thing: I slept with the one person who could complicate things.

"Your text made me feel like I wasn't good enough to be broken up with in person. I know when I fall, I fall hard, but I deserved more than that. At least I think I do." I push around the sushi in my tray with the chopsticks.

He sighs and rests his sticks against the side of his container. "You do. You deserve more than I could give you. It was weird though, I found myself coming home from work and wanting to call you to tell you all the ridiculous things that Moe did."

Moe. A laugh escapes me. Moe is Matt's assistant manager at the restaurant he manages in the city. He's the type of guy who will randomly burst out in song while serving customers, or be the loudest to sing "Happy Birthday" to the guests and make up a little dance to go along with it. I've met him a few times and he's the sweetest guy. "I miss hearing about Moe. How is he?"

"The other day, he jumped on the bar and started singing that song that Heath Ledger sang in *Ten Things*—"

Laughter fills my lungs and suddenly it feels as if we'd never taken this time apart. Matt's hearty chuckle and my joyous laughter blend, causing my heart to pound a little too fast in my chest. I hate that I've missed him. It didn't hit me until now.

"Are you interested in trying again?"

I nearly choke on the tofu from my soup. I slap my chest and stare at him. "I don't know. You said you weren't looking for anything serious. What made you change your mind?"

He shrugs, but as he speaks, his eyes never leave mine. "Coming home and having no one who wanted to know about my day hit home. I've found myself scrolling through the directory on my phone and landing on your name, wanting to hear your voice."

I put my spoon down into the container of soup and sigh. I don't know how to answer him. Would I like to try again? Sure. Am I in love with him? I don't know. Is he someone I'd envision spending my life with? Maybe. Matt and I were good together, we had fun. The sex was okay, but that's not why I was in a relationship with him.

"I don't think it's a good idea right now." I pause.

His eyes turn downward.

I shouldn't feel bad, he was the one that broke up with me. "I need to get through the week before I make any decisions about where my life is going."

He nods and reaches a hand out. I allow him to take mine, letting it fill me with minimal warmth, not like Logan. I need to erase his touch from my mind, because in a week it will all be over.

"I think I can handle that." His smile is enough to light up the room. "So," he continues. "What did you think of that new *Roswell* episode?"

My eyes grow wide. I could talk about the remake for hours

and he knows it. I love how he doesn't hang on to the conversation about our relationship. He's aware that my heart and my mind are at war with each other, and a change of subject is exactly what I need. It's not that I wouldn't love to fall back into this pattern with Matt, but my heart seems to be elsewhere at the moment and I'm not sure which direction it will take me.

CHAPTER 10

*M*ona Valentine lived in one of the big houses down by the water. She was that person who threw parties when her parents were away. We usually didn't attend these types of parties, but Charlotte begged Logan to let us go with him. We were sophomores at the time, and although other sophomores were invited, we never were. Mona was cool about it, because she was actually a nice person; it was everyone else I was worried about.

Charlotte didn't seem nervous. The moment we pulled up to Mona's beautiful mansion on the Great South Bay, Charlotte had started rambling on about how one day she would live on the water (if only she knew).

Logan was in between relationships at the time, so taking us wasn't such a big deal. He parked a few houses down, in front of a large, gated home set among mature trees and bushes. He turned to us. "If at any time either of you feel uncomfortable or you're ready to leave, let me know. Especially you." He pointed to me. "Your mom would kill me if she knew you were here."

It's true. Mom and Dad would have had a fit. Although it was at that point that the fighting started to escalate, so maybe they wouldn't have even noticed. I had told them I was spending the night at Charlotte's and they didn't question me at all.

"Got it."

It was hard to keep a straight face, because Logan was dressed up as Captain Jack Sparrow for the party. He also looked one hundred times better than Johnny Depp, but there was no way I could say it out loud. Not after what happened with Charlotte and Arthur.

"How do I look?" I asked Charlotte as we walked up the sidewalk towards the white sided two-story home.

"You make a bad-ass T-Swift," she said.

I had dyed my hair blonde, but it wasn't Taylor blonde. It worked though, at least I thought it did. When Mom and I went to the thrift store I found a beautiful gold sequin dress and black cowboy boots. It matched perfectly. Charlotte had helped me make my hair wavy like Taylor's, and I was pretty sold on the costume. I think Logan was too. When I had stepped out of Charlotte's room he came out of his and stopped short. I watched as his eyes wandered up and down my body. I kept that secret to myself too.

Charlotte decided on a costume depicting the fashion of the 1980s. She pulled it off well with her curly hair, bright neon shorts, and top.

The party started off great. Charlotte found some beer bottles and snuck away from Logan to drink them. There was a light nip in the air, as it was now late October, but it wasn't awful. On the plus side Mona's backyard had a stunning view of the bay behind it.

We didn't talk much to the other guests. We hung around each other and danced to the loud music pounding through the speakers. We were having fun, but then it all went downhill.

The last two people either of us wanted to see started to walk towards us. Carrie and Sophie.

"I'm surprised you're not a Jonas Brother. Who are you supposed to be anyway?" Carrie giggled.

Charlotte grabbed onto my arm. "Ignore them."

I nodded, and tried my hardest. When I didn't answer they ignored me for a moment, then decided to hit me hard.

"I think she's supposed to be T-Swift." Sophie peered at me through the mask of her Catwoman costume.

"No way." Carrie tossed her red hair behind her. Her costume wasn't any better. She was a sexy cheerleader. So unoriginal.

"Ellie, I'm sorry, hon, but you're way too ugly with all those braces in your mouth to be Taylor. Maybe you should stick to the Jonas Brothers."

My lips quivered, and tears welled up immediately. Back then I had no backbone. I wish I could go back and tell my fifteen-year-old self that those two would never amount to anything. In fact Carrie ended up in jail right out of high school for stealing, and according to gossip Sophie has cheated on every one of her boyfriends, including one ex-husband. They were the type of girls that made fun of others to make themselves feel better. I wasn't their only target.

Charlotte squeezed my arm. "Don't let them get to you," she whispered.

"Oh," Carrie put her hand on her mouth. "Were you trying to impress Charlotte's brother? We all know how much you love him. I'm surprised he hasn't come to your rescue. She's got such a crush on him. Too bad you'll never have him. I've already had my tongue down his throat, and let me tell you that boy can—"

"Shut the fuck up!" Charlotte shouted.

I jumped at the sound of her voice. She was also a target of theirs, but she never let it bother her, like I did. She got into their faces and started to tell them off. They kept throwing my crush on Logan in her face, and that I was too ugly for him. The words hurt a lot back then.

I had to run, because I didn't want them to see me crying.

Charlotte called my name as I ran back into the house. The kitchen was the first room, and there were bodies everywhere. It was hard to pass through even though the room was huge. From there I veered into the living room. I thought I heard someone say my name, but I kept going until I slammed hard into a warm body. His arms snaked around me and from only that single touch I knew it was Logan.

He ushered me outside on the front lawn where the sounds of the party were muted. His hands found my face as he cupped my cheeks and made me look at him.

I can still remember the way it felt as his thumb glided over my skin. It's the same way it feels now when he touches me. It sends a spark through me and that night it was so strong that I wished I could have taken back the pact I made with Charlotte. That alone made me feel guilty enough to sob.

At that moment Charlotte ran up and when I wouldn't talk she explained everything. Logan dropped his hands and held them in fists at his side. You could tell it was taking everything in him to not go back in there and tell those girls off. Instead he turned his attention on me and tucked a stray hair behind my ear.

"Let's get you out of here. Okay? You're gonna be okay." He held his hand there as he spoke. "You are beautiful inside and out, Ellie. Don't let anyone tell you any different. Do you understand me?"

I went to shake my head to tell him no, but he wouldn't have it. He grabbed my face again. "Ellie. Look at me."

And so I did.

"Don't let them get in your head. Okay? You're perfect the way you are." For a moment he looked up at Charlotte. "Don't let anyone tell you differently, either. Okay, Char?"

She nodded too. He let go of my face and wrapped his arm around my shoulder, while he took Charlotte under his other one.

"This calls for some ice cream. What do you guys say?"

It was at that moment that I truly realized how much I liked him. I knew nothing could be done and that I needed to forget about it, but deep down I'd always want that one thing I couldn't have. I resisted the urge for Charlotte, because I loved her more than anything. So what in the world was I doing now?

It's been a day. I can't begin to comprehend what happened tonight between Matt and me. Only a week ago he told me I was getting too serious, that I wanted too much, and there he was standing in the same takeout line, ordering his usual, and telling me he thinks he made a mistake.

I don't have the mental capacity tonight to even form coherent thoughts about the subject, so I'm shutting it out of my head for now. Instead, I'm on my hands and knees in the cool damp basement attempting to drain the washer for the hundredth time this month. This machine has seen better days.

The gray concrete walls and small rectangular basement windows make it feel like a prison. It took me years to get used to being down here by myself with the constant noises from the burner and everything else. My brother, Arthur, used to tease me, and one time locked me in here and shut the lights. Not fun. I still get creeped out.

The door to the upstairs opens with a bang, my heart leaps into my chest.

"Mom?" I glance behind me at the old creaking wooden stairs. I don't get an answer, but coming into view are a familiar pair of acid washed jeans and manly bare feet. Definitely not Mom. "I thought you were in Pennsylvania?" I question him.

"I'm back early. Are you not happy to see me?" Logan's voice snaps with a flirtatious bite. The last two stairs moan under his weight. He steps down onto the cool slate-gray concrete floor and pads over to me. "What on earth are you doing down there?"

He raises a brow, then crouches down beside me, a stellar grin crossing his face.

I stare up into his eyes. His smile barely reaches and there's a bit of a haze behind those deep eyes, but I don't ask, because I don't think I can handle another deep conversation today.

"The washer keeps yelling at me that it can't drain."

For a few minutes he focuses on me, then straightens himself. As I continue to drain the tiny hose into a small bowl, he heads to the back where the line into the washer is. I can't see over the large white machine, but he's definitely tinkering around with something.

"One of your hoses was at a weird angle. Should be okay now." He comes back over and gets down on his knees and takes over, grabbing the small hose from my hand. He finishes draining it for me, then dumps the remaining water, checks the filter, cleans it out with some towels, and puts it all back.

He stands and brushes his hands together. "There. You can finish your load now."

"Thanks. I could have done it."

I walk away and over to the slop sink in the other corner of the room. He follows along, washing his hands after me. It's quiet as he finishes up and I rerun the load inside the machine. As I press the start button, his hands grip tight on my hips and he spins me around.

Without warning, his lips crash into mine with a force that backs me into the front of the washer. I grunt, and he releases me ever so slightly. He wraps his arms around me, and lifts me up onto the washing machine without breaking the kiss.

His mouth opens as he invites me in, I give him my RSVP and allow him to slip his tongue into my mouth. His hands search my back, my face, and my hair, like he's desperately trying to find something he's lost. I'm not complaining, it feels amazing, but I'm a little confused by how much passion he's putting into the moment.

"We can't have sex on my washer…"

He chuckles into my neck, then nips along my collarbone. I'm not wearing much, there's only a silk rose pink tank, and shorts— shorter than I'd ever wear outside the house—covering me. His hand slides under the tank, cupping my left breast. I throw my head back, as he slowly pushes the fabric aside, lowers his head, then grips my nipple between his teeth.

"Oh shhhhhhhh." I can't even finish my sentence without my underwear feeling a bit moist.

"And why can't we?" he questions, tugging harder with his teeth.

I groan and squirm under his touch.

"Your mom left for work. She was the one to let me in. I was coming up the driveway as she was leaving. We're all alone, if that's what you're afraid of."

I shake my head. "No, it's not that." I'm barely able to speak, out of breath from the multiple orgasms he's given me by paying attention to my breasts. "This place gives me the creeps." I finally find the words, but nearly scream them out as his other hand dips into my shorts, teasing me.

Laughter bursts from his chest. I smack him hard on the arm, and even though he whines "Ow" he's still shaking with laughter. "Should we take this to your bedroom?"

"We should." I nod as his finger dances near the edge before slipping inside of me. I hiss with pleasure as he slips a second finger up.

A satisfied grin crosses his face. "Are you sure you're not interested in doing this on the washer? Could get interesting during the rinse and spin cycle."

"Uh-no."

He chuckles, removes his fingers, then lifts me.

"Do you always carry women to the bedroom?" I wrap my arms around him and bury my face into his neck.

"No," he whispers. "Only you."

His words catch me off guard, but I'm rendered speechless by them, and instead of commenting, I say nothing.

❧

I don't know what got into him tonight, but his approach was slightly aggressive with a mixture of something more. It was like he wanted to prove something, maybe to himself, maybe to me, I'm not sure. Either way, whatever happened between us for the past hour was fucking magical, and I'm on board to do that all over again.

I walk into the room after cleaning up a bit. Logan's lying on my bed, his head propped up in his hand.

"So, did I live up to the fantasy that you dreamed of all those years ago?" He wiggles his eyebrows and it takes everything in me not to shave those suckers off. He's always trying to be all sly and sexy with that wiggle and it drives me crazy. Freaking hormones.

"Don't be so full of yourself. I never used you as my go-to when I needed to relieve myself."

"Joe Jonas." He coughs.

I throw him the bird as I walk towards the bed. His laughter fills the room, and I plop down next to him. I lay my head on the pillow and roll over. "Lily asked if we wanted to go on a date with her and Jett. She thinks we're a couple, and it was hard to say no to her."

He smirks. "And are we going?"

"I don't know." I shrug.

His dark gaze focuses on me, the smile on his lips dances up to his eyes. He's intrigued by the idea, it's obvious by his amused grin. "It could be fun, pretending to be a couple."

I don't trust that evil look on his face.

"I could call you baby—"

"Don't," I point my finger at him, tapping his nose, "ever call me baby."

His laughter shakes the bed beside me. "Why not, baby?"

I shiver. For as long as I can remember I have hated that pet name more than anything. It sounds weird calling someone a baby, because they aren't a baby. "You better watch yourself, or I'll take away your privileges."

Instead of answering, he rests his hand against the side of my face, and holds it there. Leaning forward he presses his lips against me, like he'd do everything we just did all over again. I'm not sure what his intentions are, but his kiss is slow and steady, like he's trying to savor the moment. He pulls away.

I narrow my eyes at him, confused by the sudden change from playful to kissing me like I mean something. This last week has messed with my head so bad that I'm plagued with a continuous light throb in my temples.

"We should do it. It could be fun. I'd like to officially meet Lily, instead of having her gawk at me from a distance."

Laughter fills my lungs. "She thinks you're a hottie, but don't go getting a big head over it now."

He smiles, and pulls away, resting his head back on the pillow. "You sure?"

"Yeah, why not," he shrugs, closing his eyes. "Did we just fall into a rom-com trope?"

I put some space between us. After that last kiss my brain can't seem to comprehend what it meant. "Yeah, but the only difference is we can never fall in love," I say.

"I'm pretty irresistible. Are you sure about that? And isn't that what the heroine always says?"

I shove him hard and he chuckles, rolling into a ball. I get to my feet and stalk across the room, shutting the lights. I'm exhausted. Sure, he's still in my bed and we never discussed him staying, or what it means for him to sleep in my bed, but I'm too tired to think.

I slide in beside him and tug the blankets over me. He's still lying on top so it's hard to get comfortable. "You can stay if you want. And if you sneak out at the crack of dawn, lock the bottom lock on the front door."

He sighs and snuggles under the covers. My eyes might be closed, but I can feel his stare at the back of my neck.

"No sneaking. I'm good." He adjusts, rolling to the other side, leaving a large gap between us. I'm thankful for it. I don't mind him staying, but I'm in need of space tonight.

CHAPTER 11

My house rarely smells like a diner during breakfast hours, but as I stretch my body and roll into the empty space beside me, the scent fills the room. The door to my room has been left ajar. Images of last night replay in my head. Confusing to say the least. Apparently, Logan was telling the truth and he hasn't left.

I throw the covers off. It's way too hot to cover up and he's seen so much of me already. The short shorts and nearly see-through tank are nothing out of the ordinary.

A mixture of sugar and bacon grows stronger as I saunter into the kitchen. Standing at the stove, looking way too sexy for seven in the morning is Logan, in his skin-tight jeans, shoeless in front of the stove. He turns as the floor creaks below my feet. "Got hungry."

I shake my head. "Plan on sharing?"

"With you? No."

When I reach him, I hit his arm, causing him to drop some eggs on the counter as he tries to be slick by flipping them with the entire pan. He leans into me, smirking as he sets the pan back down on the stove.

I hover over him for a moment longer before shuffling around the kitchen for plates and utensils. I reach for the plates to the right of where he's standing, in the top cabinets. He shifts over, and then moves back when I finish. I place the plates on the counter beside the stove. He shuts off the stove and I hold the plates up for him to slide the eggs onto.

We silently work side by side as he makes the rest of the pancakes.

"There's a lot of batter in there. This could take a while. Where do you put it all?" I tap on his rock-solid stomach. He grabs hold of my hand pressing it hard against him, then lowers it over the center of his jeans. I grab hold and grin.

"Now, this is something I could get used to."

I let go and shove him again, trying to ignore the flutter in my stomach. I try to put the image of what could be out of my head. Him saying things like that only confuses me even more. How does he expect me to forget these moments? I lean my back against the counter and take in the sight of him. From the lingering dark scruff lining his face, and the way he purses his lips while he cooks—like he's deep in thought.

I make myself look busy, keeping my focus on the counter space, trying to look at anything other than him. While he finishes with the pancakes and bacon, I wash some of the lingering dishes to make it easier later.

"So, tomorrow after we finish the second coat, I have a surprise for you," he says over the sizzling of bacon and the water running.

"Oh, really?" I ask loudly. "Should I be worried?"

He chuckles. "Nah. I think you'll like it."

"Tomorrow I'm working inventory at six in the morning, so I'll be out by ten."

"That's plenty of time."

We work like this for the next few minutes, him finishing up the cooking while I do dishes. Every once in a while I check behind me, gazing at him sliding back and forth between the pancakes on the griddle to his left and the bacon on the right.

He shuts the burner with the bacon and I come over, grabbing another plate. He slides to the side again, then we switch without a word to each other. I lay the bacon on a sheet of paper towel on a plate and allow it to soak up some of the grease. We stand side by side, our shoulders touching as we go about doing what needs to get done.

I bring the pan to the sink, and start to rinse it off.

"Ellie?" Mom's voice rings through the house.

"Hi, Mom, in the kitchen," I yell as I shut the sink.

"It smells good in here!"

I turn to find her in the entryway. Her hair is thrown up in a messy bun after a long night at the diner. There's heavy bags under her tired eyes, but that doesn't stop the grin that spreads across her face. My cheeks burn, like we're two teenagers being caught.

"Good morning, Logan." She draws out his name as she says it. Her eyes linger between the two of us. She's not oblivious to what is going on around her, and now she definitely has an idea of what went down under her roof while she was at work. I should run or hide, or both.

"Good morning, Amelia. Would you like anything?" he questions.

She shakes her head. "Thank you, Logan, but I'm exhausted." Her eyes dart back and forth again. "I'm going to head to bed." Her attention lands on me, eyes narrowing like she's telling me we'll have a conversation about this later. Under her gaze I feel like I'm fifteen again, sneaking around. Although I never had a boy in my bed, EVER. Not even Matt.

"See you later, Mom."

As she turns to leave, I cross the room to Logan so I can help with putting the food onto plates. In the corner of my eye I catch her glancing over her shoulder one last time before leaving us alone.

❧

"Your mom is so suspicious." Logan chuckles as we stand on opposite sides of Charlotte's room painting.

He is perched on an old wooden ladder that is caked with paint splatters. I cringed when he brought it out of Charlotte and Bryan's basement. It didn't look very steady and was probably left behind by the last owner with how old and rickety it was.

"I know. Ugh. I'm not even sure what to tell her after Sunday. Maybe I can lie."

He snorts.

Yeah. There's no way I'm lying to my mom. I'll have to explain it to her, she'll never let it go. This would have been much easier if I didn't live at home. Moving out won't happen any time soon, even with all the money I've saved up. It's nearly impossible to find a decent place to live with my income.

"Tell her that you couldn't handle all of this." He points to himself, and the ladder wobbles.

I nearly drop my brush, expecting to have to run over and catch him before he hits the ground. Only, somehow, he keeps himself balanced.

"That's what you get for being a smug asshole."

He throws me a toothy grin. "I might be smug, but you know I'm right. You'll crave me when I'm gone." The ladder wobbles.

"Your head is so big that you can't seem to keep control of that ladder. I'm not catching you if you fall."

"You always catch me, Ellie."

I'm not sure how to respond, so I ignore him and continue painting my side of the room.

Through the wide open window, a summer breeze flows. We're trying to vent out as much of the paint smell as possible.

The old window was a bit hard to open. The new one should be here tomorrow and he plans on putting it in as soon as it arrives. I'm excited to see the finished project, but the thought of it being finished leaves a knot in my stomach.

I take another peek at Logan while he's not watching. My heart thuds in my chest, banging against my rib cage. What if he goes back home and forgets me again? Of course I can move on; but do I want to is the question.

A silence lingers between us. The sounds of the outdoors waft in with the south shore breeze.

"Hey, can you grab me another can?" He steps down from the ladder, then wipes his brow with a pink rag he's got draped over his left shoulder.

I place my brush down and grab the can from the center of the room and lift it towards him. "Did you lose your ability to take a few steps across the room?"

He purses his lips as he sets the rag back over his shoulder. Dark eyes settle on mine. There's so much going on inside that head of his, I'm not sure what his next move will be. He reaches up, his hand dangerously close to my cheek. I hold my breath as his fingertips throw an invisible electric charge in my direction.

"You've got some paint." He casually dips his finger inside the green-ish paint, then smears it across my face. "Oh, I think I made it worse."

I put my hand on the bottom of the can and tip it forward. It splatters onto his shirt, pants, and shoes. With the mess we've made he takes some of the glob and fights back. I step backwards, attempting to get out of his grasp, but I'm too slow and he wraps his arms around me with his paint covered clothes. I spin in his arms and face forward, tugging to be released from his arms, but not getting very far. He's pressed against my back, the bulge in his pants overly excited to be close to me again.

"Stand down," he whispers in a growl against my ear, forcing a shiver down my spine.

"Never." I grit my teeth, and bump my backside into him, causing his breath to hitch.

He releases a hiss, and spins me back to face him. His painted hand rests along my cheek as he desperately catches my lips in his. With each tug on my lips, I thrust my body into him, wanting to feel more. He lowers me to the ground beside the tray of paint. I reach over, grab a big glob and smack it into his hair.

Logan pulls back, his eyes wide, mouth hanging open as the cool, dripping paint cascades down the side of his face. He reaches for the tray attempting to cover me in paint but instead it splatters between us with a thwap. His hands reach for my side. As he tickles me, I roll into the paint. At this point we are in desperate need of a shower, and have wasted a bunch of paint.

Instead of caring, he crashes his lips down to mine. I close my eyes to savor the kiss, when I catch his eyes open, watching me with a fire I've been hesitant to see. It's moments like these, I question everything I know about him. I want to believe that this is nothing more than a fling, but the more time I spend with him, the realer this becomes, and I honestly wish it didn't.

❦

I'm not sure when the clouds rolled in or when the earthy scent of rain leaked into the room, but we were completely wrapped up in the moment that we never even noticed the change. I shiver beside Logan, covered in paint splatters and sweat.

He reaches over and wipes a spot on my face, smirking as he whispers, "You had some paint." He holds his touch there for a few more seconds. His eyes steady on me.

"What are your plans when you return home?" I question, propping my head with my hand as I roll onto my side to face him.

He shrugs. "School starts in September, so I'll probably spend the next few weeks prepping for that."

"How did you end up being a gym teacher? You used to try and forge notes to get yourself out of running the mile."

He chuckles warmly. "Running is fun, when you aren't forced to spend it on a track going around in a circle. What kid didn't try to make an excuse to get out of it? I was going for a personal trainer and I don't know, this kind of fell into my lap."

"Do you love it? Do you regret moving?" I'm rambling, because I need to think of something else aside from what we've been doing together the past week. My head and my heart are too busy fighting with each other for me to make sense of it all. One is telling me to stay strong and the other is succumbing to the Logan Fields charm.

"What's with the twenty questions?" His tone is light, but there's something in there that tells me he'd rather not have a real conversation.

I shrug. "Can't a girl ask a friend she hasn't seen in four years questions about their life?"

"Friend?" He raises his brows.

"You've always been my friend, Logan. At least, I've considered you one. You might have been a few years older, but I thought of you as more than my best friend's brother."

"We should finish up," he says in a cold tone.

And there it is. He's shutting me out, because God forbid I ask him real questions instead of being flirtatious or allowing him to fuck me. The shift in the air around us isn't from the change of weather, it's from Logan's cold dark heart. The one who likes to bring someone in close and then push them away when they start to be pulled into his charm.

In silence, we clean up, get dressed, and prep the rest of the paint. We go back to painting our own walls. The only noise is the steady loud rain pounding on the roof, and the thudding of my heart pounding loudly in my ears.

CHAPTER 12

"And this candle is for my best friend, Charlotte."

My hand shook as I raised a sweet sixteen candle towards Charlotte. Talking in front of people was not my favorite thing to do. I tried to convince Mom that it wasn't for me, but when I saw the smile on her face that night, she looked proud, and that made me happy.

Charlotte stood up from her spot in the corner of the small hall Mom rented for my party.

"Charlotte and I met in pre-K. She was the girl who swapped a cheese stick with me for Jell-o during snack because I hated cheese. I couldn't ask for a better friend. You mean the world to me."

Charlotte's beautiful purple ball gown from her own sweet sixteen swayed as she walked forward. I handed her the candle and she lit one of the white ones displayed on the table in front of us.

I didn't have sixteen friends to hand out candles to, so I gave them to relatives who were important to me. I even had individual candles for Josephine and Henry. And of course Logan.

114

"This next candle." I had to pause, because my heart was beating so fast that it was almost hard to speak. "This one is for Logan. He may have been forced to know me because of Charlotte." There was some laughter from the guests. "But he's always been there for both of us as if he were my friend too. From the ice cream incident." Logan's cheeks were bright red. "To memorizing Jonas Brother lyrics for me. So, Logan, this candle is for you."

Sixteen-year-old me practically drooled over Logan that night. Josephine had forced him to wear a tuxedo and although he wasn't happy he wore it with a smile, because it was for me. He even styled his hair, which was usually a mess. I handed him the candle and our hands brushed. Before he leaned in he glanced at Charlotte who stood to my right. I caught her smile, and then he leaned in and kissed my cheek before lighting one of the candles.

It took me a good solid thirty seconds at least before I could continue. After I got through each candle the DJ played a special song for Dad and me to dance to. Dad wasn't too thrilled he had to dance: he hated the attention. I had tried to make it worthwhile by playing one of his favorite Beatles songs, but that didn't even help. Right before the song ended Logan tapped him on the shoulder.

"Excuse me," Logan said, "may I cut in?"

My dad was so relieved to be off the dance floor. Instead of going back to sit with Mom, he excused himself because he had taken an extra shift at the hospital he worked at then. I tried not to dwell on it.

Taylor Swift's "Today Was a Fairytale" came on as Logan swept me into his arms. He held me close and put his hands low on my waist. The moment his hands moved, I tilted my chin and his eyes found mine. After all these years Logan's smile has never changed. It's the one where the edges of his eyes crinkle slightly, and a small dimple appears on the right side of his cheek. I get lost in it every time.

"Hope you're having a good time," he whispered into my ear.

I shivered and hoped that he didn't catch on.

"I am now."

Shining lights flashed around the party hall. He chuckled, but it wasn't like he was making fun of me. At that moment he held me tighter and allowed me to rest my cheek on his chest.

Charlotte watched us as she danced with my cousin Vincent. She had told me he was cute. She thought he looked like Robert Pattinson from *Twilight*. I guess he had the same hair, but his face was nothing like Robert's. She was having fun, though, and that's all that mattered.

"I'm having a great time too. The candle thing was sweet. You're a good friend, Ellie."

That statement crushed sixteen-year-old Ellie, but I kept that to myself. For the rest of the night I danced with Charlotte, and made the best of it, even if my father bailed and Logan only looked at me like a friend.

Waking up at the ass-crack of dawn to run inventory before opening is the worst. Being that I beg for more hours, I'm usually one of the chosen ones lucky enough to work. At least Lily is here, but all she can talk about is our date tomorrow. I want to be excited, but it's hard with the looming thoughts of yesterday in my head. It's been ten days, and with each passing one, my heart grows a bit fonder of the guy who's taken up residence there.

"So, I found out that tomorrow night is cover band night. How exciting is that?" Lily says.

We were assigned to help count in the men's shoe department. I check off the number that the inventory employee has written on the yellow ticket, and sign my name, signifying I got the same amount.

"Oh, that's cool."

I continue down the line. My brain is trying too hard to focus on counting. I rub the right side of my head in a circular motion. I've had more headaches in the last week during this secret relationship than I've ever had in my life. I chalk it up to stress.

"Did you and Logan have a fight? You seem a little down today?" Her eyes meet mine as she stares up at me.

"No. Yes. No. Maybe."

Lily chuckles lightly, then places her hand over mine against the metal shoe rack. "I'm not Charlotte, but if you need to talk, I'm here."

I sigh. "Thanks, Lil. It's not that I don't want to talk. I'm having a hard time trying to wrap my head around the relationship I have with him. Some days I can't tell if it's real or if I'm imagining it."

It's not a total lie. There are moments when it all seems so real. It started the night of Charlotte's wedding when Logan swept me off my feet while we danced. I think our feelings on that first night were completely alcohol induced.

"I get it. I've been struggling myself lately."

Lily grabs hold of a yellow tag three shelves below me, and signs her name to it. Her eyes narrow on the work in front of her, her brows wrinkling slightly, like she's trying to piece together in her head how to explain what's happening between her and Jett.

"With what? You and Jett seem happy."

"Oh, we are." She stops working for a moment and checking to see if Maryann is on the prowl. When she's sure there's nothing to worry about, she turns back to me. "Sometimes he pulls back from me. On occasion we will both find the same females attractive. He's cool with it, but I think he's a little jealous, which I understand. I want him to know that I'm in this with him and no one else. He's the first man that has made me feel loved."

I smile, because it's easy to see the love in her eyes. I didn't realize her relationship had gone down the serious path. I'm happy for her. She focuses on the shoe in front of her like she's daydreaming.

"Have you ever discussed it with him?" I ask.

We shuffle down again, and Lily goes back to counting. She stops for a moment to answer me. "No. Do you think I should?"

"I think you should tell him how you feel, so there are no secrets between you both. It's the hidden things that tear us apart."

Look at me giving advice about being honest, when I'm over here lying to, not only my family and friends, but to myself and Logan. If I had the nerve, I'd tell him about all the times that I imagined him when I tucked myself under the covers at night. There's also that small crush that's spent years growing into what it is today.

When this week is over, we'll never go back to how it was before. There will always be sexual tension, especially now that we know we can do something to relieve it.

She nods. "You're right. Maybe I will. Thanks."

"Sure. And I really am looking forward to tomorrow night. I think we'll have a lot of fun. Do you know what cover band is playing?"

She shakes her head. "Not a clue, but get your dancing shoes on, because you and I are gonna dance the night away." She smiles.

Even with the pressing weight of Logan and me hovering over me, the idea of dancing my troubles away with Lily is sounding better and better.

118

The light beat of music flows through Charlotte and Bryan's home. Logan offered to take me to work, but I made up an excuse that I had to run a few errands before coming over today. What I mostly needed was time away from him.

My purse vibrates against my side. I stop at the top step and settle down onto it. Charlotte's name appears on the screen, it's not a video chat—only a phone call. What is she doing up this early again?

Guilt shakes me when I realize she's been the one to call me and I haven't reached out yet. I expected her to be silent during her honeymoon, but she's always updating me.

"Hey." I try to keep my voice low enough that Logan won't hear me, but it carries through the empty space.

"Hey! You've been quiet. Everything okay?"

I hate that she's noticing that I'm pulling away. Trying to hide two big secrets from a friend is tough, especially when one of them could destroy everything.

"I'm okay. Tired. What are you doing up early again?"

Through the phone I can hear her smile. "I'm doing some early morning yoga. I know what you're thinking, me and yoga, not a combo you're used to."

I laugh. "Is Bryan joining you?"

"No. He's doing some kind of snorkeling adventure. My period is raging so I'm gonna stick to doing activities on land for a day or so."

"At least it wasn't on your wedding day in that white dress."

"I know, right?" Her voice is full of happiness. Something I never thought I'd hear so early in the morning. She's never been happier, and it's all because of Bryan. When I met him I knew right away that the two of them were a sure thing. They have the type of romance you read about in a novel, or watch in a movie. It's the, *I'd run through a crowded airport to stop you from getting on a flight so I could tell you how much I love you*, type of love.

"El?" she says.

I blink a few times down at the bottom step. I must have drifted off a bit. I'd blame it on the lack of sleep and waking up before the sun rose, but there's a tiny little Logan poking around inside my brain trying to throw my life into a tailspin of drama.

"I'm sorry. I just got back from inventory. Had to be at the store at six."

She's quiet for a few long moments. "You sure that's it? You've been zoning out on all of our calls."

I rub a hand over my face to fight the building urge to cry and spill everything. Logan's name sits on the tip of my tongue. "I saw Matt on Sunday." It tumbles out like word vomit. At least I said Matt, not Logan.

"You did what? Hold on, I need to sit for this one."

On the other end, there's static. The sound of something dragging across concrete is like nails on a chalkboard.

"Okay, I'm sitting. Wow," she breathes. "This view. I'm sending you a pic, hold on."

Again, static takes over. She mumbles to herself about the sky in front of her. The phone beeps and I pull it from my ear to open her message. I can see why she'd been so distracted. She's poolside but facing a large empty beach. The morning sun is peeking out lighting the sky in a beautiful shade of pink and orange. She has caught a wave as it breaks and it really captures the beauty of the moment.

"Wow! That's gorgeous."

"Right? I think Dad is here with me. I can feel it. All the beautiful sunsets and sunrises, it's like he's telling me to enjoy life, and—" she sighs. "It's today, the anniversary."

I pull the phone away again to check the date. August twenty-fourth. Four years ago Logan and Charlotte lost their best friend and father. I can't believe that it didn't cross my mind.

"I'm sorry, I got caught up," she says. "This place is so

distracting, and there was a moment when I found a shark tooth and, you know how Dad loved sharks. It's just so surreal. Anyway—"

I imagine her shaking her head to get her thoughts together. I don't mind her rambling about her dad. She's been able to talk about it without having a breakdown for quite some time. She does tell me a lot about how things remind her of him, and she always has a smile on her face as if the good of that memory overpowers the sadness of the situation.

"Now, you say you saw Matt. Like did you two—"

"Oh no, God no. Matt and I didn't do anything. That's really amazing about your dad though. I'm sure he is watching you and throwing all those amazing sunsets and rises out there just for you."

Our conversation is bouncing all over the place. I blame it on the fact that this, aside from the summer she went to band camp, is the longest we've been apart.

"I wish Logan would see that. I've been trying to call him, but he's been ignoring me. Do you think he's okay? Maybe if you call him he'll answer. He seemed happy to see you at the wedding—" She pauses, and my heart catches in my throat.

"I can check in on him for you. I'll make sure he's okay." My voice sounds stronger than it feels. It's like someone has their fingers around my throat.

Behind me, the bedroom is wide open. Music pours out into the hallway. I imagine Logan in there by himself with his mind caught up in today. The edginess from yesterday makes a little more sense.

"That would be great. I guarantee he'll answer your phone calls. It's hard to get through to him. He's my big brother and I want him to be okay. Anyway, enough about Logan, what happened with Matt?"

"He wants to try things again. He apologized and told me he

misses having me in his life. He said I was the only one he wanted to talk about his day with." I try to say as little as possible. I don't need Logan hearing about Matt, even though I shouldn't care because in a couple of days it won't matter anymore.

"Aw. What are you feeling?"

"It was so easy to fall back into conversation with him. We chatted as if we never broke up. I miss when he'd get into a heated discussion with me about a TV show. It was easy, and everything with Matt was always easy."

"Do you love him?" she asks, like she's on the edge of her seat. In my head is an image of her shoveling popcorn into her mouth with an intense stare on her face, waiting for me to answer, like one of those memes.

"I think I love him, but I'm not sure if I imagine him as someone I'd be serious about. After he broke up with me, I've had some time to mull over all of it. I can't see myself waking up to him every day or—" I pause while my head plays through the past week with Logan. Images of how easy it is to fall into a familiar routine with him flash by like a montage.

"I don't know," I whisper.

"Ellie Mae Garner, is there someone else?"

I choke on my own spit, way too loud. Thankfully the doorway to the bedroom remains empty.

"No, there's no one else."

The lie strikes me like a lightning bolt. I wince, as if there was a physical pain ailing me.

"Shit. I'm sorry, El, I have to go or I'm going to be late for yoga."

"Your instructor isn't like the 'Boom guy' from *Couples Retreat*, is it?"

Her thunderous laughter is loud enough for me to pull the phone from my ears. "Oh, God no, but that would have been amazing. Well, I'll talk to you later. Oh, and text me if you hear from Logan, okay?"

"Have fun!"

She hangs up. I sit at the top of the stairs for a few more minutes. I'm half-afraid to go into that room and see Logan. The other part of me is worried about him. I get to my feet, pad across the hallway and stop outside the door.

He's closing up the cans. A fresh coat of paint blanks the walls. He did the second coat without me. I can't explain why, but there's a tiny pinch in my heart. The floor beneath my foot creaks as I turn to bail on him. He's fine without me. I start to retreat and his eyes shoot toward me. I'm locked into place.

"So, Matt, huh?" His voice is gruff.

My mouth hangs open.

"You were eavesdropping?" I point at him.

He nods, then hammers around the edges of the paint can to seal it. Silently, he does the same with the next. He throws the brushes into the orange pan and lifts it.

"What does it matter? We're done at the end of the week anyway."

"I know." He shrugs. "I didn't say anything, did I?"

I hang my head low and shake it. He slides past me to head to the bathroom so he can clean the brushes.

I follow behind him. "So, are we done here then? Seems you don't really need any help—"

He enters the bathroom and flips on the light. I smile at the light blue shower curtain with yellow rubber ducks hanging over the tub. Logan stands at the sink, scrubbing the brushes. He's using so much force, I fear he'll snap them in two.

"The painting is done if that's what you're referring to," he says, curtly. His jaw is taut and there's a heaviness in his eyes. I observe the way his shoulders are rigid. He violently rubs the brushes bristles into the sink, the green running into the sink swirling around mixing with the light peach color.

I want more than anything to take away his pain. He's not going to tell me that the reason he's being cranky is because he misses his dad. I'll let him tell me on his own time. He needs a distraction. There's no point in making things worse by bringing up the one thing that's weighing him down.

Releasing a strong, steady breath I stride across the bathroom towards him. I wrap my hand around his and pry the brush from his tight grip.

"You told me you had a surprise for me today. You can't tease me with something exciting and then be Mr. Grumpy Pants."

I scrub at the brushes and bump my hip into his. He smirks. My shoulders loosen. Good, it's working. He watches the way I'm stroking the brush to get the paint off.

"God, woman, you're turning me on with the way you're gripping those brushes."

I look up, this time finding the Logan I love— I mean the Logan I— the— nope not even going there. He's got that nail-biting sexy grin that turns me on spreading across his face. I hit the brush against the side of the counter, then shut off the water.

"Is there ever a moment that you're not turned on?"

He taps his pointer to his lips. "Around you, I'm always turned on."

I brush off the comment, attempting to slay the butterflies before they make me feel things I shouldn't.

"So, what are we doing then?"

I spin and close the gap between us. The warmth he radiates covers me.

"How would you like to go on a day trip?" He stares down at me, smile never fading.

"Lead the way."

At first, he doesn't move. He stands there staring off like he wants to change his mind. It's as if he'd take me right here in this small bathroom squashed between the tub and sink. I take several steps back and wave for him to walk past.

He walks out of the bathroom without another word. I have

to brace myself and put my hand against the counter. He doesn't make anything easy, and he sure knows the way to make my panties wet. Ugh. Logan Fields, what have you done to me?

CHAPTER 13

"Why are we getting on a train?"

Logan pulls me through the Ronkonkoma train station towards a silver and blue double decker. Its engine growls, shaking the concrete platform at our feet as we race towards the front of the train. He pulls me in as the door closes and the chimes ding.

We hustle up a small set of stairs and onto the upper deck. It's a bit tighter up here, but the car is mostly empty being that it isn't rush hour. He finds a spot that satisfies him amongst the empty rows of blue seats, and allows me to go in first.

"This is the train to Greenport, the next stop is Medford." A robotic voice talks over the loudspeaker.

We lurch forward as we begin to depart from the station. I turn my attention to him.

"You're taking me to Greenport?" My eyes light up. I haven't been to Greenport since we were young. We would go every summer with his family and ride the carousel, eat at a restaurant in town, have ice cream at our favorite little shop, then run around on the beautiful grassy knoll near the carousel. His dad was really into trains, so we'd drive all the way to the Ronkonkoma station and board there.

"We had a lot of great times out there, so I figured today would be a good day to visit."

Deep down, I know he's thinking about his dad. The memories associated with Greenport all involve him.

"At the wedding, you mentioned you missed eating at the little diner where we would order chicken and fries to annoy Charlotte. She never understood how we could eat the same thing every time."

I smile. "Remember the time when she ordered the same thing two years in a row—I think it was the turkey sandwich or the BLT—and we called her out on it?"

His laughter fills up the empty train car. His shoulders shake and rub against me with every movement. He rests his hand on my thigh, warmth spreads over me.

"She was pissed for the rest of the day, and then she pushed me in the water when we went over to the beach."

Tears roll down my cheeks from laughing so hard. I don't mean to make fun of Charlotte's quirk, but it was funny. She told me later that night that she wasn't really mad at me, only Logan.

"Remember the year Dad took us to Shelter Island on the ferry at Greenport?" His demeanor changes slightly, the crinkles in his eyes disappear, but a small smile remains.

"I do. I think it was the last year we were there. You capsized our kayak, and your dad jumped in, because I was—and still am —a terrible swimmer."

From underneath my hand, he curls his pinky up and around mine, squeezing it. I cup my hand and slowly tighten my grip too.

"So, what are our plans for today? No kayaking, I hope."

He chuckles. "We are strictly staying in the village. I'm thinking by the time we get there we should go order some chicken, then take a walk by the docks and ride on the carousel."

"Don't forget ice cream." I nudge him.

He focuses on our hands together, then shifts his attention back on me.

"They have the best—" we both say at the same time and pause. "Mint chocolate chip." Another pause. "Jinx!" We yell at each other like we're ten all over again.

The train ride out to Greenport is a little over an hour. Our time is spent chatting about what we plan on doing. I'm still in awe that he's gone through all the steps of being romantic and spontaneous, all for something that is meant to end in a few short days. Which has my mind wondering, what will we be when this is all over? Will he ever talk to me again? Can we co-exist without the lust between us getting the better of us?

I try not to dwell, because as we pull onto the small one-track station in Greenport, my excitement over the day grows. He never lets go of my hand as we make our way back down and out onto the platform. We follow the small group who made the trek out to the end of the line with us, and as we pass the train, the beautiful Peconic River comes into view.

Water laps up against the dock, gurgling in a rhythmic tune over the grumbling train engine. Without thinking, we head in the direction of our favorite little restaurant. It sits on a crowded little corner, and from the edge of the street you can look straight down by the docks with all the boats bobbing in the choppy bay water.

"They changed the name." I'm only half disappointed by this new development. His shoulders droop and I understand the sadness that he's feeling. Not only was this our favorite spot, but his dad's as well.

"We could try somewhere else—"

"No. Things change, life moves on." He sighs.

I hate the pain in his voice, and the way it cracks at the end of his sentence. I shift my hands so that my fingers slip inside of his. He releases a trembling breath from my touch. He blinks away the hesitation in his eyes and reaches for the little red door with his free hand.

Inside, the place is fully renovated, but still holds that small charm it did back then.

"It's cleaner," he whispers.

The last time we were here the floor was in desperate need of a revamp. Even mopping it wasn't enough to sweep away the build-up from all the traffic.

"Look, it's our booth." I point to the empty spot all the way in the back corner, near the bathrooms. The restaurant wasn't ideal, because we all didn't fit in one booth. So we took up two. The one at the back was where Logan, Charlotte and I sat, while his parents had the next one along.

"Excuse me," he asks the waitress in a red dress. "Is that booth in the back open? It's kind of sentimental." He lifts his arm, unhooking our hands to throw it over my shoulder.

"Yes. It's all yours." She smiles, then waves her hand for us to follow.

We sit down in the booth across from each other. She hands us each a menu and tells us someone will be with us shortly. It's different, usually we seated ourselves, but I'm glad Logan asked. It's like I can feel his dad's presence all around.

"We should have told her to save the menus," he says, giving me a Logan smirk.

I nod. "Right? We already know what we're ordering. Remember the crayons they used to keep here?"

"I still am holding a grudge over that summer you two beat me at hangman."

"Hey, supercalifragilisticexpialidocious is a real word."

He shakes his head. "That was unfair!"

"Hello, can I start you two with any drinks?" A young waitress wearing mostly the same get-up as the last stands over us. Her eyes flutter towards Logan as she plays with her mousy brown hair, twisting it with her fingers. She could have stepped off the modeling runway with her long legs and perfectly plump breasts.

Being Logan, he throws in his charming smile. The only difference between this one and the one he gives me is that when he smiles at her, it never reaches his eyes.

"We'll both have Dr. Pepper, and we don't need these." He lifts the menus and hands them to her. "We'll have the chicken tenders and fries. Honey mustard on the side, please, for both orders."

She doesn't even glance at me. She holds on to the menus, Logan still holding on too. Her eyes are focused on him as she giggles over their exchange. I wait for him to make a flirtatious comment, but he doesn't. He lets go and she nearly drops the menus. His eyes return to me with an intensity so full of desire, I have to cross my legs to fight the twitch between them.

With a defeated sigh, the waitress turns and walks away.

"We should go buy those little yellow ducks. Do you still have your collection?"

My jaw hangs open. I can't believe he passed up flirting with the waitress.

"What?" he asks, narrowing his eyes.

"Nothing. Yeah, can't go to Greenport without buying some rubber ducks."

After walking around to digest, we end up behind the carousel, staring off into the bay and across at the shoreline of Shelter Island. Logan got up a few minutes ago to find a trash can, and he still hasn't returned. I stand from the old wooden bench that sits in front of the docks. Turning, I scan the open green lawn surrounding the carousel. There are families scattered all around. Some on blankets eating, others chasing toddlers. A little further up there's a group of young kids with a soccer ball kicking it around. A plaid black and white shirt catches my attention. Logan.

He's standing beside a boy who looks maybe around eleven or twelve. It's hard to tell from this far back. I head towards them to get a better look. One of the boys playing kicks the ball to them and Logan cheers the boy on. The ball doesn't get very far, and the boy's shoulders sag. Logan holds up his hand, says something to the other boys, then jogs to the ball and retrieves it.

As I stand beside a small tree that looks newly planted, I keep watch over at Logan and the young boy. It must be the gym teacher in him. He's explaining something. I can just barely hear his voice from here. He points to the inside of his foot and shows off some easy kicks. He kicks the ball to the boy and the boy kicks it back. Logan cheers, and then has him kick it towards the group who is patiently waiting. The kick is amazing and the boy jumps up and screams, Logan high fives him. The rest of the group urges Logan to play, and for a few minutes, he does. He goes around giving pointers and they all seem grateful.

As he helps a taller boy score a goal, he scans the area and his eyes find mine. I hold in my breath at the soft smile on his lips. My heart is doing ridiculous flips inside my chest. Leave it to Logan to always be helpful.

He jogs over and takes my hand. "Ready to ride?"

"I think I've had enough time to digest, let's go!"

We are the oldest on the carousel, apart from a few parents holding on to their toddlers. Logan chooses a brown horse and I choose a red one. No matter how dizzy this ride made me, it was always so much fun, because it's one of the fastest carousels I've ever been on.

Once we're done going on twice, because Logan is a child at heart, we head over to get ice cream and to check out the store with the rubber ducks in the window. There are so many I don't have, especially since we haven't been here in a while. I accumulate ten more ducks for my collection, including a vampire, batman, a duck shaped like a carrot, and a cupcake duck.

After we get our ducks, we head to the best ice cream shop in town and order our favorite ice cream. The best flavor from here is the mint chocolate chip.

We take our treats to the docks at the end of the block and lean over the railing. Sometimes there's a large ship docked here that looks like something out of a pirate movie. Today it's not here so we have a clear view of the bay.

"This was a great idea," I say, while licking off a huge chunk of mint ice cream. "I miss coming out here every summer. It broke my heart when we stopped."

"So, let's do it," he says. "Next summer, you, me, Mom, Charlotte, Bryan, even your mom. We could start the tradition again."

"So, you're planning on coming back every summer?" I stop eating the ice cream.

The early evening sun is bright and hot, causing a little bit of sticky cream to roll down the cone and over my fingers. He doesn't face me; he keeps his eyes trained on the choppy water below, and the skyline above the island across the way.

"Yeah, I think so."

I want to ask him, where does that leave us? Now that he's planning on returning annually. I can't help but think for that short time when he returns he'll expect us to dive back into whatever this is. No strings attached, random sex, but I'm not so sure that's what I want.

"Your family would really like that," I say. My voice is barely above a whisper.

"And what about you? How does that make you feel?" he asks, softly.

Now it's my turn to not look at him, while his eyes beat down on me. I shrug, because I can't let him know that my heart is having trouble distinguishing between real and fake.

"Why does it matter how I feel?" I make the mistake of glancing over.

He shoves the rest of the cone into his mouth and chews while watching me. His eyes narrow like he's about to say something to make my heart melt, instead, he says, "You know you're gonna want more of this."

I bite down on my lower lip to fight the urge to smack him. I throw out a fake smile and respond, "In your dreams."

He smirks. Whatever sentimental moment we were having floats away with the soft breeze that blows through.

"Train leaves in thirty minutes; we should wrap it up," he says.

"Okay."

I need to distance myself from him, to get my head on straight, but there's no way I can now. We have our fake date tomorrow with Lily and I don't want to cancel. We also have the furniture coming tomorrow. Before the date, we plan on putting down the new floors and installing the window. There's no escaping Logan now. I'll have to put my big girl panties on and get through the week.

CHAPTER 14

Their fight was bad the day Dad walked out. I found myself in front of Arthur's door. I knocked and hoped he would answer. I still remember his red rimmed eyes. He didn't even make one of his snarky comments. He took my shaking hand in his and pulled me into his room where we sat on the edge of his bed and waited out the fight.

Even with the door closed we could hear them. The sound of Dad's footsteps jarred us both as he stomped past and went into their room. We heard a lot of movement through the wall, and Mom was crying in the hallway.

Arthur and Dad were kind of close. He worked a lot and rarely connected, but they had their father-son bonding moments.

"Please don't go," Mom had said. Her voice broke and it killed me to hear.

The front door slammed and we were left with the sounds of Mom's cries from her bedroom. Arthur held me. We said nothing, only kept each other company. It was one of the only times he'd been there for me, and I could tell this had affected him too. We still have never talked about that day. The worst part

134

is a few hours later he was back to his usual self; and I suddenly didn't matter anymore.

We were eighteen when it happened and I had my own car. After the commotion I slipped out of the house and went to Charlotte's. I never expected to find Logan's car in the driveway. He hadn't been around much, because he'd just found a new girl and it was kind of serious. Or I thought it was.

Their dad stood in the doorway with a concerned look on his long, narrow face. He was the spitting image of Logan, from his hair to his eyes, only his hair had a hint of gray. "Ellie sweetheart, are you okay?"

I shook my head and he invited me in and wrapped me in a hug. He was such a kind gentle soul. Inside he led me into the dining room where everyone was eating lunch. Logan and his girlfriend, Diana, looked up. He shifted in his chair ready to get up, but held back. With Diana around things were different. She nudged him to look at her and then twirled her fire red hair around her long finger and smiled.

Charlotte got up and came round the table. She held on to me while I cried in their dining room. Josephine ushered the two of us out and sat with me in the living room while I poured my heart out to both of them. Josephine immediately got up and called Mom, while Charlotte stayed with me.

"I'm not sad that he won't be around," I sniffed. "I'm angry because he hurt Mom."

"I am so sorry. Maybe we should take your mom to go get her hair or nails done. When she feels better. Give her something to look forward to."

Charlotte's love for others was always my favorite thing about her.

"I think she'd like that."

Logan cleared his throat as he walked through the room. Diana was at his heels. He started to come over, but she grabbed his arm and tugged him back. "We should go," she said.

Our eyes met briefly. He looked at Diana, then back at me, but chose her. Of course he did. He was just Logan, my best friend's older brother who saw me as a little sister and nothing more. He went to walk away, then stepped towards me again, but she yanked him away. It hurt that he didn't comfort me that day.

Charlotte, Josephine and I baked a nice lasagna and then brought it back to my house. Mom never came out of her room, but I made sure she ate some.

The whole thing took a toll on Mom. Seeing her in such a fragile state hurt. The strong woman I had looked up to my whole life was crumbling before my eyes. It was nice to have the support of the Fields, especially when Arthur left with the intent of never returning.

Mom's voice carries through the house as I slowly start to wake up. I stir, listening to her muffled tone dance around the hallway. She grows louder, then softer every few seconds. She's pacing the hallway outside my room.

I lie there for a moment ignoring whatever conversation she's having, and glance up at the ceiling. It could use another coat or two of paint and there's spots that have been peeling for years. Thinking about paint reminds me of Logan.

Yesterday's events are fresh in my mind. Logan shuts down so easily when things get too serious. The thing for me about relationships that's more important than anything is being able to have a serious conversation if need be. He can't even handle three seconds.

There's a soft knock on my door. I sit up in bed. "Come in."

Mom sticks her head around the edge of the door. "Are you decent?"

"Yes, why?"

136

"Your brother skyped me." She holds the phone at a distance attempting to do something with the settings.

I sigh. "What are you trying to do?"

"Flip the camera." She narrows her eyes at the device in her hands. Her fingers tap loudly at the screen while she tries to find the right button.

"Mom, you're using a filter," Arthur says, in a dull tone.

She squints, and jumps, eyes wide.

"Mom." I roll my eyes and groan. I set my feet on the floor and walk over to where she's paused in the middle of my room. I lean in and turn into some kind of weird gothic princess. I exit the filters for her, and she breathes a sigh of relief.

"What's a filter?" she asks.

Arthur and I stare at each other through the camera, and a small understanding passes between us. A sibling moment, if you will. We may not always get along, but the twin "telepathy" thing has never vanished. Not actual telepathy, but we have this thing where we can look at each other and have some idea what the other is thinking.

"Hi, Arthur," I say, my voice falling flat. I'm not too thrilled to be talking to my brother. He's the last person I wanted to speak to this morning.

"Hi, El."

It's early in the morning in California, but Arthur keeps a lot of strange hours when he's working on a movie or TV show, so it's not uncommon for him to call early. Like Dad, he only calls when it suits him.

"How are you?" It's easy to hear how uninterested I am in this chat.

"Good. I want to introduce you and Mom to my fiancée."

"Your *what*?" I blink several times, wondering if it's the weariness from sleep, or if I heard him correctly. I mean, he is my twin so a part of me does love him, but I'm in awe that anyone would want to date him, let alone marry him. He's not easy to

137

live with. Aside from leaving the seat up, he literally never cleans his room. I swear Mom and I are still finding silverware all these years later buried in random spots in that room.

"Cassie, come here." He waves his hand.

Mom's eyes fill with tears like she's so proud of him. He's the one who took his dream and turned it into some kind of reality. He left, made himself a life, and now he gets the happily-ever-after too.

My stomach clenches as a wave of nausea hits me hard. I offer him a weak smile. It's all I can muster. How Arthur found himself a life before me baffles me.

A beautiful actress-like woman settles beside him. She twirls her bouncing blonde locks between her fingers. Arthur adjusts the phone so we get a better angle of the two of them. They are outside on what looks like a deck, with the Pacific Ocean waves rolling in the darkness behind them. Her face has not one imperfection on it.

"Mom, El, this is Cassie. We met on set about eight months ago."

"Hi, nice to meet you." Mom beams, her cheeks rosy with excitement.

Cassie's voice is about as fake as the tan on her olive skin. I muster up another smile, trying to not be jealous that my brother has his life together more than I do.

"When do you plan on getting married?" Mom asks.

"Oh, we're not sure yet. Might just do the courthouse. Nothing fancy." Cassie glances over at Arthur.

I bite down, my jaw tensing and aching from the tightness. I move away from the view of the camera so they can't see me. "She's pregnant," I whisper to Mom.

Mom hushes me, throwing her hand up for me to stop.

"That's amazing, honey. Isn't it, Ellie?"

"Yeah, great, Arthur. Congrats." I stick my head in for another moment.

Mom starts babbling to Cassie, and exits the room with the phone. I'm grateful for her taking the conversation elsewhere. I'm over here fucking someone for fun, while my brother is settling down. God, I need to get my priorities straight. My phone vibrates on the bedside table. I hop into bed and grab it. Logan.

Picking you up in fifteen minutes. Be ready. Don't forget to pack your stuff for tonight's sleepover.

He sends a second text inserting an emoji with a tongue sticking out and an eggplant. He's so immature sometimes.

Dropping the phone, I bury my face into the pillow and scream. The muffled sound vibrates in my ear. I shake whatever emotions off that I need to. If I'm going to have the life I want, I have to be the one to get off my ass and create that life. Instead of moping around, I get to my feet and head for the shower to clear my head and prepare for the crazy day ahead.

❧

By the time I get downstairs, Logan and Mom are already having a light discussion. Laughter fills the air as I head into the kitchen. On the table is a brown bag filled with bagels of every kind, and Logan and Mom are sitting across from each other chatting.

They both turn when the floorboard below my foot creaks. Logan's eyes are heavy, like he didn't sleep well, but he still manages one of his usual smiles.

"Logan brought bagels. Come eat. They are the softest bagels I've ever eaten." Mom takes a bite of the dark pumpernickel bagel in front of her. I grab a water bottle from the fridge, then slide in next to Logan, bumping him with my hip.

"Logan says you two had quite a day yesterday."

If that's what he wants to call it. I'd say it out loud, but I don't have any energy to be sarcastic. All of my sarcasm was swept away with Arthur's big news.

"Yup. Even bought more ducks for my collection," I manage to say instead.

Last night after I came home, I placed all of my new friends on the shelf above my bed with all the other ducks lined up. I'd been collecting for so many years that they almost didn't fit. It's a silly collection, but brings back good memories.

Logan reaches under the table and grabs hold of the hand I've left between us. I swallow hard. He squeezes and lets go, leaving my hand cold and my heart doing out of control flips. I don't allow my hand to linger there in fear he'll do something like that again. He lifts an everything bagel from the bag and shows it to me.

I nod. "Thanks."

"How much more work do you have on the place? I think what you're both doing for Charlotte and Bryan is amazing. They will appreciate it for years to come."

"Today we're finishing the Pergo flooring and the window," Logan says.

"Charlotte is getting a new arch window that she always talks about," I chime in. Mom's eyes light up.

"You know, Logan, I'll pay you to put one of those in my living room—"

He chuckles and takes a sip of his coffee. Of course, he's drinking out of my favorite mug with the words, "fucking Trevor" written on it from the *After* series.

"Hey, anytime you need something done I'd be more than happy to help out."

His attention remains on Mom and the mug of coffee. I wish he wouldn't make promises he can't keep. Like the other day, offering for me to come up and spend time with him in Pennsylvania. How can I believe him? All he does is run.

"In fact, we should probably head out in a minute if we want to be done with it all before tonight."

"Ohhh, what's tonight?" Mom asks. Her eyebrows wiggle as she sips from her #1 mom mug that Arthur and I got her for Mother's Day one year.

"Well, her friend from work thinks we're dating." His smirk grows.

Wide eyed, I stare at him.

"What? You have to admit, that's funny." He holds my attention for a heartbeat longer before turning to Mom. "She invited us on a double date tonight."

I can feel Mom's eyes on me, but I'm too busy glaring at Logan.

"I mean, we do make a good-looking couple." He turns to me with a devilish gleam in his dark eyes. "Right, baby?"

I growl, literally a feral growl, like a wild animal. "What did I tell you about that name?"

Mom sits quiet for a few moments, her eyes darting back and forth between us like she's trying to figure out what's going on. "Well, you two have fun. I have another long night of work ahead of me. Oh. Logan, that reminds me, your mom said something about dinner Friday."

"Oh, right. We're going to my mom's for dinner on Friday night." Logan parrots Mom.

I shake my head and blink a few times. "We are?"

I love Josephine and of course don't mind having dinner with her, but with everything going on, the idea of sitting in front of her and lying too, almost causes me to lose my appetite.

He nods. "Yeah. I'll take you to work and pick you up so you don't have to drive. You said you're working day shift, right?"

"Yeah..." I vaguely remember telling him that several days ago. His ability to remember pieces of my life is confusing.

"So, then it's settled. Do you need a ride, Amelia?" He turns to Mom.

"Oh no, dear, thank you. I'll be coming straight from work myself. You two have a great night. I'm going to catch some Zs before my shift." Mom slides out of the chair and stands. As she passes me she narrows her eyes, and I know I'm going to have to explain everything the next time we're alone. I sigh.

I set the bagel back down onto the plate. With my pointer, I very slowly start wiping off some of the seeds and other hard pieces of seasoning off. It's my favorite part, but I need to do something with my hands, and holding Logan's is *not* the thing I want to do.

"Hey."

I snap my neck in his direction. Without warning, he rests his hand against my cheek, pulling me into him. His lips brush gently against mine. A shiver rages through my entire body making my toes curl.

"We're good, right?"

Why does he do that? How can he keep pretending like there isn't something there. He can't go around touching my face like that. I tilt my head up to find any kind of explanation as to why he's being so touchy-feely. I realize he didn't even kiss me yesterday, and the lack of his touch sends my body into a frenzy, and casts this wild and hungry look in his eyes.

I'm tempted to say, *Why does it matter? In a few days you'll be gone,* but I bite my tongue instead. "Fine. Why?"

His smile has been wiped away. All of his attention is now lingering on me. "You're snippy," he says. He moves his face so close that if I move even slightly our lips would be touching. It's overwhelming enough that I have to fight the urge to do it.

"Maybe I'm on the verge of menstruation, or maybe it's because Arthur called right before you got here."

Logan gives me his complete attention. He's aware of how my brother and I are. That one minute we were best friends and the next all hell breaks loose. It's normal for siblings, especially twins, to have squabbles, but sometimes it feels like more than that when Arthur and I go at it.

"How's he doing?"

"He's engaged." A hollow laugh escapes my lips.

Logan watches me, but says nothing. It's hard not to be upset when my brother was the screw-up and now I'm filling those shoes instead.

"He's engaged, and seems to have a steady gig. It's like his life is falling into place while mine is tearing at the seams. I mean, how long can I live with my mom? I can't even get my own place." My eyes sting with the threat of tears. I blink several times to keep them at bay.

"You're only twenty-four, Ellie," he says, softly. "You have plenty of time to find out who you are."

I scoff. "Charlotte has a real job, a husband, a house; even you have a real job. Look at me, I'm a sales associate working at only slightly above minimum wage, living at home with my mom." I pause to catch my breath and settle my thoughts. "I'm a failure." My lips quiver at the word failure. "My life is a joke. I can't even get a guy to fall in love with me. Matt doesn't count: he only misses the idea of me."

"My sister has been planning her wedding since she was in diapers. She always wanted to be Cinderella. I can remember her always watching it on repeat and asking when she was going to find her prince."

I half-sob, half-laugh and snort. Logan's hand finds its way to mine without even looking, and well after I hid it under my leg so he wouldn't touch me.

"We said we'd get married together. I know it was some stupid fantasy that I didn't even believe would happen, but seeing her find the perfect husband first hurts a little."

"Fuck who society believes you should be at twenty-four." He says it like he's just proclaimed something passionate. His chest

143

puffs out and he straightens his body. "It's your life; some people don't find their passion until they are fifty."

His eyes soften, never breaking their contact with me. The longer the silence between us, the closer he gets, closing the small distance between us.

I blow air from my lips. "That doesn't make me feel any better."

He shrugs. "It should. Ellie, you are perfect the way you are. You should know that. I've been telling you since we were little."

"I know," I whisper.

"You don't need a so-called 'real' job, or a steady boyfriend. You've got so much time left to find a career and settle down. If you ask me, I think you're doing fine."

He always knows the right things to say. I lift my hand to wipe away a tear that broke free, but he's quicker than I am and swipes it away first. His hand lingers on my face and I lean into his touch with everything I have.

For a few long, lingering moments I rest my other hand against the one he has on my cheek, and shut my eyes. I make myself take several deep inhales to relax. When I open my eyes, Logan is there, like he's always been, right by my side when I needed him most.

I slide out of my seat first, and he follows. As I reach the entryway of the kitchen, he grabs my hand and pulls me into him. Burying his face into my neck, he leaves kisses along my collarbone. I want to enjoy it, but I can't, not with my mom so close by.

"Save that for tonight, lover boy." I push against his deep gray tee.

When I glance up and catch his eye, I can't help but smile, because he's Logan. Sometimes he can make me so angry, but at the same time he's also somehow captured my heart in ways that I can't explain.

Without another word, he steps around me and heads out

first, grabbing the bags I left at the door on the way out. This day is going to either go really well or it's going to blow up in my face, either way I brace myself for impact.

Ready and willing, I follow him out to the car. We spend the first ten minutes fighting over the radio, followed by a ten-minute mansplain about how to lay down Pergo. It's going to be a long-ass day.

CHAPTER 15

I've never in my life ached the way I do right now. I've been on the floor on my hands and knees for the past three hours. Logan acts as if it hardly affected him.

"What's the matter, old lady? Can't get up?"

He stands over me grinning. Other than my body hurting all over, our day together was not as bad as I imagined. While we worked, the two of us talked about nonsense things, like how if the *Cobra Kai* universe was real, he would be team Miyagi-Do and I would be team Eagle Fang.

I reach up to grab hold of his hand, but instead of getting to my feet, I tug him down to the floor with me. He lands in front of me on his knees, then pushes me back slowly, laying me down on the freshly installed Pergo. He places a hand behind my head as he lowers me to the ground.

"What time do we have to be at the pub?" he questions, lowering his fully clothed body over mine.

"Seven, which gives us enough time to shower and head out."

"Are you ready to be my girlfriend?"

His earnest tone causes my body to freeze up, but my pulse has other plans. It rapidly beats inside of me, throbbing in various points loud enough to thump in my ear. His lips lingering over mine are not helping the situation, and making it hard for me to decipher if his words have some truth to them.

"Hah." There's an uneasy brittle sound to my voice. "We should break up in the middle of the pub. Cause a scene. It would probably be your fault." I ramble on in a high-pitched squeal. My feelings have a mind of their own.

He's quiet as he starts to nibble on my neck like he was this morning in my kitchen. It catches me off guard and gets me all hot and bothered.

"Mine? Why not yours?" He pauses for a moment to lick my collarbone.

A low, guttural moan escapes my lips.

"You're the one sneaking around with your ex," he says into my neck.

"Hey! I am not, and what does it matter? You shouldn't eavesdrop on phone calls." I throw my head back as he makes his way up my jawline, kissing along the edge. "Or maybe it was you." I poke him in the chest. "Maybe your ex was the one who came back into the picture. Or you were only dating me to get ahead in your job."

He chuckles over my lips, his warm breath dancing over me. "Not sure that would quite work, with me as a physical education teacher."

"You could get me out of running the mile," I wink. I snort, then wrap my hands around the back of his neck and pull him down into me. His mouth opens the minute our lips touch. There are way too many clothes between us, and we could probably make it by seven if we took this little party in the shower. I don't know what's come over me, but his deep hungry kisses have me squirming under his weight.

He pulls back. "Okay, I got it. You're the nerdy girl that I've transformed into a beautiful butterfly—"

"No," I say, biting on his bottom lip.

His moan echoes around the empty room.

"Whatever it is, can I do a fashion montage while I try on the outfits I brought for tonight?" I ask.

He moves to the right, nestling his face beside my ear. "Will you parade around in lingerie for me?"

I love the growl in his tone, and so does my body. I squirm again. He lowers himself, lifting the hem of my shirt to expose my stomach. His lips travel over my belly button as he carefully opens the fastening on my shorts. As his lips touch right above my pantie line Charlotte's ringtone plays from my phone.

We both freeze in place. I can't tell if the pounding between us is his heart or mine.

"We should get ready," I whisper, stopping the moment out of sheer guilt.

He watches me from his position between my legs and sighs. His jaw tenses, and I expect him to tell me to ignore the call, but he crawls off me instead.

I jump to my feet to answer my phone, but miss the call. Instead of attempting to call her back, I head downstairs to gather some of my things to shower. As I'm about to walk out of the living room I get a text. I double-back and check the message. It's Charlotte.

Why did my brother comment on the selfie of you with flames and a wink emoji? Do I have to kick his ass? Is this because you called him the other day to check in? I'm sorry he's a creeper.

I laugh at the last line. I fear if I don't text her back she might get suspicious.

You know how Logan is. He's probably doing it to annoy you. Love you, hope you enjoy your last few days in paradise.

He and I are sleeping—Erase. *It's not serious or anything, but*

Logan and I are—Erase. Closing my eyes, I grip the phone in my hand. Typing out the words I realize that our days together are winding down, and I hate that the idea leaves me on the verge of tears.

Before I reach the bathroom upstairs, the water squeaks on, and steam drifts out of the room. I catch Logan as he closes the shower curtain. As I step in behind him, he's got his head tilted back and his eyes closed, allowing the water to fall over his head. His body is as taut as his jaw.

My eyes dart around the small, enclosed space while I wait for my turn. On the wired hanging shower caddy I catch sight of a yellow rubber duck.

"You're showering with the duck you bought yesterday?"

He lowers his face towards mine, beaming. "It wasn't a problem for Ernie."

I snort. "I hate to break it to you, but Ernie's a puppet."

He places a hand over his heart, shakes his head, and narrows his eyes. "Way to ruin my childhood."

I shove his chest. The laughter between us evaporates the tension in the air.

I reach behind him where he's placed his own bar of soap and lather it into my hands. Instead of washing myself first, I reach over for him and rub the soap all over his hard body. He keeps his eyes closed as I cover him in white suds. He grabs the soap, then lathers it all over me. We rotate in and out under the hot water, moving in sync with each other as we go.

It's strange how it's like the way we maneuvered around each other in the kitchen. One more thing that falls naturally into place. I'm going to need some kind of intervention after it's all over, that's for sure.

"Ellie!" Lily calls over the loud music.

149

The cover band on stage is playing a rendition of One Direction's "What Makes You Beautiful". The atmosphere is dark and smoky; even with the no smoking laws, there's still the stench lingering off the guests.

Lily and Jett have secured us a booth in the corner of the pub. It's right across from the band. It will be hard to talk, but maybe that's a good thing.

"Hey, guys." She smiles. Jett reaches over the table to shake our hands.

I shake his large rough hand first, then he shakes Logan's. Even sitting down you can tell Jett is well over six foot. His long black hair hangs at his chin, and he's the spitting image of the clean-shaven Ben Barnes with long hair. Lily sure knows how to pick 'em.

"This place is great. I think I saw some girl stumble out of the bathroom with her boob hanging out," Logan yells over the music.

Lily laughs as if it were the funniest thing she's heard all day. Her giggles are loud enough to overpower the music. I force a smile. I don't want Lily to think that I don't want to be here with her tonight. With everything coming up in the next few days my mind is frazzled.

"We ordered some apps. I hope that's okay. Mozzarella sticks, some nachos, a bunch of random shit," Jett says.

"Oh that sounds delicious." My stomach growls in response.

He winks. "Lily says you two are kind of a new thing. Last time I saw you, Ellie, you had that fella named Matt, was it?"

I nod. "Yeah, that didn't work out. Logan is—" I stare at him, realizing we never made a plan about how we met.

"I'm her best friend's brother."

My jaw drops. I jab him in the ribs, he grunts, but manages a smile anyway.

"Wait, what? Oh my God!" Lily beams. "Why didn't you tell me?"

I scratch the back of my neck. My mouth goes dry, and my throat aches from the smoky air. Before I can form an answer our waiter with spiky blonde hair comes over to hand us the appetizers. While he's here I order a sex on the beach. I'm going to channel my inner Tessa Young and get wasted like she did in the beginning of *After We Collided*. The waiter takes the rest of the orders, then walks away.

"Wait, did you two hook up at the wedding?" Lily's lips curve upwards as she starts putting two and two together.

My leg shakes under the table as I search for the waiter. It's only been thirty seconds, but I'm craving that drink.

Logan places his hand on my trembling thigh, his thumb lingering between my legs. He flicks it up and down a little. I gasp, and nudge him again. He's going to have bruised ribs by the time this night is over if he doesn't behave.

"You caught me. We fell in love, and here we are," I say, gritting my teeth.

"Oh, that's so wonderful."

"How did you two meet?" Logan asks, slowly moving his hand closer with each second.

Lily leans back and bats her eyes at Jett. When their eyes meet, even under the dark lighting, I catch a glimpse of his flushed cheeks.

"He came in for a tux." Her eyes don't leave his. "And I showed him where the section was. I may have even helped Viggio in the suit department." She giggles, and touches his chest. "I know nothing about suits, but I sat there while he did this clothing montage, and I think he valued my opinions, even though I was a stranger."

Jett leans forward and kisses her on the tip of her nose. My heart stutters at the sight of the two of them. There's a fire in their eyes that captivates me, but at the same time there's a burning in my chest, a desire to have the same passion in my life.

"Anyways," she says, after a few long moments of silence. "I walked him back to the front of the store and he left with my number in his pocket and a brand spanking new suit."

Lily turns to face us as the waiter returns with my drink. I'm thankful for the large glass of liquor in front of me. I lift it and down nearly half of it in one go.

Then I take a smaller sip, and breathe a sigh of relief. All eyes are on me. I need this drink if I'm going to make it through the night. There's a shadow lingering over our table, and an extra set of eyes watching over me.

The waiter stares blankly. It takes everything in me to tell him, the nineties wants its hairstyle back. He clears his throat. "Is anyone ready to order?"

Logan and I turn to one another, "Chicken fingers? Jinx," we say in unison.

"Stop jinxing me." I push him playfully.

He turns to the waiter. "We'll both have the chicken fingers and fries basket."

The waiter nods, then focuses his attention on Lily and Jett. They are so lost in each other that they don't notice him waiting to take their order. I down the last of my drink. The sweetness lingers in my empty stomach, sending a wave of nausea through me.

"Can I get one more of these?" I point to the empty glass.

The waiter watches me wide-eyed at the finished drink in my hands. "I uh—yeah sure." He stutters. "And what can I get you two?"

Lily finally looks up. A small blush creeps up her cheeks as she and Jett give him their order. They get different meals. Is it weird that Logan and I got the same? It's never bothered me before. It's always been our thing, but then I realize it's something we've only done around his family. It's a stupid thing to worry about, but my emotions have clogged my judgment so much that I can't think normally anymore.

While we wait for our food and my drink, Lily drills Logan

about his job and him living in Pennsylvania He talks about his job as if it's his favorite thing in the world. While he talks he slips little things in to make it sound like we are together.

"You're still planning on making the trek to visit me in September, right, babe?" He smirks.

I scowl at him, but a light smile plays on my lips. My head is light and fuzzy. My leg shakes again, but calms as the waiter drops my second drink on his way to another table.

"Yes, of course I'll be there." I bop him lazily on the nose.

His eyes narrow downward as he shakes his head.

"You know what Logan did yesterday? Oh my God, he's the sweetest." I tilt my head and flirtatiously bat my eyes at him. "While we were in Greenport he found a group of kids playing soccer. One boy seemed to have trouble. Logan went over to the boy and helped him. It must have been the coach in him. It was the sweetest thing. It's no wonder I love—" I start to say, but am interrupted by an unwelcome hiccup.

I rest my head on his shoulder, numb to anything happening right now. I haven't eaten much today, so this alcohol is going to go right through me faster than it should.

"Aw, Logan, you're such a doll," Lily mocks playfully.

Logan eats it up and says in the proudest voice, "Yeah I know." And it causes Lily and Jett to laugh, me too, maybe a little too hard.

Bringing up soccer opens up a whole conversation between Jett and Logan. The conversation lasts as our dinner and my third drink arrives. Logan eyes me as the waiter slides it in. The third doesn't sit well, so I take my time taking slow sips so I don't wind up in the bathroom puking my brains out.

As I shovel the last chicken tender in my mouth a familiar tune fills the room. Logan glances over at me right away. "Jonas Brothers," we say in unison.

"Dance with me?" I ask him.

His brow lifts in amusement. Sober me would never ask him

to dance. He slides out of the booth and holds his hands out for me. Lily and Jett join in the fun. We take the dance floor together, and dance like no one's watching.

My back is turned to Logan. I sway my hips along with his, while his fingers dance along my sides. Logan pulls me close, omitting any space between us. His hard body grinds against my backside. I have to close my eyes from the pressure building low in my belly.

His voice singing into my ear makes me shiver. I don't know if it's the alcohol, but the sound of his voice is comforting.

The song bleeds into a slow country song. Logan takes me, spinning me into him. I rest my head on his shoulder as he takes me by the waist and holds on tight. Between us our hearts beat together. I can feel mine picking up speed, and can hear his thumping in my ear.

His voice is loud enough for me to catch over the band. Logan's eyes meet mine. I'm not sure why I do it, but I get on my toes and plant a kiss on his lips. He tenses under my touch, but doesn't stop swaying to the beat. I hate to say it, but I'm almost ninety-nine percent sure this stopped being fake a long time ago. Maybe in the morning I'll forget that thought even crossed my mind.

As the night goes on we enjoy some dessert, I devour another drink, and we do a little more dancing. Hanging out with Lily and Jett has been a breath of fresh air in this mix of smog that's clogging my brain. For the rest of the night I don't think about what if or what could be; instead I live here in the moment.

I allow myself to enjoy every peck on the cheek, every lingering touch of his fingertips on my skin, and every squeeze when he holds me close. When I come off this buzz I know what I'm feeling will vanish and life will return to normal. For now, I'll let it go and let the night steer me in whatever direction it decides to take me.

CHAPTER 16

$\mathcal{I}$ giggle up the walkway to Charlotte and Bryan's. Logan stands beside me, his arms out waiting to catch me. I drank to compensate for the way my heart stuttered every time he pretended to touch me as if I were his. He can't just go around touching me that way, but I let him, so I'm at fault for that.

He walks ahead to open the door. While he does I study the outline of his shape, from his wide shoulders, to his thick, muscular runner's calves, and all that's in between. How is it even possible that someone is attractive from their backside too? And I'm not only talking about his ass. My drunk self sure has a lot of feelings tonight.

With a twinkle in his eye, he jogs down the steps to where he's left me. Without warning, he scoops me up into his arms. The world sways. I'm far too drunk for this. If he rocks me once more I might vomit all over him.

"Uh, what are you doing?" I ask, unable to stop the giggles.

"Making sure you don't trip up the steps. Last thing we need is for you to get hurt on the job."

"Oh right. I'm your, 'apprentice'. Teach me all the things, Master Logan."

155

"You are so wasted." His laughter shakes my body.

In one swift movement, he swings open the screen door. It slams behind us as we enter the mud room.

He sets me down on the floor. The paint fumes have somewhat subsided, but are still faintly obvious. I stumble into the living room where we plan on spending the night on the pull-out couch. Bryan says it's not the most comfortable thing in the world, but it's only one night.

I'm absolutely wrecked, not only from the drinking, but from the anticipation of Charlotte's arrival on Sunday. The closer it gets, the more anxious I feel. She'll see right through me the moment she lays eyes on me. How will I keep this from her, especially when we spend a good portion of our week either together or chatting on the phone.

Trying to forget about my feelings, I decide we should get the bed ready. Inside one of my duffel bags I packed extra linens. I start to rummage through my stuff. Logan preps the bed, pulling it out, and removing the coffee table while I get the sheets.

"Fitted sheets can suck it!" I stick a finger in the air and point to absolutely nobody. I tuck the sheets under my arm, then haphazardly throw them onto the bed.

I expect Logan to be disgusted by my childish drunken behavior. He stands on the opposite end of the pull-out bed. He shakes his head with his usual grin.

"What? I'm serious, whoever invented these should be fired. Or they could have at least given some instructions. Like, maybe tabs or something. I don't know." I flail my arms. "Like this one goes in the top left corner and this one goes—" I'm cut off by his soft lips pressed against mine.

How did he get around the couch so fast? And why did he do that? Being intoxicated aggravates the butterflies in my stomach. There's an angry mob of them swarming around in there. I refuse to have sex with him again while I'm drunk, it didn't end well last time, and it won't end well this time. I need to be sober for any type of sexual activity.

"What did you do that for?" I ask.

He pulls away, resting his head against mine. I blink several times to make sure I'm getting the full picture. Along with his smile, his eyes are closed.

"You like to babble when you're drunk. I was saving you from yourself."

"I don't need saving, Logan Fields." I poke lazily at his chest.

His right eye opens, wrinkles forming at the sides from his turned-up lips.

"You had to go and get yourself wasted, didn't you? You're no good to me now."

I growl and step back, crossing my arms. I'm half offended, but at least he's not planning on taking advantage of my drunk state. We don't need a repeat of the wedding night. All the memories come rushing back in. Asking him to dance, taking shots at the bar, sneaking away to the bathroom and whispering for him to follow me. I am as much to blame as he is. He could have said no.

My temples throb, causing my drunken smile to fade. "That's rude, Logan," I pout.

He chuckles. "I'm trying to be the adult here."

A loud, bellowing laugh slips from my lips. It tickles my whole body to laugh this way. He closes the small gap I've created. He pulls us onto the half-made bed. Wrapping me in his arms, he kisses me again. I grant his tongue permission to enter and that's a big mistake. I'm going to blame my state on the fact that every kiss tonight had this intense electrical sensation tacked on. Like he's lightning and I'm the tallest tree in the wood. I press a hand to his chest and whisper, "No." It's the only coherent word I can manage.

We lie side by side, our bodies pressed up against one another, way too many clothes between us, but I have to put my foot down.

"Not tonight," I whisper, gently running my hand down his chest.

"You know what? I have a better idea." He jumps to his feet and crosses the room. He rummages through his bag, and pulls out a familiar rectangular object. I sit up to make sure I'm seeing it correctly. His father collected movies on VHS, any and all genres. The four of us, Logan, Charlotte, his dad, and myself would spend one Friday a month watching them.

"Is that *3 Ninjas?*" Eyes wide, I stare at the box.

He nods. "It sure is."

"Where are you going to find a VHS player?"

He places the VHS beside the bag, then kneels down and digs in again, producing a player from his bag.

"Brought it back with me. I wasn't sure when the right time to break it out would be."

I cross my legs at the edge of the bed and glare at him. "You went all the way to Pennsylvania for an old VHS."

He chuckles. "No, that's not the only reason I did."

"Was it to see her?" I slap a hand to my face, it makes a loud thwap as it hits.

Logan tilts his head, furrowing his brows at me. He's confused by my question, so I decide to elaborate.

"The night we went to Home Depot, Marisol texted you while we were in the car. Something about when you got back—"

"Ellie Mae Garner, are you jealous?" His voice drops an octave into a sexy baritone that drives my lady parts mad. Did I just say lady parts? I'm well past the buzzed stage that's for sure.

"Pshh, jealous. In your dreams, Logan Michael Fields."

"Oh, so now we've moved on to middle names." He grins.

I stand, and wobble on my feet. In a matter of three seconds, he's across the room gripping me at my waist. His hands dangerously close to my ass.

"I doubt you'll remember what I'm about to tell you. I went back to cut ties with her. She's the one who broke it off with me before the wedding. She texted and apologized, hoping to make amends. We were contemplating trying again, but plans changed."

I swallow hard, nearly choking on my spit. I can't look him in the eye, not now, not when I sound like a jealous girlfriend. I want to ask him what kind of plans have changed, but the silence that hangs in the air is too thick for my liking. We need a subject change ASAP.

"Do you remember when we used to sing the 'Rocky Loves Emily' song from the *3 Ninjas* movie and change it to Charlotte loves Rocky, and it annoyed her?"

Logan grins then swallows hard, his Adam's apple bobbing with the motion. He slips his pointer finger under my chin, and carefully tilts my face up to meet his gaze.

I'm caught up in his dark stare. My cheeks warm under his watchful eye. With each passing second, he moves closer. More than anything I want him to kiss me. In fact, I wish he would ignore that I'm drunk and have me again. I hate that we're running out of time, and I need to think of another topic before I do something I'll regret later.

"I loved that your dad had a huge VHS collection. The older movies were so much fun to watch."

After a few beats of silence, he finally speaks.

"I'll see if I can get this monster to work on the TV; why don't you make some popcorn."

"But we don't have—" I start to say.

He steps away, leaving a draft in his wake. I shiver and hold myself as he digs back into his bag and pulls out a microwaveable bag of popcorn.

"Bryan says we can use the kitchen as long as we clean up."

"I think I can handle some popcorn." I cross the room and snatch it. He grips my hand tight and tugs me into him, pressing his lips to mine. What's with all the random kisses tonight? I'm not complaining, but it's unlike Logan to steal a kiss without wanting something more. He pulls away, smiling. I'm speechless.

While I keep an eye on the popcorn to make sure it doesn't burn, my mind wanders to the events of the past few hours. Between "fake dating", the stolen kisses, and then him breaking it off with Marisol, I'm starting to wonder what his exact intentions are. Can *he* really let go after two weeks? Or will he be one of those guys who calls you every time they are in town just to get some. I sigh. My stomach twists at the thought. Nausea creeps up my throat, but I push it back down.

The kernels have nearly stopped popping. I shut off the microwave and tug the bag out, hissing at the heat against my skin.

"Are you okay in there?" he yells from the living room.

"Ah!" I let the bag drop to the floor and suck on the sore spot on my finger.

Logan peeks his head around the entryway and glances between the bag of popcorn and me. "Can't trust you to do anything, can I?"

He finds his way to me, bends, picks up the popcorn, then straightens. His body barely leaves enough space between us. He grabs my hand and leads me back into the living room. In the four minutes I was gone, he somehow managed to set up the VCR, and fix the fitted sheet. The lights are off, the only thing illuminating the room is the light from the TV.

"You're a fitted sheet master," I whisper into his ear.

He chuckles. "And you're still incredibly wasted."

I smirk. He lets go of my hand and throws himself onto the bed. The popcorn bag lands at his side. Wrapping his legs around me he pulls me down with him. I almost land on top, but roll off. He sits up and I follow along as we settle into the pull-out bed. He opens the popcorn, and we shift around until we're both comfortable.

With the remote in hand, he presses play. A few minutes into the opening credits he throws his arm around me and pulls me close. Resting my head on his chest, I don't question the gesture, I embrace it. I shouldn't, but I do. I'm officially sucked into Logan Field's world and unfortunately, there's no recovering from the fall.

❧

A soft streaming beam of light filters in from the side window. It jets across the bed, over the sheets. I blink to clear the sleep from my eyes. I'm warm, but not too hot. Logan's body is wrapped around mine. One leg and one arm are draped over me. As my eyes adjust to the morning light, I glance down at our hands connected at my stomach, as if I'd been holding on for dear life.

Behind me, Logan stirs. His face is nestled into the back of my neck, his softs breaths tickling me with each release. The cable box on the shelf by the TV reads 10:29am. Charlotte arrives in two days. This is it, today the project ends and life will soon return to normal. I squeeze his hand.

"Logan. It's nearly ten thirty. The delivery should be here soon."

They told us it would be anywhere from ten to noon. Behind me Logan moans and snuggles in closer even though there's literally no space between our bodies.

"Please don't fart again," I tease.

The small laugh causes a slight throb behind my already aching temples from too many drinks.

His laughter grazes the nape of my neck. I spin in his arms and now it's my turn to bury my face into his chest. As I lift my gaze his eyes flutter open. I'm pulled in by his presence and I start thinking maybe it wasn't the alcohol clouding my brain. He's still holding me like there's something there. He opens his

161

mouth like he's about to say something when there's a knock at the door.

We pull away what feels like faster than the speed of light. He rolls off one side and I roll off the other. I fix my hair like they're gonna care, and check to make sure my bra is still intact. It is. Logan pulls on his jeans and hustles to the door. I need a moment before I can move, because I hate the way I liked how it felt to sleep with him and wake up in his arms.

❧

"Just move that over a smidge," I say.

Logan and I shimmy the dresser under the flat-screen TV in the bedroom. I step back and check out our handy work. Around the room everything is assembled. I've put a new set of pale green sheets with a matching comforter over the new bed, and matching curtains over the window. I never imagined loving wicker furniture until now. It reminds me of a room at a B&B. The soft colors fade into one another. The light that dances in through the window brightens up the room to make the space feel large—yet quaint.

The window that Logan installed looks amazing, the shiny new Pergo flooring does as well. I'm enthralled by the work he put into this project. Again, it's another way he's showing his love. Logan Fields doesn't love the way most do. He won't say it out loud, sometimes he may come off as cold, but he'll do things for you out of the kindness of his heart.

"I didn't realize how handy you were."

He takes a step back and falls in line with me. "Dad taught me a lot growing up." His voice trembles, so he clears his throat.

Logan stares off at the wires that he neatly bunched together between the TV and dresser.

I slip my hand into his, and I swear he holds his breath. Admitting that he's hurting is not something he can do either.

Like his response when his father died was to flee, because feelings are all too much for him.

Talking about his dad is hard for him. He's only been gone four years, but it somehow feels much longer. There are so many memories I have of him, and although he wasn't my father, he and Josephine both cared for me like their own: all those concerts and school events he drove us to; or the time when my dad had back surgery for an old injury, and Henry took a few days off from work to help out while Mom had work and I had school.

I don't expect to feel Logan's grip tighten on me, but when it does it's like he's reaching out to tell me he needs the comfort.

"Dad let me do a lot of the basement renovation. The one we worked on the summer before he passed. It was tough work, but it was the first real project he let me really take on without guidance."

He blinks several times, his eyes not leaving the spot on the wall. I shuffle to the right and press the side of my body against his.

"I'll never forget how proud he was of me. He told me if I knew how to do all of these things I'd make a woman really happy one day." His laughter falls short, like it's hard for him to hold himself together.

"Remember when I came by after it was all done? We played pool and you and your dad won."

His lips twitch, but the smile doesn't reach his eyes. "I do. I remember kicking your ass pretty good. You and Charlotte were awful."

I nod. "Yeah. We sure were, but then you gave me some lessons afterwards."

I finally get a smile out of him. It's not full, and doesn't reach his eyes, but it's something. I'm not shocked to see a sparkle in his dark eyes. I reach up and with my thumb wipe along the edge of his lashes to clear away the moisture that pooled there.

"I think you did an amazing job with this room. He would

have been so proud of you, Logan. It's beautiful. Charlotte and Bryan are going to absolutely love it!"

"I couldn't have done it all without your help." His body shifts so that he's facing me. There's not a single inch of space between us.

My hand lingers on his face. "So what now?" I whisper.

He shrugs. "No clue." His eyes narrow down at me, at my lips, and my body pressed against his. His hands find my hips and hold on. I've suddenly got that stomach falling sensation you get on the first drop of a roller coaster. I can't help that his lips are distracting and I'd love more than anything to take hold of them between my teeth.

Our heads lean forward. His slow and steady breath dances along my bottom lip. Our heads tilt in sync. We go in for the kiss as music plays from my phone. I recognize the ring tone: it's Charlotte's, again. She sure knows how to pull us from a moment. Maybe it's a sign. Without thinking, I drop my hand and step back. The gap between us becomes dark and cold.

I don't say another word as I race into the room to answer it. I'm thankful for the distraction: who knows what would have happened if she hadn't called at that moment.

It's late by the time we pull up to my house. The smoky scent of a firepit looms in the air through the open car window. From here the floodlights in the backyard shine over the driveway. Mom hasn't broken out the firepit since Dad left and that was over six years ago. This can't be a good sign.

Dad rarely reaches out and if he does it's because he wants something. First it was the house, six months after the initial separation. Then he backed off. After that it was because he claimed that the car was his. But lo and behold, it was in Mom's name. What could this man possibly want after six years?

Logan looks over at me. The car engine has ceased, and I'm not sure for how long. His warm hand covers mine. Glancing up, I catch his narrowed eyes.

"Come on, we'll go check on her together."

Logan remembers the fights; he'd heard some of them. The whole neighborhood had. Dad was never abusive, they just fell out of love, or at least Dad did.

Logan lifts his hand and settles it on my cheek. For a moment I fall into his touch. He was so lucky to have two parents who loved each other and showed him and Charlotte what real love could be like. It's a shame that his dad's life ended too soon.

Before things get too awkward, he moves away and steps out of the car. I follow, our doors shutting in sync. I meet him around the front and he links his hand with mine. I crane my neck to check his expression. Eyes locking on me, he nods.

In the backyard Mom has a roaring fire going in the stone firepit that Dad built forever ago. There were some good memories associated with it, and I think that's why she's here. Arthur and he spent a whole weekend building it, while Mom and I went shopping for s'mores and went to the camping store for tents. We spent that last night of summer under the stars. I may resent my dad for never keeping in touch, but we did have some good times together.

Mom has a somber look in her already heavy eyes. I release my hand from Logan's and walk across the grass towards her. The firepit is in the center of our lawn away from the fence.

The camping chairs sit around the flame, like how we used to have it set up. I come and sit in the sky-blue one.

"He asked to see us. He said he had news."

I grab hold of her hand. Logan comes and settles in the chair beside mine. She stares into the fire. Even after all these years and all the distance, I know she still loves him. It sucks to love someone who doesn't love you back, especially after they vowed till death do you part.

"He wanted to move back."

"After six years?" I mumble.

My shoulders tense. They are so taut that I'm pretty sure I've pulled a muscle in my neck. Logan's hand settles on my back like he knows. I suck in a breath quietly as he rubs right in the spot that hurts.

"He says he's had time to think about it."

"And you told him to screw off, right?" I hate the way my voice jumps an octave and wavers. Logan's grip on me tightens.

"I told him we were doing fine without him." Her voice is calm and collected, but all I feel is rage.

Her eyes land on Logan's hand, but then focuses back to the roaring hot fire in front of her. She blinks trying to force the tears away, but they fall anyway. I rest my head on her shoulder.

"Why does he think it's appropriate to fuck with your feelings? He can't just waltz back into our lives as if nothing happened. I wish I'd been home when he called, I could have—"

"I handled it," she squeaks. "I should head to bed. Can you make sure the fire goes out?"

I lift my head, immediately regretting my outburst. She leans down and softly brushes the top of my head with a kiss.

"Goodnight, Amelia," Logan says softly. "I'll hang around to make sure the fire is good."

"Thank you, both of you." She throws a sad smile at Logan and shuffles off towards the sliding glass doors leading into the house.

My body shakes as I hold a breath. "He's such an asshole. If he came back it would be like before. They always fought. There was not a day when he didn't run out of the house slamming the door like a child throwing a tantrum. I should call him, tell him off. We don't deserve his bullshit."

Logan quietly observes me. I release a harsh, shaky breath and lean forward towards the heat of the flame.

"I'm sorry." My voice barely reaches above a whisper. "I'm

over here angry with my dad, while you're mourning yours. That's so shitty of me. I should be thankful he's alive, and that I have a dad I can hate, but he—"

"Your dad's an asshole. More than ever, I realize that I'm more like your father than I am mine. Mine would never leave when things got hard, he'd fight till the very end. Me?" A sad laugh leaves his lips. "I do exactly what your dad does, leave. I leave behind the people who need me the most, because I can't get my shit together."

I watch him over my shoulder. His cheeks are red, and I don't think it's from the heat of the fire. His eyes flick over to mine.

"So, no, don't feel bad for hating your father. You have every right to hate him. You don't deserve to be treated that way, neither does your mom."

A long grueling silence falls between us. I settle back into the chair only for him to tug me enough so that I stand and wind up on his lap. I wrap my arms around his neck and rest my head on his shoulder. My legs dangle off to the side.

"I hope one day you find a man that treats you the way my father did my mom. She always came first. He never once raised his voice to yell at her unless they had one of their petty normal arguments that couples have. You deserve a man who understands the value of love."

There are so many things I want to say back. Logan may not stick around, but he is nothing like my dad, not in the slightest. Instead of voicing that, I hold on tight and let Logan gently run his hand over my hair.

Something inside of me stirs. It warms me like a blanket, and it's not the fire. He rests his head against mine as I burrow deeper, and nestle my face into his neck. His breathing slows like he's relaxed. My breathing mimics his. "The man who gets your heart one day is a lucky bastard," he whispers.

And what happens if I want that man to be you? I don't say it out loud because it can't ever happen. I've already crossed one line; it

167

won't end well if I cross the other. I sit there in his arms, enjoying what is probably our last night together like this before he leaves.

"You don't have to stay for the fire," I say into his neck.

He inhales deeply, sucking in his entire middle, then he slowly releases. "I want to stay."

Logan and I sit by the fire until the last ember burns. It's well after midnight by the time we say goodnight and I head to my room. I don't watch him leave, because that would hurt far too much.

CHAPTER 17

$\mathcal{I}$ open the front door with my toothbrush hanging from my mouth. Logan stands there with a playful smirk. I'm still in my towel, so I only have the door open, enough for him to step through. Our time together is coming to an end. If I don't put some distance between us, ending this will be harder than it has to be.

"Sexy," he teases.

I say nothing, only brush and stare him down. Stepping aside, I allow him in. His footsteps don't stray far behind as I make my way back into the bathroom. I flick the fan off as the steam has subsided from my shower, and spit the toothpaste into the sink.

"So, Mom said she'll have dinner ready by the time I bring you over tonight."

"Cool," I say between gargling water and spitting.

I reach into the wooden cabinet to my left and pull out some Q-tips to clean out my ears.

"Didn't your mother ever tell you that you shouldn't put something smaller than your elbow in your ear."

I shrug. "My ears bother me if I don't clean them."

I toss the Q-tips into the trash, and shake my hair out of my

169

towel. I'm well aware of the way he's watching me. I grab my brush and comb through the knots. He reaches over, grabs the brush from me and starts carefully working his way through.

"I'm staying at Mom's tonight. You can stay, but—"

"I'll go home with my mom," I snap.

He stops the motion of the brush briefly, and meets my eyes in the mirror. Why I've suddenly gone from flirtatious and fun Ellie, to angry emotional Ellie.

He places the brush on the marble counter, then spins me around. Leaning down, he brushes his lips against mine. I close my eyes trying to ignore the bubbling tickles that make their way through my body. Resting his head against mine, he hums, while blowing out a soft breath.

"What's wrong, Ellie? Talk to me."

I sigh, refusing to let my eyes open. Butterflies linger low in my belly. *Make them go away, please.* I try to reason with my heart, but it has no desire to listen. Logan pushes his head into me. He steps closer, pinning me against the counter.

I jump when his hand presses softly against my face. He rubs his thumb over my skin. It's impossible to not want more.

"I'm fine," I squeak.

"Ellie," he tries again.

"Logan, I said I'm fine." I grit my teeth. Why doesn't he stop? I don't mean to be sharp with him, but he's making this harder than it has to be.

His shoulders deflate. I'm thankful he doesn't press me anymore. His lips meet mine and I allow it. He reaches around and grabs my ass. There's barely any fabric between us and no matter how confused I am, I enjoy the way this feels.

"Can I steal you away tomorrow at least?" he asks when he pulls away.

"And what would you be stealing me away to do?" I allow my eyes to open. Wrong move. He's watching me with an intensity that makes my insides squirm.

"I don't know, maybe enjoying the feeling of your body against mine. Or we could—you know—uh—go rollerblading or something," he stutters, and that confuses me. Logan Fields never has trouble finding his words.

I snort. "Rollerblading?"

"Uh-duh, only our favorite thing to do."

I smile, feeling less tense than a few minutes ago. "My rollerblades have been in the back of the closet for a while, I can't remember the last time we actually did that."

"You were in your junior year, it was summer, and I raced you and Charlotte at the park."

How does he have exact moments like these stored away in his memory? I didn't remember it until he said it. Now it slowly trickles back.

"Oh my God, yes. And I tripped over a stick."

He chuckles. "And then I had to carry you in my rollerblades to a bench."

That was the first time he carried me somewhere. Thinking about it, it's kind of funny. For a few moments things feel okay between us. Sure, there's sexual tension, and a tingling sensation between my legs. Bantering with him feels nice. And normal.

"So, what do you say? Tomorrow we blade?"

There's hope in his eyes. I don't want to take it away from him. After everything he went through, he deserves a little happiness.

"Fine."

"And then maybe we can do some of this too." He bends down and kisses along my neck.

I suck in a breath, wanting to capture this feeling so I never miss it. The way he does it is so sensual. I almost lose myself as he slips a finger up my towel. His slow, steady movement has me teetering on the edge of an orgasm.

As he kisses me he whispers something, but it's muffled in my neck, I can't be sure I heard him right. It almost sounded like he said, *What am I going to do without you?* There's a stinging in my eye, the build-up of tears is coming on way too fast. I clear my throat, then pull away. "I have to finish getting ready for work. I can't be late."

He reluctantly steps back. A small smile on his lips. "Okay," he whispers. "But later, you're mine. Okay?"

The car ride to work isn't so bad. We sing along to the awful songs on our local top forty radio, and chat about where we will rollerblade tomorrow. I like that it feels normal, I wish it could stay that way, but I know it can't.

⚜

"So, Wednesday night was interesting," Lily says.

We both got stuck folding jeans over in the petite department. The assistant manager is on today instead of Maryann, so we don't have to be as cautious about getting caught chatting.

"Yeah, sorry. I got a little wasted."

"Oh no, honey. You were so funny. I'm also a little jealous," she says, folding some shorts in the clearance section.

"Jealous?"

I pick some jeans up off the floor. People are pigs: they can't even clean up after themselves.

"I've been saying it since that first day I caught you two chatting. He's so in love with you. The entire night he didn't look at anyone else. It was like we didn't exist."

My cheeks burn under her stare. Hands shaking, I attempt to fold the second pair I picked up from the floor, but the tremors are so bad that I lose my grip several times before completely giving up.

"Sweetie, what's wrong?" she asks, making her way around the fixtures and over to me.

I push some jeans aside and sit on the edge of the table. I pinch the bridge of my nose trying to fight the itching sensation.

"He can't love me. We aren't really dating."

I hate that I've lied to her too. Some of the heaviness on my shoulders deflate, but not all of it.

"What do you mean?" Her forehead crinkles.

"We're friends with benefits. It's supposed to end on Sunday when Charlotte comes home." I sigh, burying my face into my hands.

"Oh." She pauses. "Ohhhh." She puts her arm over my shoulders and holds me tight. I don't feel the urge to cry, but there's this sadness building inside of me that I hate. It's painful and I never meant for it to go this far. It was supposed to be nothing—just fun.

"I never meant for it to turn into something more. He kind of—"

"Swept you off your feet?"

I sigh. "I'm a terrible person."

Instead of crying, I want to scream. There's no pillows here to muffle the sound. I close my eyes and take a deep breath, trying to calm myself.

"You can't help who you love."

Love. Is that what this is? Is it supposed to hurt like this when you love someone? I roll my neck trying to ease the tension.

"What do you want from the relationship you've formed with him? Do you want to be friends?" She removes her arms.

I glance up at her like she has all the answers, even though I know she doesn't. "I don't know if after this I can be his friend. This won't end well, and it will be painful. I'm bracing for impact. I never even cried when Matt broke up with me, but this—this is fake and it hurts a thousand times more."

She sighs. "It hurts because you were never in love with Matt. You liked the idea of love, he was there, and so you took it. Logan, he's it for you. Not only did I catch it in his eyes, but yours as well. Your banter is cute too."

My face grows warm as my pulse speeds up thinking about

173

our crazy little relationship. Logan and I have always gone back and forth making witty remarks at each other. He's also always been there, even when I didn't need him or ask him to be, he just was. I run a hand through my hair. "What should I do?"

"Do what you told me to do. Talk to him. Secrets can break you."

I inhale. "You're right."

It was only a few days ago that I told her to go for it with Jett. I said secrets are not good to hold, and I was right. This one is eating me up inside.

A giggle across the store catches my attention. I'm taken aback by what I see. Matt is standing in the women's department. His arms covered in clothing as a woman around my age leans forward and kisses him while draping another item of clothing over his arm. Well, I guess he found someone to talk to about his day.

Like he can feel my eyes on him, he looks up. He puts a hand on the girl's shoulder, and nods at me. She lets him go, and he starts walking towards me.

"Holy hell, is that Matt?" Lily questions.

"It sure is."

He crosses the aisle, jogging over to us. "Hey."

"Hey," I repeat.

"Um—About that, I—"

"It's fine," I say. "You look happy."

His face pales, like he's been caught doing something bad.

"It's fine, Matt. We wouldn't have worked out anyway. Now get back over there before she gets suspicious."

Matt's hypnotizing eyes find mine. They're easy to get lost in, but they most certainly don't make my insides squirm like Logan's do.

"Thanks. It was really good to see you. I hope everything works out with the other guy."

I release a shaky breath. "Thanks."

He gives us both a wave before jogging back across the store towards the girl. I don't bother to look after them. I turn to Lily.

"Well, that was awkward." She smirks.

I laugh, because it's funny how life works out. Staring at Matt with another girl, I feel nothing, not even a twinge of jealousy. When Logan was texting with Marisol I wanted to trek to Pennsylvania and wring her neck. I wish I didn't love Logan, but I think I always have.

"You know what you need?"

"What's that?"

"We need to have some dip and dots ice cream on our break." She smiles.

Dip and dots, the tiny little balls of ice cream that taste like magic in your mouth. I could use some magic right now.

"Like, for lunch?"

She nods. "Can't go wrong with dip and dots for lunch."

Laughter bubbles up inside of me. I hope once Charlotte returns that Lily and I can spend more time together too. Or maybe we can all go out together. These two weeks haven't been all awful; Lily and I have grown closer, and I've enjoyed my time with her. She's a good friend, and I'm lucky to have her in my life.

I pull my phone from my pocket. It's nearly twelve thirty. There's still five more hours until Logan picks me up. Ice cream will definitely be needed if I'm going to survive the rest of my shift and contemplate what to say to him. It will be a long five hours, but at least I have Lily and ice cream.

CHAPTER 18

$\mathcal{I}$'ve never been nervous to go and have dinner with Josephine Fields and her family. They've been like a second family to me. The thought of sitting there beside her while I'm lying to, not only her, but to Charlotte (even though she's still on her honeymoon), Tommy, and worst of all, my mom, makes my stomach churn.

Work is nearly done for the day and Logan is picking me up in under twenty minutes. I'm on the sales floor folding more jeans that have been ransacked by customers. I sometimes wonder if people are slobs like this in their own home. Sometimes, they don't care. I could be standing right over them and they still mess up every pair of jeans, or every neatly folded shirt. It drives me crazy. Anxiety makes me ramble.

"Hey."

I turn around and come face to face with Ethan.

"Hey, what's up?" I finish folding a soft red cotton tee and fluff the pile, before turning back to him.

He pushes up his black round glasses and scratches the back of his neck. "Ian wanted me to return these to your department." He holds up some dangling hoop earrings.

176

I take them from him. "Thank you."

He runs a hand over his bald head. He hesitates to leave. His brown eyes flicker in all different directions. There's more he wants to say and for some reason, I think I know what it is. Leave it to Ethan to wait until the moment when my heart was at its weakest.

He swallows hard, his Adam's apple bobbing against his skin. "I don't mean to be nosy, but are you still, um, dating that guy?"

Wow. Ethan is bolder than I thought. "It's, uh, it's complicated. I'm not in the right frame of mind to make any future plans."

What is happening here? How did I end up in some weird love quadrangle? How is it that I spent my teen years awkward with very little interest? Why now, when my heart feels like it's about to burst, are men finally finding an interest in pursuing me?

His shoulders slump like the tiny bit of confidence that allowed him to ask me out was taken from him. I'm one-hundred percent sure that after Sunday, Logan and I will go our separate ways, but I want to take some time to fix whatever will break in the aftermath.

"Right, yeah, of course. I'm sorry that was really dumb of me to assume things." He shifts on his feet, and then reaches back to scratch again.

Before he turns to walk away, he takes a quick glance over my shoulder. Eyes wide, he ducks his head and spins back towards the men's department. I check behind me to find Logan strolling over. His eyes narrow on me like he's determined.

He glares over me, and I don't bother looking back, because I know it was meant for Ethan. Logan pauses in front of me. I tilt my chin up. As his eyes meet mine, I hold on to a breath. His hand brushes against mine, sending a strange electric current between us. I swear he feels it too.

I clear my throat to try and clear the tension in the room. "I'm off in ten."

"I parked at the food court entrance, meet you over there?" he asks.

I nod. As I go, I swear he reaches out for me. It's a light enough graze that it could be my imagination. Ignoring it, I slip away back to where Lily is ringing up a customer. I rest my hands against the counter facing the back wall.

"That looked intense," she says, pulling the ink tag from a pair of jeans.

The machine used to pull them off is on the same side of the counter. Since we aren't facing customers, she leans in. "Are you okay?"

I shake my head. She rests a free hand on my shoulder while placing another magnetic ink tag on the machine. "You'll figure it out."

I wish I could share her viewpoint on that. I don't think I will figure it out. I can barely figure out my life without guy drama. How will I ever manage with what's going on now?

Tension is high in Logan's car as we drive to his mom's house. He reaches over and I allow his fingers to intertwine with mine. They rest on my lap. His grip tightens. He moves our hands together to the center of my lap. My long, gothic-style black lace skirt trickles down past my knees, but that doesn't stop him from releasing my hand and dancing his fingers underneath. I hiss at the sensation that tickles my insides. I squeeze my legs together, but his wandering hand pulls them apart.

He's still concentrating on the road ahead, even as his fingers slide in through the side of my panties and rub lightly against me. I suck in a breath and thrust my body up. In the corner of my eye I catch his lips turn into a smile. Anger leads to want, and then I'm grasped by a need so strong, I almost yell at him to pull over.

He somehow manages to take his pointer and push it up

inside of me. A soft moan escapes my lips. I grasp onto both sides of the seat.

"You're always so ready for me, aren't you?" His deep velvety voice is enough to send me over the edge.

I nod, the words never surfacing. There are too many of them raging in my head, I'm not sure I'd say the right ones.

"I'm gonna—" He stops mid-sentence as his phone goes off. Sighing, he hits a button on the steering wheel to answer. "Hey, Mom."

He releases a shaky breath as he reluctantly tugs his finger out of me. He leaves his warm calloused hand against my thigh, which burns from his touch. The flame that had been flickering ignites. I have to control it, because we still have dinner to get through.

"Logan, sweetheart is Ellie with you? Have you picked her up from work yet? We're all here waiting."

"Yes, she's right here." He squeezes my leg. "Should only be ten minutes as long as Sunrise isn't bad."

We are going the opposite way of most commuter traffic, but that doesn't mean we won't run into unexpected delays.

"Okay. We'll see you soon. Drive safe. Love you."

"Love you too," he replies.

The speakers on the car click, signifying her hanging up. He remains quiet and never lifts his hand from my leg. Logan might have this naughty side to him, but he's also a big mush when it comes to his mom. He loves both his mom and Charlotte more than anything in this world. One day he'll make a woman happy because of how deeply he loves. I hate that I wish that woman could be me.

When we arrive, Logan excuses himself to the bathroom to wash his hands, and I settle down into the recently renovated dining room. It's still small, but the freshly painted tan walls and white molding lightens the room as opposed to the dark blue it was in the past. A cherry wood oval table sits in the center of the room; above it is a crystal chandelier with sparkling white crystals dangling.

Mom and Tommy, stand to greet me. Their seats face the beautiful screened in porch with gorgeous wooden louver doors.

Tommy reaches out to shake my hand. He's the tallest one here, and shoots over Logan by at least four inches. The man has to be somewhere over six foot. I take his hand, then walk around him and into Mom's embrace. She wraps me in a hug. Even though I saw her this morning, being in her arms is nice.

Josephine comes in from the kitchen with a large pot of pasta. I step around Mom and slide the tomato sauce over to make room for the pasta pot.

Josephine's warm brown eyes, almost identical to both Charlotte and Logan's, find mine. "Thank you, sweetheart." She places the pot on the table, then turns and hugs me too. She's always been like a second mom to me. I can't count how many times I spent the night here and the number of family vacations I stowed away on with them. She has always been welcoming.

"New haircut?" I ask.

For the wedding she had grown it out so she could do a beautiful updo that brought out all the beautiful features of her oval face. Even now with the short brown bob, she manages to look stunning.

"Yes. Do you like it?" she asks, touching the sides.

"It's gorgeous."

She smiles. She doesn't even have to hear him to know Logan's in the room now. "Logan, dear," she says, but is facing me. "Be a doll and go grab the rolls from the oven."

He doesn't say a word, but retreats to appease her. As we all settle in, Logan appears with the rolls and sets them down between the pots of pasta and sauce. Josephine's sauce is the perfect blend of a hearty meat, with the right balance of onion and garlic.

I find a spot across from Mom, and Logan sits beside me and to the left of his mom at the head of the table.

"So, how did the renovation go?" she questions, dropping a heaping helping of spaghetti onto her plate.

Logan grabs a roll. "Really good. We put the finishing touches on it yesterday. I'd say we did a good job, wouldn't you?" He winks at me.

I can't help smiling at the satisfied look in his eyes. He didn't have to stay two extra weeks, but he has. There are things about him that show how selfless he is. But then I think about him from a relationship standpoint and he really has never been able to keep hold of one girl for more than a few weeks.

"The wicker furniture came yesterday, and you know I really wasn't sold on it," I chime in. "But with the color scheme she chose it really makes the room pop. I can see why she wanted it."

I twirl the spaghetti in my bowl with a fork. As I lean over to take a bite, Logan's hand finds my leg again. I try not to choke and concentrate on chewing my food. His little stunt in the car left me with an intense throbbing between my legs. One I plan to get rid of later. My emotions may be all over the place, but I couldn't ride this one out, even if I tried.

"I'm so glad you two could work together. Charlotte is going to be shocked!" Josephine says happily as she rips apart her roll.

Shocked is an understatement. My body tenses and I have to remind myself to stay calm.

"So, Logan, have you heard anything about the job interview?"

I drop my fork and it falls with a loud clunk. He squeezes my leg tighter. "Interview?"

"Oh, he didn't tell you? He was thinking about maybe coming back to Long Island to work full time."

"Oh." My voice squeaks. "Really now. What happened to, 'Oh, move to Pennsylvania, because you get more bang for your buck.'?" My attempt to imitate him gets a laugh out of everyone at the table, including him.

181

He shrugs and holds my leg tighter. I gasp. "I might have found a reason to stay."

For a few moments, I'm lost in his eyes, and I have to remind myself to pull away. I stare back down at the plate in front of me, wondering how Logan could forget to mention that tiny detail.

"How—How long ago did you find out about the interview?" I ask.

He returns his attention back to everyone at the table instead of me, but his hand lingers, warming me up.

"I got the call for the interview on Monday. I did ask Mom to keep it a secret. I wanted to surprise you— surprise Charlotte." He stumbles over the words.

Josephine blushes and flicks her wrist at him. "I couldn't help myself, having you home will be the best birthday gift."

"I didn't get the job yet," he says.

"I know." She smiles. "But you will."

"I'd love to spend some time together," Tommy interjects, looking at Logan for a reaction.

He concentrates on his food, pushing it around with the fork in his hand. He mumbles what I think is "Mhmmm," but I'm not sure.

"That would be just wonderful." Josephine is beaming. "Having my whole family together again. It's like a dream."

Tommy takes hold of Josephine's free hand that rests on the table. He lovingly lifts her hand and kisses the back of it. Logan tenses beside me. His jaw is set tight as he sucks in a breath. There's a slight tremor in the hand he has wrapped around mine. Josephine is so caught up in her romance bubble that she doesn't notice the way her words affect her son. It's not her fault: she deserves all the happiness in the world, but I truly feel for Logan. His feelings are valid, because there's always going to be that small hole in his heart.

Conversation shifts over to Tommy chatting about a new project he's working on at the advertising firm he works for in the city. Logan grows quiet. He's still getting used to the idea of his mom having a boyfriend. In his eyes, his father was the only man good enough for her.

I cross my arm over his and rest a hand against his shaking leg. I'm not paying attention and with the flowing white cloth blocking my view, I end up over the bulge forming in his jeans from my touch. He straightens his body.

His mom stands and we both remove our hands, each banging them against the underside of the table. It stings, but I bite my lip and smile like nothing's wrong. Mom shakes her head, a smile inching across her face.

Logan clears his throat and excuses himself to the bathroom again. While he's gone, I help bring the dishes into the kitchen where I'm shooed away and told to go relax by Josephine. Mom steps in and helps with the dishes while Tommy disappears somewhere outside.

I linger in the living room where the stairs call to me. I set my hand on the newly painted white banister and start to head up. I know what's up here and I have a feeling his lingering disappearance means he wants me to go find him. So I do.

CHAPTER 19

$\mathcal{A}$t the top of the stairs my eyes follow the familiar path of the thick beige runner that takes up the length of the hallway. I stand before Charlotte and Logan's childhood rooms. They are opposite each other and there were many pranks played during sleepovers with the rooms so close, like Logan tying a string between both doors and watching us from the steps struggling to leave the room. The memory jars a smile out of me.

I head for the bathroom to check on him, only to be distracted by the door to his old room slightly ajar. He is sitting on the edge of his old bed atop a plain gray comforter. He's facing the window on the other side of the room and is unaware of my presence. It's nearly dark, but the light from the setting sun beams across the room, making a streak across the bed.

Everything in here is mostly preserved from his teen years. The only difference is there are no posters of bands or half-naked pin-ups on the slate-gray walls. And on the oak wood desk the messy array of papers has been replaced by a sewing machine and a variety of fabric is draped over the back of the matching chair.

I knock softly while opening the door. He glances up. His

dejected eyes worry me. Subconsciously, I know what I'm doing as I shut the door separating us from the noise of the dishes being washed, and the muffled voices of our moms' conversation. He doesn't even smirk or make a snide remark.

I settle down beside him on the bed, keeping my body close, letting him know I'm here for him. He grabs hold of my hand, pulling it onto his lap. Gently with his pointer he draws lines up and down the back of my hand. My body responds with a shiver.

"You okay?" I ask, staring down at our hands.

"I'm sorry, it's hard for me to see my mother happily flirting with another man. It's been four years and she should move on and be happy, but—" he pauses briefly. "I'd be lying if I said it didn't hurt."

"Have you told her how you feel? You know, without yelling?"

He shakes his head. "No. I can't. Not with the way she smiles around him. I haven't seen her that happy in years." He only half-smiles.

His shoulders slump with a heaviness I've never seen him display. It's odd seeing him this open with me. I like it, maybe a little too much.

"You're allowed to have feelings, Logan. You can speak to her without turning it into an argument. Be open with your mom, I've known her almost my whole life too, and you know she's not going to go off the rails if you tell her how you feel. I see how much you love her and Charlotte. You'd do anything for either of them. They are so lucky to have you in their lives."

He sighs, and runs his free hand through his short locks. There's a stillness in the air. His dark, warm eyes fill with glimmering adoration. Like two strong magnets, our faces grow closer until there's a connection. I hiss at the softness of his kiss. It's usually all hot and heavy, but this kiss is filled with emotion.

His hand frees from mine and lands on my cheek, covering the entire right side of my face. I lean into him, enjoying the warmth of his touch. The tiny caress with his thumb sends shock waves over my entire body. His hand on my cheek slides back, cupping my head, he slowly lowers me down into the softness of the mattress below, keeping me from hitting the headboard.

He plants soft, gentle kisses over my mouth. My eyes flick open as his lips nip at the bottom of my chin. He focuses on my face, like he's memorizing everything about it and holding on to the moment so he can keep the memory when our two weeks are over.

My shirt is the first to go. His fingertips glide up my sides as he tugs the fabric off my body. I reach for his next, enjoying the way his hard abs feel under my touch. With our shirts off he lowers himself over me, allowing our naked bodies to collide.

Slow and gentle, he places a trail of kisses along my bare chest. He reaches under me, unclasps my bra with the swift move of his hand and throws it to the floor. Pressing back down he settles his lips between my cleavage, then carefully makes his way down. Every few seconds he lifts his brow, letting his eyes fall on me. I shiver at the intensity of his stare.

He reaches my stomach and removes my skirt, shimmying it down. His lips find my inner thigh, and my insides scream with pleasure. I bite the back of my hand to keep from yelling out. Keeping his head down he lifts his hand to find my face, then blinks up at me through his lashes. After a few more earth-shattering kisses below, he straightens himself and then lowers onto me.

We never lose sight of each other. It's like our bodies are in tune enough to calculate the next move. Is this how it feels to be loved by Logan Fields? If it is, I need it in my life. It's the perfect combination of passion and lust.

There's a tenderness in all of his caresses along my skin. He shifts his body this time burrowing inside me. We gasp in sync, sharing a breath with every kiss. Our eyes remain open and locked on each other. I always thought having them open during sex was creepy, but this—this is not what I expected.

As we move together, he raises our hands up behind my head, clasping them together like a missing puzzle piece finding its mate. I arch up into him, tilting my chin back. He kisses my jawline, then takes my ear in his mouth and nibbles lightly.

We moan in unison. In one strong, swift movement he lifts me. Straightening into a seated position, I wrap myself around him. His grip on me is tight. *Please don't let go*, I think. It's almost like he hears me. He burrows his face in my neck, resting it there like he needs a moment to collect his thoughts.

My nails dig into his skin. He hisses as we rock together, his steady arms keep me from falling back. We stop kissing and rest our foreheads against one another, stilling for a moment. My eyes flutter closed, but not for long, because I don't want to miss a beat.

With our attention locked on each other, he lowers me back. His shimmering eyes line with a fiery passion that I never want to forget. When my head hits the fluffy pillow, he buries his face into my neck again and gasps. He's still as he lets his lips sit unmoving on my neck. Our breathing falls in sync like we're one person.

I'm not used to him being quiet. He usually encourages me with his dirty words, but tonight, it's just his soft moans, and my name.

"Ellie," he whispers for only me to hear. "Oh, Ellie. My Ellie." His voice catches in his throat.

A warmth spreads over me at his words. *My Ellie*. The way it sounds on his lips covers me in a warm blanket of what feels like love. It's new and exhilarating and I want to be his. My eyes sting with the threat of tears. I don't want this to ever end. Two weeks is not enough time to have him. I need him longer.

I push him gently. As if he knows what I need, he rolls us around so that I'm the one in control. I lay my body over his and roll my hips around and into him. I watch the way his jaw clenches every time I move. As I study the shape of his lips, he cries out my name pushing me into an intense orgasm that I feel all over.

He lets out a strangled gasp at the sound of my moans. I wish this could last forever. Every thrust feels as good as the last. I feel myself clenching around his hard erection buried deep inside of me. For a moment, he pulls back and places his hands on my cheek. There's no smile there, but the intensity of his stare tells me all I need to know.

Again, he takes me carefully in his arms and swaps us back over. I don't protest as he lowers himself and pushes into me with everything he's got. I lift my head back, but even then our eyes never stray. Right before I know he's about to finish, he runs his thumb along my jawline. I quake underneath him as we finish together. He lets out a relieved sigh, lightly moaning as my body continues to orgasm for several seconds following.

He pulls himself free, but instead of leaving, he lies down beside me and scoops me into his arms. His heart beats in a steady, quick rhythm against me, and his rapid breathing tickles my neck as he snuggles close.

A light tap at the door is the only thing that makes us both jump up. We reach for our clothes.

"I have dessert if you're hungry," Josephine calls.

"Be right out!" he yells as we scramble to get ourselves together.

I reach for the tissues on the desk and wipe down a bit before shrugging my underwear up my legs. He's quick to put on his jeans and get himself together.

There's a dark cloud looming over the room. He hasn't looked at me since it happened. Which only makes me believe that the entire moment we created together was nothing but a lie.

A knot forms in my throat.

"I'm going to head down first. You should follow a bit after," he says, as if what happened between us was no big deal. Like it was just another fucking session and nothing more.

"Mmhmm." It's the only coherent thing that I can say. I don't trust my voice.

He carefully observes me shimmying on my shirt, but doesn't say a word. Once I'm decent, he leaves. I take several deep breaths before crossing the room. I stop at the door collecting the memory of what was, and should have never been.

As I head for the stairs, Charlotte's closed door calls to me. I wonder if she took all of her stuff to the new house. Curiosity gets the best of me and I cross the hallway to her room. I swallow hard and push the door open. I find the light switch to the right and flip it on. Everything is as she had left it before she moved into the apartment with Bryan a year ago. The purple walls are mostly bare though, she took a lot of the artwork she'd bought through the years. She loves art museums, and paintings. There are some boxed items on the floor, but it's mostly still all there. I lift my gaze. Hanging on the violet wall is a corkboard with our friendship rules tacked on.

The paper is crinkled, the edges folded. There's a coffee stain over the center from one of our Starbucks trips where we wrote rule nine and ten. The rest is filled with different colored markers, some items crossed out, others rewritten, but the one that sticks out is rule # 5. We promise NEVER to fall in love with Logan or Arthur. Beside the rule are our initials, as if it were an actual contract.

My chest constricts, and the tears I'd been holding back no longer want to stay in. Thick warm droplets fall, some so fast and furious they drop to the floor in a mad dash to leave my eyes. My knees grow weak enough that I have to lean against the door frame to keep myself from crumbling. I can't do this anymore. I can't lie to Charlotte, and our families. She and I made a promise and I broke it. It doesn't matter that we were fourteen when we made it, it was never meant to be broken. EVER. I don't care that we still have two more days of whatever this is, it ends now.

I back out of the room forgetting to shut the lights, because I can't think straight. My eyes are so blurry that I almost tumble down the stairs. I catch myself before it happens. When my heavy steps reach the living room, I'm not expecting everyone to be there. All of their attention is placed on me.

I ignore him and look at his mom. "I am so sorry, Josephine. I can't stay for dessert." I redirect my attention to Mom. "Mom, can we go home?"

Logan's intense stare startles me, and I try not to look.

"Please. I'm not feeling well," I beg, desperate for space.

Mom pulls her attention between Logan and me. "Of course."

"I'll be in the car." I turn back to Josephine. "Thank you for dinner."

I would hug her goodbye, but I can't breathe in here. My throat feels as if it were closing up. Through the sobs I start gasping for air, needing to get out of there quickly. Loud thunderous steps follow behind me. I make it to the grassy area of their front yard when a hand reaches out and pulls me back. I stumble into his strong arms as he embraces me.

"What's going on?" he questions, eyes flicking over my face.

"I can't do this anymore." I finally take a good look at the man standing before me. The one who I've fallen in love with.

"Do what?" His eyes glisten, with a knowing look. He wants to hear it from me.

"Us. This. I thought I could do no strings when the truth is I can't. I've fallen and there's no turning back. Plus I can't lie to Charlotte anymore. I'm done, Logan. I need to walk away, it's already become too much. And what we did up there—" I pause to check his reaction. There's wetness now pooled at his bottom lid waiting to spill over. "What we did up there, that was not emotionless fucking and you know it."

"I—I—I can't be with you like that," he says.

His lips tremble. He wants to say more. The grip he has on my wrist burns and I hate it. I tug my arm away as Mom appears on the brick steps out front. I hold my wrist to my chest like it's been scorched by flames. Shaking my head I start to walk away. He steps forward and reaches out.

I mouth a silent *No*, before retreating into Mom's car and locking the door. She rushes to the car and it's only seconds before we start pulling away. In the side-view mirror, Logan runs a hand through his hair and looks up at the sky. Josephine jogs down the steps and it's at that point that I look away. It's over, and I need to forget that it even began.

CHAPTER 20

$\mathcal{I}$'m good at hiding my emotions during work hours. I've somehow made it through my shift without a single breakdown or tear.

As I settle into my car, I turn my phone back on and put it on the passenger seat. I had shut it off so that I wouldn't be tempted to check my messages, or take a call from Charlotte. There is no way I could handle that right now. I'd break down on the call and then I'd have to tell her everything. I did send her a text early this morning wishing her safe travels home. I mentioned working, and said I was sorry if I didn't respond.

I turn the key in the ignition. The radio comes to life with a Jonas Brothers song, the same one we danced to on Wednesday night. My hand darts out fast to turn it low.

My phone starts up and I count ten or more dings to inform me of missed messages. Closing my eyes, I inhale deeply, trying to center myself before I look. Mom knows to call the store in an emergency, so I'm not expecting them to be from her.

I reach over, not opening my eyes until the phone is in my hand. There are about fifteen missed calls and ten texts. Logan's name takes up my entire screen.

Ellie, please talk to me.

I'm so sorry.

I'm worried about you, please send me some kind of sign that you are okay.

Okay, I deserve your silence, but in my defense, you promised no strings attached.

I didn't mean to sound like an asshole in that last message. Ellie, please, I need to hear your voice to make sure you're okay.

I messed up, but I'm not going to discuss this over text. I wish you'd talk to me.

There are a few more messages like this, but I can't bear to look at it anymore. I silence my phone, and put it on the passenger seat face down. I pull out of my parking spot and head home. Hopefully tonight I'll get some sleep.

I park in the driveway behind Mom's car. It's late, but the lights are all still on. She's probably waiting for me. Another text comes through as I grab my phone. Logan's name again appears.

Hope you got home safe from work. See you tomorrow.

In my head I hear his deep voice through all these texts. The sound of it, even in my head, causes my stomach to flutter. The urge to reach out is there, but I can't keep playing this game, because to me, it's something more. It always has been.

I was never a girl who could be detached with someone I was having sex with. To me, having sex means you're in love with that person. I don't know how I convinced myself that attempting a friends-with-benefits relationship would work. In the end I got my heart broken. This break felt different than the rest. I've known Logan almost my entire life. He was the one who, even though he'd play pranks and act like he didn't care, was always right there when Charlotte and I needed him the most.

I recall the first day of mine and Charlotte's freshman year.

He was a junior. I was trying to open my locker and struggling. A few junior girls came waltzing by and saw me in my favorite Jonas Brothers shirt. They decided to mock me. As luck would have it, Logan was passing by and ushered the girls to move on. They hesitated until he wrapped his arm around me and started belting out "Burnin' Up".

"Honey, is that you?" Mom's voice pulls me from my thoughts.

Concealing the pain at work was easy, but with Mom I can't hide it. I slip off my shoes and place them on the rack. It's well past 10:30 and Mom should be sleeping. We didn't have much of a chance to talk yesterday. When we arrived home, she gladly gave me space while I spent the evening in my room tucked under the covers rereading *After* for the millionth time.

"Yeah," I manage. "It's me." My voice is thick, and I have to clear my throat to rid it of the knot forming.

I find her sitting at the kitchen table reading the newspaper. She lays it flat, then pats the spot beside her. Without hesitation I sit and rest my head on her shoulder. I take deep, slow and steady breaths to calm myself.

"How was your day?"

I'm glad she didn't start with *Are you ready to talk about it?* I know I'll have to explain everything to her. I just need to work myself up the courage to do so.

"Exhausting. Julie from shoes got ill and I offered to take her spot. I've only worked in that department once or twice, but it was a lot of work jetting back and forth between the cash-wrap and the stockroom. We had a mad rush after dinner. My feet are so angry."

Her chuckles jar me, but I continue to rest my head on her shoulder.

"How was your day?" I'm afraid to ask about Dad. Mom is like me, she'll talk about it when she's ready, so I don't push her to discuss it.

She shrugs. "We have a new server and she's a mess." There's a melancholy tone to her voice, and I hate that she's in pain too.

"Worse than when I tried waitressing?"

Junior year I took up a waitressing job so that I could save up money for a car. It lasted a week before they fired me for dropping things, and mistakenly dumping a whole bowl of pasta in a customer's lap.

She laughs. "I don't think anyone is that bad."

Her jab at me brings a smile to my face. The room grows quiet, except the soft hum of the refrigerator and the banging of the washing machine sputtering in the basement below us. I stare off at a small dark brown knot on the table in front of me.

"Charlotte returns tomorrow," I whisper.

"Oh?"

I sit up and spin my body to face her, positioning my right leg under me. Closing my eyes, I exhale a long quaking breath. At the sensation of Mom's hand against my leg, tears prick my eyes.

There's not one ounce of pity on her face. She grows still, carefully assessing my mood and lending me her ear.

"I've lied to my best friend for two weeks." I finally get out, and once I start there's no stopping. I tell Mom everything. From the night of the wedding to yesterday evening. I won't go into *full* details. She's my mom and it feels weird describing the moment fucking turned into making love, but she understands with the amount I give her.

"That boy has always had his eye on you, but I noticed it more when I saw the way you two acted around each other the morning he came over and stole your cereal. If you want my opinion, I think he's afraid to love."

I nod in agreement, my mouth dry as if I'd been wandering a desert for hours.

"Logan is like a son to me. One thing I do know is that he would never intentionally hurt you. He's already sent me several texts asking if you were okay. He even texted a few minutes before you pulled up to make sure you made it home from work. Sweetheart, that boy is head over heels, but I agree, he needs to grow up a little."

"Is he like Dad?" I ask, my voice quivering.

I immediately regret asking the question. She holds her breath for a long moment before blowing out air. Rubbing her temples, she regards me. "He has some of the same tendencies, but your father never looked at me the way Logan looks at you. Dad would have never ridden his bike all those miles in the hot sun to deliver an ice-cream cup."

My lips twitch with the desire to smile, but they don't quite get there. "You knew about that?"

"I saw you two out the window. There were many other instances while you two were growing up. Like prom. We were all at Charlotte's, you and your prom date—what was his name?"

"Winston O'Donnell."

Winston was like a prize that I somehow had won. He was kind of popular, but hung out with almost every group. He was the type of person you'd call a "social butterfly". He didn't stick to one group, and we'd done a lot of improv together in theater class. His promposal in front of the entire class (who were in on it) was choreographed to "Can I Have This Dance" from *High School Musical*. It was sweet, and although our relationship only lasted a month, we ended on good terms, and sometimes still comment on each other's Facebook posts.

"Yes, Winston. There was this look in Logan's eyes while he was helping Josephine take photos. You could tell he wished it was him."

"You can't know that."

Mom purses her lips. "Josephine brought it up later that night, so it wasn't only me who noticed."

I sigh. Thinking back, sure I did have that huge crush on Logan, but I never noticed him noticing me in that way. Mom and I sit in silence as tears continue to fall.

"It felt so real," I whisper. I blink my blurry eyes and stare at my hand on the table.

The tears turn into angry sobs again. The urge to punch something rages through me, but dissipates when Mom wraps her loving arms around me. I don't know how long she holds on. I lose track of time and of myself. There's a part of me that wishes I could go back to the wedding and erase all the shots I took that night, and most of all, I'd take back accepting a dance with him.

CHAPTER 21

I pull up to Charlotte's house on zero hours of sleep. After my chat with Mom, I went up to my room with the intention of sleeping, but only ended up tossing and turning instead. I got maybe ten minutes before my alarm went off so I could get here on time.

Logan's car is already outside. The blood drains from my face. I stare at the paler version of myself in the rearview mirror. I don't want to go in yet, I should wait. Josephine is picking the newly-weds up from the airport and we are meeting here to surprise them. Today was supposed to be a happy occasion. I can't let it get to me, because this moment is all about my best friend starting her new life, but for some reason that doesn't make me feel any better.

I'm happy for her, truly, I am. She deserves the world, but the idea of my friend starting her new life while I'm steadily falling backwards hurts more than I ever imagined.

I rest my head against the steering wheel. The car is already heating up since I've cut the ignition and I have my windows closed. The late-August heat cooks me from the inside out, but I'm so tired I can't move.

A loud knock at the driver's side window makes me jump. I gasp and turn to find Logan's narrowed eyes on me. He tries for the handle, but it's locked from the inside. My shoulders fall as I flick the lock open. He tugs on it, bends to get eye level with me, and carefully observes me. His lips are taut and he pushes them out like he's contemplating saying something.

I lift a hand to my chest to relieve the pressure building up inside. It's no use: the longer he's in front of me, the more it hurts. What kills me most is the way his eyelids appear as heavy and swollen as mine feel. Underneath them are dark purple bags. His breath is uneven as he watches me.

He opens his mouth to speak as someone drives up and honks their horn. Saved by the horn! I have nothing left to say to him. He steps aside and that's when Charlotte's wide brown eyes find mine. Her smile is brighter than ever. Bryan leans over from the other side and waves at us.

Josephine pulls into the driveway. Logan remains silent, but holds his hand out for me to take. Ignoring it, I grab my black purse, put it over my shoulder, and leave the car without saying a word to him.

Charlotte's shriek pierces me as she gets out of the car and runs to meet me halfway. You'd think by her reaction we'd been apart for years. She takes me in her arms and I have to fight the urge to cry. She's tall like Logan and towers over me. My lips tremble as she sheds a few tears of her own, but they're happy, unlike mine.

I take a deep breath and flip to a smile as she pulls away.

"What are you doing here?" she asks.

"Would you believe me if I said I missed you?" My voice sounds off. Shaky, and way too high-pitched for me. Her brows furrow and she's about to open her mouth when Bryan calls her over.

Charlotte grabs my hand and tugs me along with her to the car. Logan has disappeared into the house. I help them take their luggage inside. Charlotte is one of those girls who packs as if they were never coming back. We all chip in with the exception of Logan.

Inside the house, the faint smell of paint lingers in the air. If Charlotte notices she doesn't say anything.

Logan leans against the railing of the steps leading up to their room. He props his foot up on the wall and crosses his arms, observing the scene before him. I try to avert my attention. It's hard enough to be in the same room, but every time he looks at me I feel as if I'll crumble.

"What are you all doing here? I only expected Mom. I thought you went home already?" She turns to Logan, a questioning look on her face.

"I was going to, but I was conned into staying, by your husband. Oh, and Mom said if I didn't stay and help she'd never send me her famous blackberry pie again."

Josephine's laughter carries over from the kitchen where she's preparing the lunch she picked up from the deli on the way over. The plan was supposed to be for us to all have lunch together. I'm not sure I can handle lunch with my best friend after lying to her for two weeks. I'm going to need some time to process everything that's happened.

"You know I don't like secrets." She pokes Bryan's chest.

Her words leave me breathless, and a small gasp escapes my lips. I ball my hands into fists at my side. The hairs on my arm stand and my eyes find Logan's. We hold each other's stare for a few seconds before he turns away, biting hard on his lower lip.

My attention lands back on Charlotte and Bryan. He bends over and grazes the top of her forehead with a sweet peck. She looks up at him with dreamy eyes. Most couples go through a honeymoon phase at first, but eventually it vanishes over time. Not Charlotte and Bryan. Their love is eternal. Those two will spend every moment together until their last breath. The thought alone of my friend finding happiness does ignite a spark inside me. Being jealous and happy at the same time is confusing.

"Yeah, but this secret is something you're going to love," he tells her, planting a second kiss in the same spot.

Charlotte smirks, then passes a look between all of us. "What's going on, you guys?"

I clear my throat, trying to make this moment about her. It's hard to focus on anything with how Logan regards me with a longing stare. I wish he'd stop; it's not helping.

"You guys!" she whines.

"Follow me and you'll see." Logan smiles genuinely at his sister.

She walks up to him, puts a hand on his chest, then turns to me. "Are you in on this too?"

I nod. "I might have had a small hand in it."

"It was more than a small hand," he says.

I swallow hard. Her eyes dart back and forth. She purses her lips, about to say something, but instead, she shoves Logan up the stairs to see what we've been keeping from her.

I want this to be a moment she won't ever forget. Logan and I worked hard to give her exactly what she wanted, and I can't wait to see the joy on her face when she sees the room.

"I swear, you two are the same person. She knew more about your personal tastes than I did," he says.

Charlotte laughs. "That's because you don't pay attention, brother."

"Come on, this way."

He urges her on. I allow Bryan to go before me and follow behind them. We all stop at the closed door. I'm furthest away, trying to keep my distance.

"Is that a fresh coat of paint?" Charlotte places her hand on the bedroom door. She leans forward and sniffs.

"Wait—" She turns to Bryan. His cheeks are a deep shade of red. "Is it? Did they?"

Bryan shrugs. A killer smile graces his round face.

"Open it already."

He chuckles. "All right. Here you go." With one hand on the knob, he twists and pushes it open, revealing her new bedroom.

Her gasp echoes through the house. Mouth open and eyes wide, she steps inside. "You guys, you?"

She turns as I enter the room. I step further inside closer to the bed, away from where Logan keeps himself perched by the door.

Charlotte spins around, doing a complete 360. She's speechless, something that is rare for her. Her eyes shimmer with tears. They cascade down her pink cheeks and land on her upturned lips. She covers her mouth and gapes at us.

"My window," she cries, pointing upwards.

I knew the window was going to be her favorite feature of the room; it's definitely mine. The light pours through leaving a streak between us.

"The arch! It arches at the top. Oh my God, you guys!"

Bryan hasn't seen the room yet either and I watch him taking it all in. "You know, that wicker furniture is not as bad as I imagined," he says. "I expected it to be too girly, especially with the wall color. This works. Thank you, to both of you. Logan if there is any way I can help you pay for your hotel—"

"No, man. Don't worry about it. You're family, I got it covered." Logan's genuine smile kills me inside. He might be someone who leaves when things get tough, but this man loves his family with all his heart. There's no denying that.

There's some mist in Bryan's eyes. He blinks several times to clear it. "That means a lot, Logan." He turns to me. "Ellie, thank you for putting up with that one." He jerks a thumb over towards Logan. "And for taking the time to make this perfect for my girl."

"Of course," I say. "Anything for Charlotte."

"Aw, guys, I'm blushing." She wipes the tears.

She heads to Logan first and wraps her arms around him. He

grunts at the impact and chuckles, but the smile he has at her reaction doesn't reach his eyes. I study them and how he holds on to her and closes his eyes. He's a very passionate man when it comes to the women that mean something to him. If only he'd be like that in a relationship.

The lump in my throat returns and I have to sneak that I'm fanning my eyes with my hand to conquer the tears. Luckily, Logan and Charlotte are too busy hugging to notice.

"You're the best brother ever!"

"I'm your only brother," he says in a teasing voice, rolling his eyes.

She chuckles and hits him playfully as she backs away. Charlotte turns and looks straight at me. She's too excited to notice my rigid posture. She bolts forward and stumbles into me the same way she did Logan. I take the impact and nestle into her arms.

I can't stop myself and as she wraps her arms around me the tears start flowing. She's holding on tight enough to make me think she doesn't want to let go. I lift my head, rest it on her shoulder, not facing her. I don't want her to see the tears. The truth I've withheld from her falls heavily on me.

The hairs on the back of my neck stand on end. It's like we are connected somehow. My eyes flick open and I gasp at the sight of Logan's warm eyes set ablaze like they were Friday night. There's a longing behind them that seems so real, but after what he said, I know it's fake.

"Hey. Hey. Are you crying too?" She pulls back.

In the corner of my eye, I catch Logan attempting to step towards me. I shake my head at him but make it look as if I'm forcing the tears to stop.

I wipe my eyes. "I missed my best friend, that's all."

"Aww, I missed you more. Oh! And I got you so many souvenirs." She squeals.

I chuckle, trying to wipe the tears away. Logan's eyes continue to linger on me, but I refuse to look up.

"Also, how did you deal with my brother? Ugh. I'd go mad doing a project like this with him. He can be so bossy. I apologize for his bad behavior."

She smirks at him. He responds by sticking out his tongue, releasing another sad attempt at a smile. She turns, her teeth shining bright. All I can give her is a sorry excuse for a smile. There's an intense throbbing in my temples that feels like a jackhammer is drilling into my skull. I reach up and press my fingers directly on the spot that hurts.

"Gosh, guys, I'm so speechless, I don't even know what to—" She starts to scan the room again, but instead her attention lands back on me. "Ellie? Ellie, what's wrong?" She narrows her eyes at me.

Logan's attention and everyone else in the room snap to me. I wave my hand at her. "I'm okay, why?"

"I know that look, El."

She rarely calls me El, unless she disagrees with something I've said or suspects something is bothering me.

I make the mistake of looking up. That magnetic pull is more intense than ever. He watches me intently through glistening eyes and knitted brows. I'm the worst friend in the entire world, and I want to apologize to her a million times over for ruining this moment. My heart is having a hard time processing the mess I've made.

"I have to—I need to leave. I didn't get much sleep, but can we hang out this week?"

She wraps her hands around mine. I suck in a trembling breath and try to fight the building sob growing in my chest. This shouldn't hurt this much, but the pain grips me like a giant claw digging in deep. It's all still too raw. My eyes can't seem to focus on anything but him. Charlotte takes notice, her attention flickering between Logan and me.

She sighs. "Of course, we can."

I muster the best smile I can, let go of her hands, wrap her in my arms, then silently walk towards the door. As I pass Logan I make sure to leave a wide gap, but he closes it, causing me to brush against him.

"Ellie, please don't go," he whispers only to me, but the room is silent enough that it's as if he's screaming the words.

A lightning bolt surges through me at his touch, only making me want to get out of there faster. His eyes flutter, leaving some moisture on the edges.

"We can fix this." His trembling voice is almost enough to make me stay. I shake my head. I can't. I need space and time to think things over.

As I leave, I hear Charlotte say in a low-pitched voice, "What did you do now, Logan?"

I don't bother to wait and hear what his response is. I hurry down the stairs and jog to my car. Once inside, the tears don't have any mercy; they fall furiously again. I can't let this consume me. I have to pull myself together. There are plenty of other men out there who are worth my time, like Ethan. Yeah. I should go on a date with Ethan. I have to move on and forget Logan. You can't love a man who won't love you back.

As I lean down to put the keys in the ignition I catch sight of Charlotte and Logan in the mud room. His curious eyes keep checking to see if I've left yet. Charlotte's hands are flailing all over the place. I don't know what they are saying and I hate that I've ruined her happy surprise.

Without any more thought, I turn the key. I put the car in drive and as I pull away I find Logan stepping out of the house and staring after me, again.

I pull into the driveway and Mom is already standing in the doorway like she's been waiting for my return. In her hand is her cell, and she's typing away frantically. The phone disappears and her attention is fully on me now. I'm not used to seeing her home so early on a Sunday, but here she is with open arms.

"Logan sent a text. He wanted to make sure you got home okay," she says as I jet up the steps and into her arms.

He sent a text; of course he did. I wish this didn't hurt so much, and that it didn't affect my life, but it does, way more than I expected it to. I've known the Fields practically my whole life. They are a staple in my world. The idea of losing any of them crushes my soul.

"Can we watch some ridiculously bad nineties sitcom and eat lots of ice cream?" I ask, pulling away.

After Dad left and Mom finally came out of her room, we spent many nights binging on old shows and junk food. It's our thing; it always has been.

"Of course we can. You let me know if you need to get more feelings out."

She's never once let me down, has always been there by my side. Even if I was in the wrong for something, she was there to tell me that we all make mistakes and that I must pick myself back up and keep going. Now, here I am worried about my relationship with Logan, when Mom has some heaviness hanging over her heart too.

"I am so sorry for the things I said the other night."

"Sweetheart." Her beautiful smile makes some of the pain go away. "You have every right to be angry at that man. Your father is a no-good rotten piece of crap. I'm okay now. Hearing his voice did some things to my heart, but I'm better off."

I sigh. "I was worried you were angry with me—"

"I could never be angry at you for having feelings. Now, let's get your mind off of this Logan fiasco."

I take a deep breath, and smile. Mom wraps her arm over my

shoulder and tugs me into the house towards the living room. I settle down on the couch while she scurries to the kitchen to grab the ice cream and spoons.

If things were different, Charlotte would be here with us, chowing down, but now I have to face the fact that Charlotte may not want to do these things with me anymore. All because I screwed up. I try to shake it all out of my head as I scroll through some streaming services to find the perfect show.

Thank God for Costco and their gigantic ice-cream tubs. In Mom's hand is one of those triple containers with three flavors in one. She sets it down on the small glass coffee table along with the spoons.

"*Saved By The Bell?*" I ask.

"You know I was convinced I was going to marry Zack Morris." She smiles and digs her spoon into the tub.

I laugh. "It's too bad he didn't get to chase zombies or vampires whatever they were for too long. He looked good in that, I mean, for an old man."

Mom nudges me with her shoulder. "Hey, young lady, he's not that old."

Laughter surrounds us, and although my heart feels like it's being strangled, there's a little tug lessening the pain.

CHAPTER 22

Josephine had caught my attention through a small crowd of people gathered in her living room. It was the day of Henry's funeral and the darkness that surrounded the family felt like a thick fog over all of us. We all felt the loss of such a great man.

She made her way over. Her eyes were rimmed with redness. She'd been crying on and off all day. She gave me a weak smile.

"Have you seen Logan?"

I shook my head. "No, but I can go look for him."

She patted my shoulder. "Would you please? I'm worried."

"Of course." I reached up to give her a hug.

She sniffled and wiped her face, then pulled away. "Thank you, sweetheart."

Charlotte was busy trying to entertain her aunt, so I didn't bother asking her about Logan. I knew if I did she'd get worried. He hadn't taken the news well at all, which was to be expected. Charlotte hadn't taken it well either, but Logan was just a shell of himself.

The guests were thinning out, but there were still a decent

number of people at the house to pay their respects. I opened the door to their backyard. The floodlight illuminated the yard as I stepped out. A shadow lay in the grass. As I walked towards him the light went out.

I got down in the grass and lay beside him. Adjusting my short black dress I inched a little closer. He reached out and grabbed hold of my hand. His breath stilled for a moment as our fingers interlaced.

It was quiet between us. The chatter from the house leaked out from the opened window, but from here it was muffled. The stars above us twinkled. I watched them in silence as we took several breaths in sync with each other.

"Talk to me, Ellie," he said.

"Came out to check on my wingman."

He laughed. It wasn't his usual Logan laugh, but it was better than his silence. He moved closer so that our bodies were touching. It was hard to be that close and not reach over and kiss him. He sucked in a deep breath and let it go. His hand tightened around mine. My heart was doing flips.

"Your grandma tried to feed me those cough drops she carries around. She told me they were candy. I had like three."

Logan rolled his head to look at me. His face was so close to mine that I could feel his breath as it tickled my lips. He smiled and gave another sorry excuse for a laugh.

"I once almost ate the whole box," he said.

"That can't be good."

"It probably isn't," he said.

We didn't say anything else for a long while. I didn't mind though. Holding his hand and enjoying being close was all I needed.

"Your breath is sweet," he said quietly.

For a few long lingering breaths we stared at each other. His dark eyes were sad, but there was a little sparkle in them as I leaned closer and my lips almost brushed against his. I wish I would have seen that he had a plan to escape. Maybe I would have kissed him that night. I got caught up in the moment and the way his fingertips gently ran over my knuckles.

There was no space keeping us apart and as he moved in a loud bang came from inside the house. It sounded like some pots and pans fell. We shot up from our position and wiped ourselves off.

"I should go check on Charlotte," I said, my heart ready to take flight out of my chest.

"Okay." He paused and I started to walk away. "Ellie?" His voice sounded so small. I wish I would have run back and took him in my arms. "Thanks."

I nodded as a knot formed in my throat. His eyes were saying goodbye. If I could yell back at my younger self four years ago I'd tell her to hold on and keep him there.

I glanced back once over my shoulder to check on him, and caught him staring up at the sky with his fists clenched. I didn't want him to catch me staring so I hurried back inside to find Charlotte. I needed to go home too, because hanging around would only get me in more trouble.

The sun filters in from the window, burning my eyes and making them ache from the tears. My shift doesn't start until later, and as much as I'd like to call out, I think it's best that I work and keep my mind occupied with anything other than Logan.

Things are going to be different now, not only between Logan and I, but Charlotte too. That was the one friendship I never wanted to screw up, and now it's hanging in the balance. How will she ever forgive me? Sure, we wrote those rules when we were teens, but that doesn't change the fact that I lied to her for two weeks.

The doorbell echoes through the house, not once, or twice, multiple times, and is accompanied by several hard knocks. Mom is at work again, and I'm the only one home. It doesn't sound like they are going to let up any time soon. On top of the knocks, my phone dings several times in a row. I reach for it off the bedside table.

Let me in!
It's Me!
I'm your best friend! Please, let me in. I swear I'm alone, Logan left to go back home. Talk to me! Please!!

The messages keep coming through and the knocking on the door grows louder by the minute. My temples throb, the pain radiates down to my neck, and as I stand the pain shoots from my head and travels downward. It's like I'm hungover, but I never had anything to drink.

It might be summer, but as I throw the blanket off a shiver runs through me. As if it were a game of Jenga, I carefully pull my light gray sweater from Victoria's Secret from the center of the pile on the junk chair. Clean, dirty, who cares. I zip it up and hold myself together with my arms.

Downstairs, the banging grows louder and the doorbell leaves a ringing in my ears.

"Please, El, open up the—"

With shaking hands I fling the door open and come face to face with Charlotte through the screen. Her shoulders slump and her mouth falls open. Unlike the beautiful smile she carried with her yesterday, today there's a gray cloud over her head. I push open the screen door, lowering my eyes to the ground as I step aside to let her in.

"What the hell is going on? Why won't you answer me? I've been texting you all night. Bryan took my phone away and made me go to sleep, but I couldn't." Her voice is full of rage, but there's a softness to it that tells me she's half upset, but mostly concerned.

I stand beside the opened door, but can't meet her eye. She shifts on her feet in front of me, and crosses her arms while she waits for me to explain everything that has happened the past two weeks. I honestly have no clue how to tell her what's been going on. I mean, I could tell her I fucked her brother and it was good, but admitting that I fell in love with him is hard to relay. Most of all, how do I tell her that I've been lying?

A familiar knot forms in my throat. I try to swallow, but can't, so I lift my gaze and find tears leaving streaks down her sun-kissed cheeks.

"I've been such a terrible friend, the worst. The reason I didn't say goodbye to you at the wedding was because I was too busy sneaking away to make out with Logan. I woke up naked in his hotel room and that's how it all began. I broke rule number five, and then I proceeded to lie to you for two whole weeks."

There's a heavy sob building up in my chest, making it hard for me to breathe. Charlotte's tears continue to fall, and if I'm not careful we'll end up like *Alice in Wonderland* floating down a river of tears.

"I don't know why I thought it would be a good idea. It was supposed to be a one-time thing, but then he came to me and said he was going to redo your bedroom. He asked me to help; how could I deny him that? I knew your dream bedroom: you've been talking about it since we were kids. I wanted to help, and then helping led to—" I pause, placing a hand on my chest. If I wasn't so upset, I'd think I was having a heart attack.

"More sex," she finishes for me in a quiet whisper.

It's hard to catch my breath, but at the same time it's good to get it all out in the open. Although, it's two weeks too late.

"I kept trying to ignore the fire inside, but every time I did he was right there and he kept wanting more, asking for it, it was like I couldn't stop."

We stand there, and I hate that she's quiet. It can only mean that she's contemplating how to end this friendship. I've invested so many years into it; if she and I are over, my heart will be ten times more shattered than when Logan broke it.

"We were kids when we wrote rule number five." She finally speaks, but her voice is thinned out and trembles with each word. "I'm not mad because you broke some rule we made over my fragile teenage heart. I'm mad because you lied."

I run a hand through my hair and tug hard at the ends. I expected it to go like this, I knew she'd hate me. There was always a possibility that I could lose Charlotte, but I never imagined losing both of them at the same time.

"I'm so sorry, Charlotte. I never wanted to hurt you or lie. It was only supposed to be two weeks. I never meant to feel anything."

I hold my hand back against my chest hoping it will help me catch my breath. The pain lingers around my heart.

"You can't deny that you've always felt something. I know Logan has. A few weeks before graduation when we went rollerblading at the park, I caught him watching. He was always aware of you and your presence, but this was different. I confronted him and he denied it, but I saw it. It became even clearer the night of Dad's funeral a few years later."

"You saw that?"

"I was looking out my bedroom window and saw everything."

I gasp at the memory, and lift a finger to my lips. "I should have told you what was happening this week, but I also wanted to keep it quiet, because of the room renovation. If you knew Logan was here you would have gotten suspicious, but that's no excuse. I've been a terrible friend." I stop for a moment to try and swallow again, it's painful but I manage. "I understand if you hate me—"

"I don't hate you, Ellie. You're my best friend. I'm heartbroken that you didn't talk to me." Charlotte sobs into her hand. I didn't mean to hurt her, I truly didn't. I got so caught up in trying to forget how my life felt stagnant that I lost sight of the big picture. I needed some excitement in there that as much as I knew of the consequences, I still did it anyway.

"Charlotte, I love you more than anything in this world. If you don't want to talk to me ever again I—"

I'm cut off by her throwing her arms around me. Her loud sobs cause mine to surface. I wish I could take it all back and fix everything that happened. It's all my fault that what was supposed to be a happy return turned into a mess. If I hadn't gotten wrapped up in myself it would have never come to this.

She holds me at arm's length, and looks me in the eye. "I hate what he did to you. My brother can be such a dick. He doesn't know how to love a woman the right way. I should have suspected something was up when I was doing all the calling." She sighs, shaking her head, trying to pull her words together.

I wait to say what I have to say, because I know if I speak now it will come out all jumbled.

"He's never going to settle down, Ellie."

"And I one-hundred percent knew that going into it." I pull back and wipe away some tears. Her eyes meet mine, and some of the tension keeping my shoulders rigid releases like a balloon losing its air.

"You're my best friend and my whole world. You can talk to me about anything. I don't care about some list we made when we were teenagers, what I care about is you."

It's a miracle that she doesn't hate me. I'd hate me. Her not being mad should take all the pain of the heartbreak over Logan away, only it doesn't.

"I'm sorry he hurt you."

My body sways as I stare at the floor. "And I'm sorry for lying to you." My voice is tiny enough that it could come from a mouse.

"I forgive you, Ellie. Please don't lie to me again."

I shake my head and now it's my turn to wrap my arms around her. "I promise. Never, ever again."

"Good," she says. "Now, let's find a way to mend that broken heart of yours."

CHAPTER 23

It's been a tough three weeks, but my heart is slowly on the mend. Logan hasn't sent a text to me directly, but he's been checking in via Bryan. Charlotte said he's only messaged her to check in about Josephine's birthday party, which is in a few short hours from now. I'm a nervous wreck at the thought that I have to be in the same space as him.

Last week I decided to dust off my resume and do something for myself that could change my life. I applied to a few radio stations in the area, mostly sales positions, but it's something. Yesterday I got a phone call that they want to interview me on Thursday. I love that Sheer Threads has been my home away from home for the past six-ish years, but I hate this stagnant feeling. I had to dive in headfirst and good news is just what I need.

For a Saturday, at one of the busiest malls on Long Island, the time is going painfully slow. It's a beautiful early September day, so people are getting in their last bits of sun before the fall weather hits. The temperatures are still around eighty during the day, but drop quickly down to sixty in the evenings. Tonight it's supposed to be cool, but not too bad, perfect for an outdoor party.

"Hey, Ellie. Can you take this over to the men's department?" Lily hands me a pair of men's jeans, folded neatly, with the belt placed on top.

"Sure. Give me all the busy work Maryann left. Is it insanely slow today or is it me?"

She rolls her eyes. "It's awful. I'm on till close, it's going to be never-ending."

I groan. "That's awful, closing shifts on a Saturday blow."

"Tell me about it, but Jett is taking me to a pub in Nassau and says they have the best beer. We'll see."

"Sounds like fun."

She reaches out and touches my arm. "You should come out with us again sometime. By yourself is cool. Or you can invite Charlotte. We could do a girls' night."

She's trying to tread lightly around my broken heart, and I love her for it. She worked with me those first few days following what happened, so she knows how much of a wreck I was.

"I could ask Charlotte. I think she'd like that."

"Great. I have to get back over to the register. Patty's by herself. She's still having trouble detaching the ink tags."

We part ways, and I head over to the men's department. It's quiet like ours, but there's a few lingering guests over in the suit area.

"Fancy running into you here."

I turn to find Ethan watching me from the fitting rooms. He's folding a heaping pile of clothing that was left behind by customers.

"Hey, just returning the favor and bringing back the goods."

His genuine smile catches me off guard, and I'd almost forgotten how cute Ethan is. Logan was clouding my mind. He's not Logan by any means, but he's the sweet type that would probably hold a door open for a woman or greet her with flowers for every date. The type of man I should probably be going for.

"Great. You can put those jeans right there. I can put it away with all of this."

I place the pants down on the small counter and step back.

"So, how are—" We both say at the same time, an awkward giggle passes between us.

"How are you doing?" He finishes the question before I can.

"Could be better, but I'm hanging in there."

He nods, his lips not quite forming a full smile. Scratching the back of his neck, he stares at me. I did promise him I'd be up to getting something to eat together. With Logan out of the picture, and knowing I have to move on, I figure why not.

"Do you wanna go get that dinner sometime soon? I mean, as friends for right now. My heart's not one-hundred percent ready, but a night out won't hurt."

"As friends?" he questions.

"Yeah. If that's okay—"

"Oh no-no-no. I mean," he stutters. "It's—it's wonderful. I'd love to go out as friends. You take all the time in the world to heal." His face burns red. He moves his hand from his neck to his arm, rubbing right where his sleeve meets his arm.

"Great. Is next weekend okay?" I ask.

"Um-yeah. I'm off Friday."

"Me too. So, Friday then?"

We mark it down in our phones and make plans to meet at TGI Fridays. Since we're going as friends, I'd rather drive myself instead of having him pick me up.

I head back to the women's department. There still isn't a line. Lily stands at the register picking at her cuticles. I rest my elbows on the counter.

"You're smiling."

"I have a 'friend date' with Ethan."

She smirks. "Ethan from men's?"

"Yeah. Is that weird?"

She shakes her head. "No way. I think it's great. You look happy."

I straighten my body. We are only going out as friends, but it feels nice to go out with a guy who I know I won't end up in a hotel room with naked and confused.

I try to take this friend date thing as a good thing. Moving on is necessary, especially since Logan was never mine in the first place. I spend the rest of the early afternoon shift putting away minor shipments and helping some customers on the floor.

When I finally get home it's a little after two. The party starts in an hour, so I plan on showering before we leave. I find Mom in the kitchen in a beautiful black sparkling evening gown. It's not over-the-top fancy, but it accents all of her curves in the right spots.

"Mom, you look amazing."

She does a little twirl. "You really think so?"

"I know so. Who are you trying to impress?" I tease.

Mom's cheeks flush. "Oh, hush you." She pauses. "You seem happy."

I suck in a breath. "I am. A little. I have a 'friend date' with Ethan from work."

Her eyes widened. "Honey, that is amazing. It'll be good for you."

For a minute, my heart flips with uncertainty. There's still that lingering piece that wishes things were different with Logan. I need to brush it away, because nothing can ever come from a guy who can't commit to love.

I excuse myself to get ready for the party. The minute I'm in my room I send a quick text to Charlotte.

Going out with Ethan from work next Friday.

I'm surprised when I catch the three dots flickering on the bottom of the screen. She's probably knee-deep in party preparations, but is still finding the time to reach out to me.

That's amazing! I want you to tell me everything when you get here.

I reply.

Of course

I give myself a few minutes before I get ready. Starting tonight I'm going to focus on my future. There's no point in dwelling on what could be. I've got a date with a great guy; my best friend still loves me; and I might have a girl date with Lily and Charlotte. Sure, I still work a dead-end job, and my heart was broken only a few short weeks ago, but things can only get better from here. I can only hope.

❧

I'm awed by the way Charlotte's backyard has been transformed into something magical. Mom and I come in through the small white gate against the two-car garage. Large white twinkling bulbs hang from the wooden fence that has been resurfaced since the last time I was here. They illuminate the entire backyard as the late summer sun begins to set.

A loud rumble of voices floats around us as we enter the backyard. The Fields have a large family, and a huge support system. It's what helped them bounce back from the loss of their father.

Charlotte is amazing at planning parties and decorating: she has always been. She even helped Mom plan my sweet sixteen. Most of the ideas came from her. Sometimes I think she should have been a party planner instead of a teacher. One day she's going to be that cool mom that throws the best birthdays, the ones with the perfect Pinterest vibe.

Along the right side of the yard are tables with a smorgasbord of food set up on them. The scent of Italian meets barbecue and sets my taste buds on fire. In the center of the grass is a makeshift cherry wood dance floor, and a DJ playing country music, Josephine's favorite.

Josephine is the first to spot Mom and me. She's chatting with a group of women who look around the same age, probably some work friends. She looks amazing in her beautiful short-sleeved bubble-gum-pink dress and matching heels. A black and gold sash falls over her shoulders that says *60 & fabulous*. She raises her arm and excuses herself to greet us. "I'm so glad you both made it." When she says it she mainly looks at me, a knowing, sympathetic look on her face.

"We wouldn't miss it," Mom chimes in for me.

Josephine reaches over giving us both hugs.

"Happy birthday." I hand her the seafoam-green gift bag.

She smiles and peeks inside. "I'm sure whatever you ladies got me is fabulous. Please, make yourselves at home. Food's hot and the dance floor is open."

She shimmies away to the beat of the music, shaking her hips to the rhythm. Mom excuses herself to go get a non-alcoholic drink. She told me if I needed to drink alcohol to ease myself into the spirit of the party she'd be more than willing to be my designated driver. I was going to decline her offer, but I scan the yard and my eyes fall upon Logan. *Keep your head up, Ellie. You got this.* I straighten my shoulders and even with my aching heart I manage to put on a smile.

Logan is standing at the DJ booth with his old high-school buddy, Keith Potter. He's sure aged a lot in the ten years since I last saw him. He always had short hair, but now he's got a shiny head. His goatee has never changed. It's one of the major things I remember about him. Keith's head is tilted. He bobs up and down to the music as he holds a pair of headphones between his shoulder and right ear.

Logan and he are chatting over the music. The muffled sounds of their voices carry over to where I'm standing. The worst part about seeing Logan is that I can't look away. I want to go over there and mostly rip his head off, but I can't, not only because this is Josephine's party, but because I did this to myself.

I hate that he looks good tonight in his tight faded blue jeans and red and blue plaid shirt with the top few buttons undone, exposing some of his chest. The images of all the ways I kissed that bare chest and ran my fingers over his muscular physique has my stomach tied up in knots.

As I plan to look away, I'm swept up by his dark eyes finding mine. *Don't let him see how he affects you*, I try to tell myself. His jaw clenches, and his face flushes in the glow of the light behind him.

"There you are!"

I'm beyond grateful for Charlotte's interruption. I spin to find my best friend looking fancy as hell in her lime-green sweetheart dress. Her hair is all tucked up in a neat little bun on top of her head.

"You look amazing." I smile.

"I know," she says playfully, rolling her eyes. "And you as well." She takes in my blue floral lace sleeveless dress.

"Thanks."

She touches my arm gently. "So, we have the best food ever here. You should go try the heroes. Like, I've never had Italian heroes that taste this good before. It's sorcery, I tell you."

My stomach growls at the mention of lunch meat sandwiched between my favorite kind of bread. "Lead the way."

She smiles, hooks my arm in hers, and whisks me away. "So, tell me about this Ethan guy. Is he cute?"

Charlotte's face glows while she talks. She's always had this pep in her step, but since she's been married it's increased. Her eyes find Bryan's amongst the crowd and she tucks her chin down then gives a small wave.

"You met him," I remind her. "We went to Applebees one night, he's the guy who..."

"Oh, the one with no hair!"

"Yes, that's the one."

She contemplates what I've said for a moment. There's more in that head of hers. I've known her almost my whole life and I know when she purses her lips and stares off that the wheels are turning inside her head.

"Oh, he was a cutie!" She licks her pointer finger then holds it out into the air and makes a sizzling sound.

I chuckle. "He's a good guy. I think I need that."

She nods. "As long as you're happy." Her tone is different, a little on edge, like she's rooting for the other guy, the guy who I want nothing to do with. As we reach the table behind the DJ booth, the hairs on the back of my neck prickle against my skin. Logan is nonchalantly staring at me. He pretends not to see me, but his eyes rake over my tight lace dress. I turn my attention to the food and don't look back.

§

Mom and I have been here for over two hours. The party feels like it's just getting started. The night sky is clear with twinkling white stars shining above. It's not easy to see stars out here on Long Island with all the light pollution, but under the right circumstances it can be beautiful.

Mom is busy chatting up a storm with one of Charlotte and Logan's aunts from their father's side. Aunt Millie was the first relative I met all those years ago. She took us to Adventureland and Logan got sick on the roller coaster after eating pizza. We were so mad at him because she packed us all up and we had to head home.

A slow song plays on the speakers. It's one of Josephine's favorite country artists, Brett Young. Charlotte jumps in front of me. She must have caught me staring off. A wide grin forms on her face. "Dance with me?"

I smirk. "Of course, my dear."

She takes my hand and kisses the back of it as I rise. The gesture makes me laugh. As we reach the dance floor we're surrounded by couples. She takes me in her grasp, and dips me. I giggle, but almost forget I've had two cocktails and I'm a little on the tipsy side. We both fall to the ground in a heap of laughter.

A familiar hand reaches down over me. I glance up as another song from the same artists fades in. A slow, familiar tune that I've heard plenty of times on the radio. Charlotte takes his right hand, while he waits for me to take the left. Bryan comes over and steals Charlotte away for a dance.

As they veer off to the other side of the dance floor, Logan takes hold of my hands. I try to protest, but it doesn't work. He lifts me and clutches me to his broad chest. Butterflies dance around in my stomach, fluttering up to the one organ I wish they couldn't touch, my heart. I'd be lying if I said I felt nothing, because I feel *everything*. The hate, the anger, the love, the lust, it's all there festering inside of me waiting to burst.

With my ear against his chest, we sway to the slow steady rhythm. "In Case You Didn't Know" is one of those songs that somehow speak to you in ways you don't understand. Goosebumps rise all over my arms as the sound of Logan's voice over the artist surrounds me.

The song lyrics take me to a place that I don't want to go.

I press a hand gently against his heart. The beats are so rapid you'd think he run a marathon, but all he's done is steal a dance with me. For a moment, my heart warms, melting the ice exterior.

I stare down at the small space between us, and can feel his eyes lingering on me, waiting for me to make my move.

"I have a date on Friday," I whisper. "You can't just sweep me up into your arms during a beautiful song and think you can make everything okay. Life isn't a movie, Logan. I'm not a fictional character. My heart is real and it's damaged."

I've run out of tears, thank God, but that doesn't stop my voice from breaking.

"I know it won't make it okay. I just. I can't," he stutters.

Holy shit. Logan Fields never stutters.

"God, why is this so hard?" he yells over the music.

He releases me and grips the ends of his hair. It's grown a small amount since the last time I saw him. In fact, even his scruffy face is fuzzier than usual, something I didn't pick up earlier. His eyes are swollen with the lingering pain of sleepless nights, and I know that look all too well, because it's the spitting image of my own.

"It's hard because you don't know what you want. You're the guy who can get a girl to sleep with him from one look into those dark, mysterious eyes. You can't fool me: I already know what's hidden behind them. And it's all a lie." I swallow hard, trying to press the knot back down.

"I'd never lie to—"

I shake my head, pressing my hand harder into his chest, trying to push him away. "I know, but I can't trust that you won't walk away. I stepped back, because I think deep down, I never wanted it to be just sex, and anything more with you would never work. Now if you'll excuse me, I'm going to go stuff my face with something sweet."

I push, then free myself from him. I make the mistake of meeting his glimmering eyes. His tears almost break me. I can't let it distract me from the truth of who he is. This is over. It's better in the long run for both of us.

He reaches out, but I slap his hand away. His brows furrow at my advance, but then he nods like he gets it. He sucks in a deep breath and closes his eyes.

"As you wish," he whispers as a tear escapes his eye.

My heart stutters, making it hard to breathe. Shaking my head, I spin on my heels, leaving him and his lies behind.

CHAPTER 24

J stab the poor innocent scrambled eggs on Charlotte's beautiful new white china. She shuffles around the kitchen searching for her coffee maker. You'd think after almost a month of living here she'd be a little more organized. Her life might be put together, but most of the time, she's a hot mess.

Bryan strolls in leaving the fresh scent of Ivory soap in his wake. As if he can read her mind, he sets his sights on the one spot Charlotte hasn't looked—atop the cool gray fridge. With ease, he reaches up and grabs the coffee maker. Charlotte turns, and grins when their eyes connect. He passes it along to her, and as they squeeze by each other he plants a soft kiss on her lips, and they continue on their path.

It's like watching one of those sitcoms set in the olden days where the husband and wife have this perfect little routine. She'd be wearing a very businesslike dress—even though she was a homemaker, and he'd be wearing a well-pressed suit that she ironed early that morning. They'd have a perfect little life.

My heart squeezes with that longing, and the memories of being in my kitchen flood my mind. I lower my gaze and close my eyes tight. I catch flashes of the way Logan and I easily navigated through the room with each other as if we'd been doing it for years. I try taking slow, deep steady breaths, but with every passing inhale, the pain becomes almost unbearable.

A cool hand slips over mine. Charlotte. Her hands are always cold. My eyes flutter to find her dark eyes watching me. They're so familiar, like Logan's.

"Are you sure you should be going on this date?" she asks.

"I'm sure." There's zero conviction behind my trembling voice.

"You can bail. I'm sure Egan—"

"Ethan," I mumble.

"Ethan will understand. I mean, he's more like a rebound anyway, right?"

I shrug. I thought it would be nice to go and enjoy a normal date rather than having a fake one. Part of me wants to move on and live my life without love. I'd even go back to before Matt. Well, before I was constantly checking the dating app so that I could catch up to Charlotte. I hate admitting there was jealousy over her relationship with Bryan. I don't need a man to make me happy, but without Logan there even as a friend, it's like there's a piece of my heart missing.

"I want to do this. I need to get back into the world and live my life as I did before—" I pause, and try to swallow the knot forming in my throat. "Before I made the worst decision of my life." I wince, because it's far from the truth.

I was doing fine up until last weekend at Josephine's birthday. I had convinced myself I was moving on, but every damn thing reminds me of him. It kills me. Even being with Charlotte, the memories of our past keep unfolding like a movie montage in my brain.

A familiar song surrounds us at that very moment. Charlotte insisted on cooking to her favorite playlist on Alexa. The device sits in front of me on the counter. The haunting tune is the same one that Logan thought would be appropriate to sing into my ear last weekend.

"Alexa, stop!" I whisper.

"Oh, darling." Charlotte rounds the marbled countertop and steps beside me, wrapping me in her arms. I don't cry; there are no tears left in me. Logan Fields will forever have this stupid hold over me. He always had, but after everything that happened recently that hold has become like the grip from a vice.

I inhale deeply and pull back, wiping my eyes, except there's nothing there, not even a drop. Maybe I have moved on. I turn to the eggs on my plate that no longer look appealing. My stomach churns like I'm going to be sick. I push the plate away. "I should go get ready."

She sighs, and spins me on the barstool. "You have my permission."

My brows raise as she holds my attention.

"You don't need my permission, but I can't stand being in the middle of this anymore. He had the same look in his eyes yesterday afternoon while Bryan and I helped him move into his new apartment. He moped around the whole time. I was only able to get him to smile when I dropped a pot on my foot, and instead of saying fuck, I said fudge."

"He made the move? I honestly thought he was doing it to rile me up."

"Well he took the job. He's going to be working out of Sachem."

Eyes wide, I stare at her. This is not the news I was expecting. I do recall Josephine questioning him when we all had dinner together, but I never imagined him actually moving home.

"He's back. You brought my brother back home." Charlotte's eyes glimmer. "He says it's because he wanted to come home, but the week before my wedding he was saying how he'd never come back. He was adamant about it, too. He'd never admit that the memories of our father are too hard for him. He wants to be with you. You're the only thing here that he truly wants."

I shake my head. "All he ever wanted was a fuck-buddy. That's all I was to him."

Charlotte grabs my hands and holds on to them tight. In her eyes, I see the truth. The idea of him moving for me renders me speechless. I keep opening my mouth to say more, but I'm like Ariel after Ursula stole her voice.

"I don't say this because I'm on my brother's side, I say it because I'm concerned. He's excited to start his new position, but there's also this sadness that looms over him. I see the same look in your eyes as you watch Bryan and me together. There's something missing in his life and he knows it. I hate seeing you both like this, it's killing me. Sure, I was pissed about you going behind my back, but something beautiful came from it."

Only Charlotte would be okay with me having a relationship with her brother behind her back. After the initial shock, and the way she yelled at me, I would have never expected her to be on board with it.

"Think about talking to him. Okay? I'm not saying to stand Ethan up. Go on your date, but think about talking to Logan. He's always loved you, even when we were younger, I knew it could potentially one day turn into something. He acted brotherly towards you, but it was different, like he knew if he waited it out he could one day have you."

I scratch at my throat, desperately trying to dig for my voice. "Okay."

"Do you love him?" she asks.

My body deflates, my limbs become limp like cooked spaghetti. I desperately rub at the ache forming behind my eyes. My weary eyes catch sight of hers, and I lay it all out for her to see. Admitting what I've been holding back is painful, but necessary. The weight of the secret lifts and it makes me feel exposed. Loving him was like breathing, sometimes it was difficult, but other times it made me feel alive.

I know I have to talk to Logan, but I can't leave Ethan hanging. I promised him a date as friends. I'll make sure to remind him that it's all it can be. I'm meeting him at the restaurant so if things go awry I can slip away easily.

I pull up to the restaurant. It's nothing fancy, just your typical Long Island date at *TGI Fridays*. My phone goes off. I've been mostly ignoring my phone calls in case it was Logan, but a strange number pops up on my screen. I've been waiting for a call from the radio station I interviewed with yesterday. I answer to be sure.

"Hello?"

"Hello, is this Ellie Garner?"

"This is she," I say. My leg bounces.

"This is Eric Long. You came to the office for an interview yesterday."

My pulse starts to race. This is it, they are going to tell me that I wasn't the right candidate. It's been way too long since I've interned for a station, I'm sure they want someone with more experience.

"Yes."

"I hope that you will accept our offer for a sales position. I know you said you have a retail job you'd like to keep part time, but would you be able to start Tuesday?"

I gasp. "Of course. I can arrange something with my boss. Thank you so much."

"Oh no, Ellie, thank you. You're just what we were looking for. We can't wait for you to be a part of the team."

Eric gives me the information I need to start, and before I know it there's a huge smile on my face. I tap out a quick message to Mom and Charlotte letting them know the good news. Thoughts of Logan pushed aside—at least for now. I put my phone away. Ethan is already standing outside. There's a calm that enters me as I carefully take in his clothing choice for the night. He's not dressed up: the dressiest part is probably his white collared shirt. I'm not any more dressed than usual either. He's used to seeing me in my simple flowing colored skirts.

He takes notice of me right away. He waves with a broad smile. As I cross the lot, my thoughts wander to my conversation this morning with Charlotte. I can't imagine me being the reason for Logan moving back home. He made it perfectly clear that what we had was nothing more than a fling.

"You look beautiful."

I stare down at the skirt gently waving in the evening breeze.

"Thanks. You clean up nice too." I give a genuine smile.

He chuckles as he grabs for the door handle and opens it for me. I nod in appreciation and walk into the restaurant. He truly is the guy that holds open doors.

We sit down in a booth in the far back. The lights in this section are always dimmed. It's better that way for now; maybe he won't catch the sadness radiating from me.

"So, what are you ordering?" he questions, peeking out from the large menu.

I smile, because despite my heart not being here, he's adorable and I hope he one day finds the girl he's meant to be with. My eyes wander down my own menu, laid flat on the scratched up wooden table. The chicken fingers are the first picture I come across. It's sad that a picture of chicken can make my eyes water.

"Hey, are you okay?"

Shit. He noticed. I sniffle to clear the tingling in my nose, and smile.

"Yeah. Sorry. Don't laugh, but chicken fingers are my go-to food."

Ethan's face lights up, his smile reaching his eyes. With a hearty laugh, he closes his menu.

"Nothing wrong with chicken fingers. It was on my mind to get it, but I'm in the mood for the JD burger."

Our waiter, a young guy with Nick Jonas hair, circa *Camp Rock*, comes over to take our order. We hand him our menus and when he walks away the silence between us is deafening. What do we even talk about? I haven't been on a date since Matt and I first went out.

"I got a promotion," Ethan says after a few minutes. "Assistant manager of men's."

Staring at him over my bubbling Sprite, I run a finger along the cool wet glass.

"What? That's amazing. I am so happy for you. What happened to Richard?"

Ethan lifts his Blue Moon beer, taking a swig. "He walked out. I was looking into positions elsewhere because being a full-time employee doesn't pay the bills."

I understand where he's coming from. It's not cheap living here. While I've always been able to pay my bills, having the money for extra living expenses is tight. I feel bad leaving Mom behind, but I won't go far like Arthur. Hopefully I'm taking the right step to getting my life back on track. "I hear you on that. I also have some job news. I'm going to be swapping part-time. I found a job at a radio station in their sales department."

"That's amazing! So happy for you. Look at us adulting." He chuckles.

I give a genuine smile. "I can't believe Richard quit though, that's crazy."

Ethan takes another sip. "I'm surprised you didn't hear. He and Thomas got into a huge argument over the till being counted incorrectly and he snapped."

"I'm surprised Lily didn't tell me."

He chuckles. "She does love her gossip. The other day she

233

came over to the men's department and started babbling about something the new girl did."

I smile. "Sounds like Lily."

We chat about some other work-related things and I try to be enthusiastic about our conversation, but as the date continues, it's hard to focus. I'm busy replaying this morning's conversation with Charlotte. Like how she told me she'd known that Logan has liked me all these years, and that she gives me permission. Then the idea of him moving here for me and being sad because we aren't together...It's all way too much.

"Are you going to get dessert?" Ethan questions.

We've both finished up our meals. The waiter stands at the edge of our table collecting our things, his eyes on me.

"No. Can we get the check?" I look between the waiter and Ethan. Ethan's smile doesn't quite reach his eyes. He knows. After we collect the check he still offers to pay. We walk out together, and he follows me to my car. We stand at the driver's side.

"I'm sorry, Ethan." I lower my gaze.

"Your heart is somewhere else, isn't it?" His shoulders fall.

I nod, glancing down at the concrete, and kicking a loose stone. I meet his eyes.

"Don't apologize. You can't help who you love."

The idea of being in love with Logan sends shivers through my whole body. "Thank you for dinner."

"Of course. I'm glad we did it. I hope we can be friends."

I wrap my arms around Ethan. His embrace is warm and friendly, but I feel nothing. Pulling away, I plant a small kiss to his cheek and get into my car. He steps aside and watches me drive off. I'm not ready to drive to Logan's. Charlotte gave me the address before I left her house. So, I'm going to go home, sleep on it, and figure out how to tell Logan that I'm in love with him.

CHAPTER 25

$\mathcal{I}$ make a left onto my block when I see a familiar blue Nissan parked at the curb in front of my house. My lungs deflate like a balloon losing air. Flutters invade my chest making my heart go a beat or two faster than normal. He's here. Logan Fields is standing on my front steps waiting for me. Is this real life?

He pushes himself from the rail and straightens himself as I pull into the driveway. Tiny rain droplets land on my windshield. Out of the corner of my eye I watch him. He doesn't move, but his eyes stay focused on the car. I grip the steering wheel with all of my might. If I were The Hulk the wheel would be crushed under the weight of my hands.

Talking to him was inevitable, but I never expected it to be spontaneous. I wanted to get my thoughts together and figure out what I needed to say. *You can do this, Ellie.* I try to convince myself that everything will be okay.

Can the man standing here provide me with the type of relationship I need? Logan's not a man who sticks around, and that scares me. If something else were to happen, would he flee again? It's hard for Logan to commit to anything; why would this be any different?

It's now or never. I step out of the car, the rain lightly tapping my head. Walking around the car I keep my sights on the white concrete at my feet. Even as I grow closer when his black and white Converses come into view, I can't lift my gaze.

"What are you doing here?"

I hate the sadness in my voice, I'd rather it be filled with anger. I don't want him to know that if he took me in his arms right now and kissed me, that I would kiss back.

"I needed to see you."

A trembling laugh escapes my lips. Charlotte wouldn't lie to me, but Logan wanting anything more than what we had for those two short weeks almost feels unreal.

"Look at me, Ellie. Please, let me see your face." His voice breaks, causing my eyes to shoot up to make sure I'm not hearing things. His mouth opens. He allows himself to inhale deeply, as if he'd been holding back the whole time.

"I want you to trust me," he says.

I shake my head, lowering my gaze to his chest. It heaves up and down more rapidly than usual. "You're going to have to give me a reason to trust you."

I yell at myself for the weakness in my voice. I've never been good at being strong.

He slips his hand into mine the way he did the last time we made love—no, the last time we had sex. If we made love he would have seen it as that and not let me walk out that door. He let me go, and now I have to know if this is real and if he's serious. My heart isn't a toy to play with.

I gasp as the tips of his fingers dance over my skin. This should be a serious moment, but my lower half has other plans and I squirm under his touch. I'm overwhelmed by the urge that comes over me. He's the only guy to ever get me on the verge of an orgasm from one simple touch. It's like he has magic fingers.

"It didn't hit me until after that night at my mom's house. It took me a while to understand why I kept you close but pushed you away. I never expected to ask you for more." He pauses to stare down at our hands intertwined with each other, as he continues to glide the tips of his fingers in circles.

"Then I started doing things like taking you to see the sunrise, begging you to paint with me, doing the things we loved as kids, and randomly showing up at your house to spend time with you. At first, I figured it was because I'd be leaving again and I loved hanging out with you, but it was so much more."

With his free hand he runs it over his face, rubbing at his eyes. He sniffles, then lowers his hand, reaching for my other one.

"Did you move here for me? Or is this what you wanted before we got together? Charlotte said you took the job and moved back. What about your life in Pennsylvania? Your home?"

He shakes his head. "That was never home, but being with you made me realize it even more. I wasn't sure if you'd talk to me, but I had to try."

He lets go of one of my hands and a cold rushes in, and it's not from the rain steadily increasing as we stand here. He runs a trembling hand through his hair.

"Ellie, you—I—" he stutters through a trembling breath. "You know I'm not good at this, but I'm willing to try because with you it feels real. I've never wanted to be with a woman more than I do with you." He pauses, swallowing hard. His Adam's apple bobs up and down. He takes three deep breaths before continuing.

"When we made love that night I ran like a scared little boy, because I knew at that moment that I loved you more than I've ever loved anyone. Loving leads to loss, and loss—" he blinks several times as a mixture of tears and rain glides down his cheek.

"Loss is something that I don't know how to handle. I know all too well what hurt and loss feels like, but didn't realize what it would be like when someone you love walks away. I know you're seeing Ethan—"

"We aren't seeing each other. I told him I could only be his friend."

"Why?" Logan asks, closing the small space between us. I use my free hand to press up against his chest. I want him close, but I don't at the same time. I fear the heartbreak that comes with loving a guy like Logan Fields.

"Because I already gave my whole heart to someone else."

As the words tumble out, the tears follow. I rest my cheek against his chest. The thumping of his heart calming me with every beat.

"I'll take care of your heart, Ellie. I can't guarantee that I won't fuck up, but I do know that there's no way I could love anyone the way I love you. All I need is for you to trust me. You're my forever, El. You've always been."

An unwanted sob forces its way out of me, causing him to tighten his grip. In his arms, I'm home. He's my safety net and it's always been him too. I trace that back to the summer we spent together when Charlotte was away at camp, everything changed then, even with the age difference, this always felt right.

His warm hand tucks under my chin, forcing me to lift my gaze to his. Rain hits my nose and cascades between the two of us.

"My Ellie. I love you."

"I love you so much, Logan. Always have." I half-smile and sob at the same time.

His laughter surrounds us as he pulls me into him and gently rests his lips against mine. Our kiss starts out slow. I finally invite him in and his hand flies up to my cheek, cupping it, blanketing me with his warmth. I lift my hands and run them through his damp hair.

"We should take this inside," I whisper against his lips.

"First you kill my washing machine fantasy, and now sex in the rain. Fantasy crusher." He chuckles, tickling my lips with his.

"I don't think my neighbors would appreciate the show."

"You're right. Keys?"

He takes a step back, leaving a small gap between us, and holds out his hand. I pull them from my purse and lay them in his hand.

"Don't move!"

He rushes up the steps, unlocks the door, then doubles back for me. He scoops me up into his arms like it's the easiest thing in the world. I throw my arms around his neck and settle into him. Through my tears, I laugh as he carries me into the house and somehow manages to shut the door behind us. Without a second thought, he races up to my room, heavily breathing with each step.

"Getting tired, old man?" I tease.

"Tired? I've got gym teacher stamina."

He puts out his foot and kicks my door. Nothing happens, and I burst into a fit of laughter at his sad attempt.

"That only works in the movies."

He glares at me with an amused grin. He tries again, this time I catch him pressing down the handle and kicking at the same time.

"Cheater," I tease.

He presses his lips to mine to keep me quiet, but it doesn't work, my giggles roar around us. He smirks into my mouth then slams the door with his foot. Once on the bed, I'm lost in the shuffle of our clothes being tossed to the side, and him lowering his naked body over me. He fits like a security blanket, tight, safe, and warm.

In my head I replay his words, *You're my forever, El. You've always been.* There's always been some kind of different love between us, even as kids, and being three years apart. He'd been the one to stand up for me when my own brother wouldn't; he spent a whole summer with me to keep me company, and even traveled across town on a bike with ice cream he knew I wanted.

I don't wish I would have known sooner though, because I'm a firm believer in things falling into place when they are meant to, and our time is now. Everything leading up to it was just the opening act, and this moment is the main event.

CHAPTER 26

8 MONTHS LATER

$\mathcal{I}$t's not perfect, it needs a lot of work; but it's the start of our new life together. Logan drops one of the boxes of Pergo. The sound echoes around the empty living room of our new brick Cape Cod.

The walls inside are made of mostly old wooden panels, aside from the kitchen, bathroom and bedrooms. Most of the baseboard heating lined around the living room is broken off, and painted with a mixture of awful green and eggshell. We ripped up the carpet here a few weeks ago when we bought the place—YES, PURCHASED! Our names are both on the deed. I can't help smiling every time I think about it.

Tonight, after Charlotte and Bryan's gender reveal party for the little nugget growing inside her belly, we plan on coming back and starting on our living room renovation.

I can't believe my best friend is pregnant and I'm going to be an auntie! I was so overjoyed by the news when they told us a few months ago. Now, we are finally ready to find out the sex, and I couldn't be happier for the two of them.

Things between Logan and I are serious. When he asked me

two months ago to move in with him, it was easy to say yes. After becoming the gym teacher at a local school, he was asked to also coach football, soccer, and wrestling. Between his job and my two we were somehow able to afford this house. It was a cheap fixer-upper and after our renovation of Charlotte and Bryan's room, we were ready to tackle something a little bigger.

"What time do we have to be there?" he questions, wiping his hands off on his jeans.

I slip my phone from the back pocket of my jean shorts. The party starts at three and it's a little after one.

"Like an hour and a half. Promised your mom I'd help. Why, what's up? Did we forget to get anything?"

Logan crosses the room, narrowing his eyes at me. His footsteps echo through the empty space. His hungry mouth meets mine as he sweeps me up and cradles me in his arms.

"I'm not sure we have time—"

"There's always time," he says in between his soft kisses.

There's no denying that Logan and I still have a very active sex life. After we decided to make this work, it was easy to fall into a simple routine of spending nights in the apartment that he moved into. It was crummy and cheap, but I didn't care as long as we were together.

He carries me through the house, and up the creaking paint peeling stairs to the master bedroom. The walls are bare, and the scratched floor beneath our feet is a work in progress, but it's ours, so we don't care. Our room isn't huge, but it's just the right size for our queen-sized bed that is currently sitting in storage. For the time being, we have an air mattress until we renovate the room.

As he lowers us, he loses his balance from the air mattress being so low. We land on it with a thud, and I swear I hear a pop.

"Oh my God, did you break the only bed we have to sleep on for the next two months?"

He laughs as if it doesn't matter, and instead of worrying,

grabs a hold of me and kisses me. Throwing a leg over my body as he settles down on top and slowly bends down.

"Are you ready to get to work tonight, my little apprentice?" He chuckles into my lips.

"Teach me all the things, Logan Fields."

We start sinking, and the mattress is no longer stiff as it should be.

"Are we going down with this ship?"

"Looks like it." He grins. That grin has gotten me into more trouble than I could have ever imagined, but it does things to my insides that I can't explain.

"It's coming out of your paycheck." I bop his nose.

He leans down, taking my bottom lip between his teeth. I wrap my arms around his neck and lower him to me. I'm overwhelmed with emotion every time we're together. When he came back to live here I never imagined it would be for me. It almost feels like I got my happy ending, but it's no fairy-tale. There are still people in our lives that aren't here to bask in the joy of what's to come. I see the look in Charlotte's eyes every time she touches that belly of hers. Her dad would have been super grandpa, and it sucks he's not here.

Speaking of dads, mine went back to being MIA, and my brother and I still can't talk without getting into some kind of tiff. He also never invited Mom and I to the small wedding, although Cassie's entire family was there. Mom acts like it's no big deal, but she'd never tell him she's hurt.

Sometimes you can't control things that happen in your life, and you have to move forward or life will take you down. Despite all the bad, I'm happy. I've got the most amazing man; Mom and I are closer than ever; my best friend is making a mini version of herself; and we are all okay. That's all I can ever ask for.

"We're still going down," he says as the mattress sinks a bit more.

"We'll go down together."

Logan chuckles, grabs hold of me, and rolls us over so I'm on top. I stare down at him, my cheeks hurting from the intense pull.

"That's right. You're stuck with me forever." He watches me like I'm his entire world.

I raise a brow. "Are you sure about that?"

"Never been so sure in my entire life." He reaches behind him, and pulls a white gold ring from his back pocket. There's a small sparkling stone mounted in the direct center, with tiny ones on both sides set into the ring itself.

"Wait, are you–?" I sit up, still straddling him.

I love how this moment isn't over the top. There's no silly flash mob or huge romantic gesture. It's him and me, in our new bedroom, on a sinking mattress. It's perfect and messy, just like us.

"I want you to be my apprentice for the rest of my life." He smirks.

I snort, and clasp my hand over my mouth. My vision blurs as wetness pools against my lids.

"Is that a yes?"

I nod, and squeak out a tiny, yes.

"I want to see your smile. Now give me your hand."

I hold it out for him. He slips the ring onto my finger, his eyes never leaving mine. My heart thuds in my chest, skipping several beats all at once. He blinks a few times, tears streaking down his cheeks.

Slowly, I lean down and press my lips to his. I taste the salty mixture of our tears running together. His kisses never get old, and the tingles in my lower half feel as if they won't ever fade. I never imagined the one person off limits would be the one I get to spend the rest of my life with, but here we are, and I couldn't be happier.

THE END

ACKNOWLEDGMENTS

To my parents, my biggest fans, for always encouraging me and supporting my love of writing. Thank you for always believing in me. To my husband, Steve for allowing me to escape into a fictional world for hours on end to finish my books, and my kids for being my number one supporters, and my cats of course, for being my emotional support animals and writing buddies.

A huge thank you goes out to my VR ladies who helped me shape Logan and Ellie's love story. They are by far the best writing friends an author could ask for. I love you guys! Kelly, Keri, Tara, May, Eilene, Nicole.

To Beth, for seeing my potential and encouraging me to keep writing. This time around, it's my turn to thank you.

Nicole and Lauren for being my shining lights during the pandemic, and for giving me an outlet to discuss romance books and all the things in between. Your support means so much.

My grandma, Maga. Thank you for humoring me as a child with a big imagination, and for playing house and watching me pretend to get married in your dining room to fictional characters from movies. I'm pretty sure that's where my love for storytelling came into play.

To the rest of my family, you all know who you are, especially my Cheetah's, Jeanmarie and Toniann, who have been following my journey, thank you for the support.

This entire book wouldn't be possible without Bloodhound Books. I'm so honored to be a part of such an amazing group of authors. Thank you from the bottom of my heart for everything.

I can't wait to see where this journey with Bloodhound Books goes. This is a dream come true.

A NOTE FROM THE PUBLISHER

Thank you for reading this book. If you enjoyed it please do consider leaving a review on Amazon to help others find it too.

We hate typos. All of our books have been rigorously edited and proofread, but sometimes mistakes do slip through. If you have spotted a typo, please do let us know and we can get it amended within hours.

info@bloodhoundbooks.com